TRANQU
IF IT I.

Mridula Koshy was born and raised .... migrated to the US. There she worked as a union and ....nity organiser. Presently, she lives in Delhi with her partner and children. Her short stories have appeared in India and abroad. She is at work on her first novel, set in Kerala, Delhi and other parts of the world. *If It Is Sweet* is her first book.

PRAISE FOR *IF IT IS SWEET*

'Here is a natural stylist, with an easy, accessible turn of phrase . . . Hers is a determined, stealthy eye, born of fierce concentration, often conjuring up a rustic quiet: "Now her pregnant beauty startles him like the fish that rustle and slip past his shins in the flooded fields of paddy he bends over to seed".'—**Rajni George,** *India Today*

'. . . beautifully spare and evocative, with turns that are riveting, surprising, and revealing of the mysteries of the human psyche.'—**Manjushree Thapa,** *Outlook Magazine*

'. . . this is absolutely rigorous and distinctive work, and there is a sound and a sense in these stories that make Indian fiction a bigger place'.—**Chandrahas Choudhury,** *Live Mint*

'What counts more than the narrative is the language—tender, poetic, informed by our mutilingual milieu. The stories retrieve to fiction, if not to history, marginalised lives around us. But they aren't shown as objects of condescending pity, but as real beings with their own joys and longings.'—**K. Satchidanandan,** *Tehelka*

'The writing is evocative, layered and masterful . . . [Koshy's] fascination with the underbelly is something she has in common with Aravind Adiga, but where his writing is terse and action-oriented, her stories delve deep into the head space of these faceless, marginalised people.'—**Sunaina Kumar,** *Mail Today*

'This riveting collection, at once nuanced and adventurous, will stay in the reader's memory for the way it probes away at the complexities of class and money, transgressions and violations.'—**Naintara Maya Oberoi,** *TimeOut*

If It Is Sweet

MRIDULA KOSHY

TRANQUEBAR

TRANQUEBAR PRESS
An imprint of westland ltd
571, Poonamallee High Road, Kamaraj Bhavan, Aminijikarai, Chennai 600 029
No.38/10 (New No.5), Raghava Nagar, New Timber Yard Layout, Bangalore 560 026
Survey No. A - 9, II Floor, Moula Ali Industrial Area, Moula Ali, Hyderabad 500 040
Plot No 102, Marol Coop Ind Estate, Marol, Andheri East, Mumbai 400 059
47, Brij Mohan Road, Daryaganj, New Delhi 110 002

First published in TRANQUEBAR by westland ltd 2009

10 9 8 7 6 5 4 3 2

This is a work of fiction, Names, characters, places and incidents are either the product of the author's imagination or are used fictitiously and any resemblance to any actual person, living or dead, events or locals is entirely coincidental.

ISBN 9789380032122

Cover design by Gynelle Alves

Typeset in Californian FB by SURYA, New Delhi
Printed at Radha Press, Delhi -110031

For my father and my mother,
Stephen Koshy and Mary Koshy

Contents

Acknowledgements

I wish to thank:
Nilanjana Roy and Prita Maitra, this book's editors. The rest of
the team at Tranquebar and Westland.

Riyaz. These stories were written with your varied sensibilities
in mind. When I failed to impress you I had your critical faculties
to guide me. I am a better writer for writing and thinking with you.
The British Council for sponsoring Riyaz.

Merridawn Duckler. You opened the door. The Attic, in
Portland, Oregon for giving me a place to start from.

Shakti Bhatt for generous encouragement and practical
guidance.

Jeet Thayil. Your close reading and suggestions have made this
a better manuscript. Your support makes me a better writer.

Samit Basu for advocating for this book.

Bhawna Sharma for friendship, and tea at Tanku's.

Shazia Mona, Rukhsana Salim and Lata Manchanda for the
grace, wit and intelligence you bring to the job of helping me raise
my children. Without you there would be no writing.

Saleem, Akshay and Surya. If I could only ever be one thing I
would be your mother. But you let me be a writer as well.

Michael Creighton, my companion in all that I am. How did
you know?

My thanks to the editors of the publications in which the following stories have appeared:

'Intimations of a Greater Truth' in *Existere*
'Romancing the Koodawallah' in *Wasafiri*
'Stray Blades of Grass' in *The Dalhousie Review*
'Companion' in *Prairie Fire*
'Good Mother' in *India Currents*, winner first place Katha 2008
'The Large Girl' in *21 Under Forty* from Zubaan and Katha: *Short Stories by Indian Women* from Saqi
'When the Child was a Child' in *First Proof* 3 from Penguin India
'Jeans' in *India* from Isbn Edizioni
'Same Day' in *Tehelka*: Original Fictions, January 2009

The Good Mother

At the end of her tenure as mother, she leaves Manchester for her parents' home in Dehra Dun to enact what she doubts they will recognise as a pilgrimage. Once in Dehra Dun, she does not have the strength to dissemble, and she compromises with herself despite the fierce conviction that she is not obliged to compromise, ever again. She compromises neither by lying about nor by revealing the truth of her planned pilgrimage to her parents. She compromises by remaining silent in the face of their questions and instructions. This is what she saves her strength for: leaving them hobbled together on the verandah, her mother holding steady her now nearly-blind father with one hand, sari-end clenched between her teeth, freeing the other hand to wave at the car pulling the daughter away through folds of brown and green mountains.

In Rishikesh, she forgets them as she has forgotten those left behind in Manchester. She does not visit the ghats. She makes herself forget her children's wild joy the year before, as they floated twinkling lights in spinning boats of sewn leaves. 'To Delhi!' they had cheered. 'No,' she had said, 'not Delhi. The Ganges doesn't go to Delhi.'

She takes the Shatabdi Express to Agra and, acquiring an unexpected companion there—a boy younger by far than herself—criss-crosses back to Delhi with him. They take the accommodation in South Extension. To their relief, it is given to them at the same weekly rate of Rs 1,000 per night, exclusive of utilities, laundry and food, that they are quoted in the Delhi Tourism office. The rooms are dusty. There is an over-large front room their host says is the drawing room, where his dead wife's numerous self-portraits hang. There is a cramped bedroom, a closet-sized bathroom, and down the hall, a kitchen they share with the other tenants of the house.

Mr Kapoor introduces them to Megha, who ducks her head in assent to everything he has to say. Afterwards, trying to picture Megha, all she can remember is the sharpness of the part in her hair, a mismatch for her plump shyness. Mr Kapoor speaks in a certain weary code: 'cancer', pointing to his wife's self-portraits in the drawing room, 'call centre worker', pointing to Megha's bobbing head, 'sleeping', referring to Arun, whose door he opens without knocking.

When Mr Kapoor leaves, she looks at Marc for a moment. Megha slides back into her room, and then they are alone in the hallway of introductions. She opens their door, the bags are pushed in and they follow, shut the door and lock it with the key Mr Kapoor has provided. For good measure, Marc slides the reluctant top bolt into place, and she pushes in the bolt by the door handle.

With a giggle, she slides her hand into his front pocket, but he, already weary from the effort of the bolt, is turning to the television. She watches him destroy the strange symmetry of cushions, balanced on point and in a row down the length of a bony sofa, in his search for the remote. A minute later, he has abandoned his failed search and is on his haunches, one hand cupping his chin and the other relentlessly depressing the channel button adjacent to the screen as he switches through a multitude of offerings.

She turns and explores the flat and feels a stirring of delight when she discovers the balcony. It is narrow and latticed in thick concrete lace. Where there should be light, there are shadows she welcomes.

She unpacks both their bags, fills the plastic bucket in the bathroom, mixes in the laundry soap and washes the dirty clothes that have been accumulating since Agra. Now it is she who is on her haunches, the long tail of her kurta tucked between her calves and buttocks. The concrete floor is free of the mossiness of the bathroom in Agra. She jettisons worries about fungal infections and relishes the feel of water on the bare bottom of her feet. When her kurta slips out as she swivels from one pile of garments to the next, she removes it and her salwar, then her too-tight bra and underwear.

When the laundry is done she carries it out to the balcony where she ties together the cords from three salwars, lashes them to a length of wire looped in the corner and stretches her creation back and forth, criss-crossing the narrow space of air. Taking care to first wipe the wire clean, she hangs his jeans, her salwars and kameezes, his t-shirts and boxers, her blessedly clean underwear. She lingers behind the gauzy window of pink that is her duppatta. The clothes crowd around her in mild movement and their gentle slaps rebuke her naked arms, breasts and ribs. In the heat of the afternoon, she shivers and thinks, I might be seen.

She has to thrust her face into the lattice and only then can she look out. She has allowed this apparent obscurity to lull her. Now she hides between the rows of clothes hanging around her and skirts all three walls, pulling items of clothing around her as she steps forward to peer through the openings. Two of the walls open to sky, and below that, a still market lane of motley shacks. The third wall, she discovers, abuts the balcony of the property wedged next door to Mr Kapoor's. She had not noticed from the outside, but the houses are built with no space between them, just the superfluity of two sets of walls in a tight kiss, so that they are suctioned, one to the other. But these houses bear no relationship of symmetry nor do they accord any thought to each other.

The balcony next door is built a good four feet higher so that she can see at eye level, through the openings in the lattice, the floor next door. It contains a jumble of abandoned cots, tools and wooden boards, a plastic container—the kind used for storing drinking water—and a few steel cups tumbled in wood shavings. The house next door appears to be under construction, and perhaps the workers have broken for lunch and will return. She beats a retreat.

Marc is still in front of the television—no longer perched on his toes, no longer seated on his haunches, but now sprawled on his front; still close enough to the instrument to control it with his forefinger. She lays herself facedown on his back. Her own back dries from the quick suck of the air conditioner that he has turned on. She thinks to clean him somehow before she begins. His clothes are stiff with the dirt of the train journey; his hair, lank and fine, smells salty to her, and in the delicate creases at the back of his young neck, little twisted rubbings of black grease alternate in the neat pattern of a feathery stalk of wheat. She licks him there, and he relents, sinks his chin from his cupped palm and releases his head. She licks methodically till he unlocks the elbows on which he is braced and lowers his chest and then his head to the floor. She abandons her earlier plan to bathe him and works against the hard floor as she digs under him for the buttons of his fly. Once unbuttoned, she turns him over. The salt-scent rising from him sharpens.

He is a selfish lover, and that is how she prefers him. They are practised in their selfishness for all they have known each other—only these nine days. She has blown him thus: tiredly now, and in the beginning relentlessly, with all of the technique and innovation at her command, to keep him with her. From Agra, she has brought him with her to Delhi.

When she is done, she moves up his length to look at his sleepy face. On the television screen, an advertisement for contact lenses urges changing the more or less fixed brown of Indian eyes. The flickering light of the screen scatters on his face, and in the late afternoon dark of the heavily curtained drawing room, he blinks in and out of her vision. She searches for the sheen of moisture that gathers in dew on the fine hairs of his upper lip.

Even after he turned three, the cut-off she had outlined to him, her younger son had insisted on continuing nursing, and further insisted on exercising this right in the most public of places and always with her seated and while standing himself between her knees. He had insisted loudly and earnestly—after a burger at the Burger King, the crumbles of meat spraying from his mouth; when they stopped to rest on the bench outside the pet store at the mall; and in the parking lot, with the driver's seat pulled back to its furthest and with his chubby back braced against the steering wheel.

And when her younger son pulled his face back from her, his sly eyes filled with laughter, and disdainful of his brother's disapproval, then there was this same sheen of spent pleasure on his upper lip, and sometimes a droplet or two of her watery offering sliding from plumped upper lip to chin. At such times she had not known what, if anything, that she felt, was truly hers. There was always the huge surge of embarrassment that they were engaged thus, at his age, and with her limp breasts. Alongside this, there was the gratitude that she could so simply satisfy such great need. And then there was also the dread of his impending flight from her on the same trajectory his brother had taken—a trajectory that allowed her first-born the distant and cool appraisal with which he had taken to viewing her. Gently, she releases the sleeping Marc's face, turning it toward the television, so that he will wake in the cradle of its oblivion.

She had met Marc outside the doctor's office at the government clinic in Agra and offered to help him with the necessary translation. The doctor had bypassed the three-step process of French to English to Hindi and back by easily communicating his expertise and anger as he gestured for the pants to be pulled down, held up the syringe, turned to her with a sharp 'antihistamine', and proceeded with a brutal haste that forced her back and out of the room. She apologised to the boy later for not staying and conveyed the awkwardness of the idea that the doctor had disapproved of her seemingly being with him, a foreigner.

They stumbled forward. In Agra, in French, she was able to say what had eluded her since her flight from Manchester. '*Mes fils*,' she said, and her eyes remained dry. Her sons can only be viewed in a hasty jerk of her head over her shoulders, so the eyes slide in a split second past the vision of two sturdy boys belted into their car seats, and then out the window of her two-door, single-mom, second-hand, Toyota Tercel to take in her car crushed into the motorway barrier. Her eyes blink, obliterating what they have seen. Her sons are distant and dwindling specks, fixed against the static horizon of that barrier, which she flees. To look too long is to be sucked back. She is on a pilgrimage, she explained to Marc, and he said he would like to be on a pilgrimage as well. Not on this pilgrimage, she replied. But it was weak, and he knew it, because he followed her to her hotel, claiming she still owed him translation services. At this, she laughed and let him into her room.

✳

From outside the drawing room, she hears the tap-tapping of hammers. There is lightness to the sound. These tools, she thinks, are made light, for smaller hands, or made cheaply, for poorer people. In the bedroom, she removes from her bag the small lota which her mother has wrapped in an endless length of fabric. Perhaps her mother had thought to stave off this inevitable scattering. Certainly the numerous knots had eluded her in Agra. She had stood with the awkward bundle, defeated in the effort to find a spot away from the crowd, ignored the curious looks of those around her and picked and picked at the wrapping. In the end, afraid of being found out for the foolishness of all her ideas about herself, above all the idea of herself as a good mother, she had wept, turned and left.

She stands at the balcony door listening to the repeated tapping, the lengthy pauses, the cawing of a crow, and then she steps out. She stands and waits in between the hanging clothes. It is a long wait, and she feels herself seized with revulsion. The hammers fall silent. Accompanied by the scuffling sounds (how many faces pressed to the lattice—she tries to see and cannot) she thinks hard about what it is that she really feels.

Dry-eyed, she unwraps her bundle. This time it is easy. The knots are not really knots, just cloth twisting and criss-crossing, and deep inside the length of cloth there is a knot that slides free, revealing warm brass which gleams in the shade of the balcony. She tips the lota to the lattice that faces the street and market below. The lip of the jar catches the edge of the narrow opening in the concrete but cannot intrude beyond. Shaking out the contents is an awkward business. The brass and concrete where they meet and scrape make a rasping sound, and there is no breeze to carry the ashes that, soft and oily, disperse only slowly. Much of it mounds into the opening, and when the jar is empty she sets it down, kneels to the floor and, bringing her mouth close, blows. Little bits swirl back and stick to her lids and lips, but the rest float out, and before she can grasp the moment they are gone. She cannot remember the words her mother had taught her to say.

The year before, when they pleaded for their sewn-leaf boats to float if not to Delhi then to Agra, she promised her boys she would take them there someday. 'To the Taj Mahal, to the Taj Mahal,' they had screamed, ambushing each other with imaginary laser guns. Having failed them, she prays, the words stumbling from her, 'Please, take them to see the Taj.'

P.O.P.

I

By the time Manish turned five Sarla had to admit the truth of her preference for him over Ajay. She continued to work at the balance in which she weighed their place in her heart, but she also forgave herself the tilt she felt toward her second born. He 'feeds me' was her explanation to her husband, Jettamal, to whom she confided even this. The elder was clever but taciturn. The younger one struggled in everything; there was nothing quick about him, but his journey was always to her centre, and his offering was never less than his soul. Until Manish, she had never known that Ajay withheld. But she was also clear that the children were formed differently, that Ajay withheld not only from her but also from himself.

Jettamal was home from the sea once every three to four months, and then only for a handful of days. Come night, it was a hardship to have the boys in their one room. The very thing that allowed her to say of Ajay, 'but he doesn't know a thing', was also what prevented her from asking him to sleep out on the footpath. To ask would be to lay too heavy a finger on his unknowing. She resented the obtuseness but also feared the fragility of its fabric. If torn away, what would be revealed? Her touch on Ajay was a gentle one. She had acquired this gentleness from her mother, who had pushed her in childhood up the trunks of trees—Sarla scrabbling at the trunk, and at the last the palm of her mother's hand firmly cupping and raising Sarla's bottom so that reaching with her arms, Sarla could grasp and hoist herself onto lower branches from where she rained plums into the spread of her mother's skirt. For years Sarla continued to sleep with the baby Manish between her and Ajay, and on her other side the eager silence of the returned husband.

When Ajay was ten, and Manish five, Jettamal came home and spread on the charpoy the thick navy-issue blanket that he carried home with him every trip. All morning, the day of his arrival, he and the boys walked the market street, stopping to greet and be greeted. Sarla's parents had moved here from the countryside when she was Ajay's age, and carried on in a narrow lane the old trade of iron-mongering passed down in their family for generations. In the city they lost the open vista of their old lives and the expertise with heavy cartwheels, tillers and yokes that had made their reputation at home. Here, instead, they accepted the joy of life lived in a crowd, the vista ever changing and bold with jostling; and here they acquired expertise in soldering handles to kitchen pots and utensils. When they brought Sarla's husband into the family fold, the dowry he was offered included a sense of being settled such that his transient life would not otherwise have afforded him. On each return to his wife he renewed acquaintance with this dowry, the privileges of which he enjoyed and feared.

Jettamal's fear sprang from his fear of names. For him there was always the moment of agony when accosted by a familiar face and its laughter—of wondering if the beard surrounding the laugh could be matched to Nathu Chacha or if it was someone else distinguished by bald chin and bald pate who claimed the name. Which would still leave unnamed this laughing hairy-faced relative—now embracing and now making mystifying reference to other relatives with their own confusion of names. Then it comes to him in a tide of relief: this spread beard carried by a belly-shelf is of course Sarla's uncle's wife's brother. Not Nathu Chacha. But Roshan Chacha. Sarla, when she was with Jettamal, made sure to greet people with emphasis on their names. So: 'Nathu Chacha, look who has come home?' This made for oddity, even rudeness in her speech, since conversation in the days of her husband's absence was unmarked by anything as dramatic or formal as the use of a person's name. But Jettamal did not live the daily life with these members of Sarla's family, and formality marked their quarterly affection for him. Fear and love was the return he offered. And real cigarettes. Early on in his marriage he learned to handle his dowry, to convey a pretext of mastering the trick of it with packs of cigarettes from the navy canteen. Among the numerous beedi-smoking Chachas, Nanas and Dadas, and even among the occasional Dadi—who having acquired the armour of age, no longer smoked her beedi while shitting in early dawn loneliness—Jettamal's cigarettes were as much a reason to pronounce him a good boy as was his habit of regularly returning from the sea to love his wife.

On this visit, wandering many lanes over from the lane of tin homes in which Sarla's family spread the length but not the breadth of the market, Jettamal came to the end of the morning. Here in a lane devoted to the sale of fish, he and his boys watched rahu and surma and king fish, silver and gray, some dead and others feebly gasping, gills desperate for the depleting oxygen of shallow plastic tanks.

Manish, horrified, said, 'Why do we have to eat them?' Jettamal, whose job in the navy was to wash and cut and keep ready kilo after kilo of vegetables, to knead and knuckle tubs of dough for rotis, but never to cook fine delicacies like meat or fish, loved nothing more than to come home and demonstrate the recipes he had learned only from observation. He boxed Manish gently on the ears and promised him he would enjoy the fish that night. Then he winked over the teary Manish's head at Ajay, and inviting Ajay's complicity in disparaging 'little babies who need to grow up,' Jettamal said, 'Son, I will put the charpoy out tonight. The weather is good and you can use my blanket. You keep an eye on this baby out there on the footpath. You never know, the mate of the fish he's going to eat tonight might be prowling the footpath looking for him.' Even this distance from Sarla, Jettamal felt something of her heat burning the back of his neck. When the bloody package of flesh and newspaper was handed to him he scowled fiercely at the fish-monger's boy and Manish and Ajay were cheered by the sight of their father's moustache, its curled tips trembling over his lips.

That night Jettamal did as he said he would. The fish was eaten by Manish who could not understand how raisins had come to be in its belly. Jettamal spun a long story about a ship full of grapes at rest at the bottom of the sea; and of fish that swam fat and sleek through the round windows of this ship. This made Sarla laugh though she was aware of Ajay silently transferring handfuls of his father's cooking to his mouth. Jettamal asked Ajay what he though of this raisin-stuffed fish and Ajay said, 'It's okay.' Soon after that Jettamal dragged the charpoy out and spread his blanket over the two boys. All in a row they slept, his boys, other boys, and men, many of them related and others friends, some on the ground, and some on beds. The rhythm of the traffic lurching by informed the rhythm of their sleep—not till its glare and noise abated at midnight-past would any of them drift to the deeps. Before he fell into an easy sleep, Ajay said to his mother as she bent over him, 'But I am longing for you and father.' Jettamal heard Sarla counsel his eldest son, 'You have to save that for the day now. You have to use that up during the day.' Again he felt that hot flush of her mounting his legs, reaching his neck.

✳

They sit on a mat spread over the dirt floor of their home, surrounded on three sides by tin walls filched long ago from the construction of the Chirag Dilli flyover. A bamboo pole lifts a bright blue tarp roof over their heads and this same pole divides their vigil from each other—Sarla on the one side of the pole and Jettamal on the other, both of them facing out from darkness to the haloed island of their sons asleep, and beyond that the busy street garlanded in headlights. He knows how to win her. 'Do you care for me?' he asks and swift comes her retort, 'I am married to you, aren't I?' Over their heads a brisk wind raises the tarp roof higher and beats it back onto the compressed air of their interior. Jettamal turns his head to hide his smile in darkness. His smile is for the familiar tone of mock dismay with which his wife is approaching him.

II

This girl who came to live in Ali Gaanv was tall and dark; her front teeth, the two sharp ones, stuck out. These two teeth of hers gave her smile a quality of something else, something that was not there anywhere else in her face. Something like the feeling when a word you hear and don't know the meaning of becomes suddenly full of meaning. Suppose if somebody tells you the meaning, then suddenly you know. These two teeth said something to me, the way they stuck out, even when she tried to close her mouth.

She smiled a lot when she came and people thought her a bit silly, given all that smiling. But everyone downstairs and everyone in all the other homes in Ali Gaanv thought her charming and Manish very lucky. She was popular with everyone and was invited to many homes. Some younger girls adopted some of her silly, show-off gestures. For example, this girl had the habit of raising her arms and pretending to adjust the chunni on her head to allow the cream and red and gold bangles stacked at her wrist to escape and slide down to her elbow, then she would suddenly drop her hand to her side and the bangles would rush to restack—a plastic clack!—at her wrists. For a few months after her arrival, girls too young to draw a chunni over their heads went around copying her—adjusting invisible chunnis, using their tongues for the 'clack' their fewer bangles could not make.

At first everyone called her 'Dolly'. Later she started correcting those who still called her 'Dolly'. The name was hers. But after her belly began showing, she felt she needed a new name, probably to better fit the dignity of her status as an expectant mother. Around Ali Gaanv it wouldn't be surprising to find any number of girls come there in marriage, never murmur two words of disagreement when mistakenly or purposely called by the wrong name, and years later go mad trying to remember who they really are. But one thing can be said about Ali Gaanv. And it is this: people in Ali Gaanv are an amiable lot. A girl may be hit for any reason. But she can also change her name for any reason. And most people here had no trouble calling her by the new name she gave herself.

Her first night in Ali Gaanv the upstairs was left empty for the newlyweds. Otherwise, normally, other than me, many of the downstairs kids, and even the landlord's nephews from next door, will crawl up there to sleep with Manish and me. The emptying of our room ended up troubling not only me but all the parents of these children who had to find places for them that night. I moved my bed-roll up to the roof, though Manish kept urging me to take the rest of my things also. But January is no time to sleep on the roof, and as I pointed out to my brother there was little in the house that was separately mine or his—even the single comb was both ours, and days he tucked it into his pocket and left before I woke, I was left to wander Ali Gaanv with a bush on my head.

That first night in Ali Gaanv it was easy to see this girl was full of fear. Probably she was first and foremost frightened of Manish. The funny thing was she was at least as tall and broad as he was. But their marriage was at the end of a bloody courtship; and Manish, ugly since birth, was uglier still on their wedding day. He had started at the wrist and in the two years he chased after her, his knife had worked its way past the inside of his elbow, up to his shoulders and laid even the chin and cheek open in shiny welts.

The cutting was difficult for Manish, but in Ali Gaanv it is a popular way to convince a girl. He begged my help. I drank with him, which is the only help I could give him. And then I watched him. Always, he was frightened, then I saw him hating himself for being afraid, then I saw him hating her for driving him to this madness. It was cursing her that he drew the knife. Often he could not control his hand and just chopped at his arm, crying and cursing. But when he was done he talked only about her goodness and could not wait to take the bus to Badarpur border where she lived.

On the bus he strained his eyes looking past the crowd of shoulders and necks to get a glimpse of the pahadi area between Ali Gaanv and Badarpur. He imagined getting to her house and persuading her parents to allow him to take her for a walk to the market. He imagined bringing her instead to the green and grey velvet of these gorges. He imagined clasping her as he helped her climb down to where water pooled between rocks. Clasping her he would refrain from any expression of pain but sensing something she would pull back the sleeves of his white shirt and seeing the gleam of a fresh wound she would look at him with love in her eyes. All this he imagined while standing in the aisle of the bus, swaying in the grip of hips tightly bound to his.

Manish is a small man. He will never understand that Dolly's parents, who were on the lookout for a tall groom for their peepul tree of a girl, only agreed to the match because he had frightened her with the fervour of his courtship. His courtship had destroyed her sleep—sleep in which she dreamt Manish brooding at the foot of her bed. Once asleep she was fearful of waking to find the dream realised, and awake she was afraid of the power of her nightmare. In this state between sleep and waking she decided the intensity of the fear she felt was the intensity of love and convinced her parents to let her go with him.

Of course there was more to it than that. When she was pregnant I took her regularly to the hospital, at first on the bus but when it was nearly time for the end then we went by auto. During one of those trips she turned to me and gesturing at everything that was rushing by outside the auto she said smilingly, 'This feels like a dream. It's hard for me to believe this is real.' I knew she was lonely, but it made me cringe to see this proof of how horribly lonely she was, of how little she must see in her days locked up in Ali Gaanv. In the years I listened to her talk endlessly about herself I never questioned the fancy reasons she ascribed to her actions. But I did come to know there was little she did that wasn't born from her loneliness. In her parents home she must have been lonely enough to have wanted to go with Manish.

From afternoon to evening, the day he took her from her parents' house, three of us kept Manish company, first to Old Delhi to the courthouse and then to the temple and then so he could give us a treat, to Haldiram's. She had called three of her friends who did not come. And her family members, who were not happy, stayed away as well. So there was only us as guests; and she couldn't have looked more frightened by the time we got to Haldiram's. Inside, nobody could think of anything to say, except for things like, 'This food is well prepared.' In fact none of us had ever eaten in a place like this and it took us a long time to understand how to get a seat or food. She did not eat till we forced her to.

Outside, it was already dark though it was only four o'clock. It felt like a dust storm was coming. Even in a fancy place like that with its air conditioning, its walls covered in tile, and its glass through which we had to point at the food to order, the windows chattered, loosening with the wind. We behaved normally as if we were used to a place like that, but our chairs kept scraping on the floor when we moved and we were all thinking about what would happen next when we took the newlyweds back to the room. We looked in one another's eyes and saw that this was what we were thinking. Then each of us looked secretly at her; and she was thinking the same thing. Then it seemed as if we somehow would all arrive together to the other side of the moment in the night we were all so intently imagining. I had to shake that idea from my head. I realised that of course only Manish and she would travel that moment, and looking toward him I could see that Manish was getting angrier and angrier at all of us that he had brought there for a treat.

That was when she smiled and said something in Manish's ear. And he laughed. And she touched the sleeve covering that arm of his, which I immediately pictured in my mind with all the scars covering it. He smiled broadly at her and turned his palm up on the table so she could let her fingers graze this bit of him that wasn't ugly. He told her to repeat what she had said and she tried and she was never able to say it loud enough for us to hear. Finally, he took over and told us; hearing her words repeated, she laughed the loudest of all.

'Feed me,' she had whispered in his ear, 'like this, everyday'. He was going to be happy with her. I knew it from that moment. We turned the whole thing into a joke. When the bill came, Manish flashed the amount at us; it was for around something like Rs 345. Manish said, 'When I get a Rs 15,000 job then we will eat here every day. Our friend Yusuf said, 'Sure, you had a job like that just last month, didn't you? Doing a P.O.P. job should get you at least that much every month.' She asked us what P.O.P was and I told her, 'It's what we say for our job. We do the work of plaster of Paris.'

I was quiet that night, not having much to say. As I said, I knew he was going to be happy. From that moment forward his happiness was assured. And though she went back to looking frightened I knew her happiness was also assured.

I won't try to explain why I dozed on the stairs that whole night, listening to their quiet breathing coming from the room that I was going to argue my way back into at the earliest. As I said before, the roof is no place to sleep in January. The stairs were no good, either. Early in the morning when I heard her coming to the door I woke and crawled, dragging my quilt, back up the twisting stairs. Downstairs the landlord and his family were asleep. All of them had come out to meet her the previous evening and looked her over, all the while thinking the same thought we at Haldiram's had shared.

That first morning after she came to live with us, I would have kept crawling up to the roof but she had already made it to the downstairs lavatory. From behind the green curtain that is hung there in place of a door I could, in the silence of all the sleeping-breathing, hear the sound of her crying. The smell of her using the toilet pushed up the stairs. Manish woke and crawled out to sit on the step below mine. He whispered to me for as long as she was downstairs, and then hearing the sound of water hitting the pot he scrambled from the steps. A long time passed and then came the sound of water churning a second time from the cistern. I couldn't imagine what she was doing except maybe more crying. I stayed back behind the curve of the stairs and after she came back to the room I listened to them making the little conversation they knew to make at that point.

✳

I like to tell the story of how this girl came to Ali Gaanv. Though I never got used to her new name I knew her for long enough to get used to how she changed and stayed the same. I have told this story a few times to a few people and many times to myself. This girl went on to have a baby boy, and when he was a little older than one, Manish and I and this girl quarrelled. It was about work and about money. I made the purchases for work, and after cutting the cost from our earnings we had always divided the money between us. One day she said I was taking too much money from them since I ate her cooking for free. I asked her if she was going to charge Manish and the baby to cook for them. I knew that sounded strange but when I thought of all the mornings I had sat in the kitchen with her after Manish left the house, the times she had talked about her days with her brothers and what they had done together, about the contest to see who could suck a pebble longest, which had ended with her swallowing hers, when I thought about all this I couldn't see how she could talk about the cost of plaster of Paris and the cost of food all in one breath. But that's the way it was. I left off living that way, shuffling between the room and the roof. The last time I saw her she was wiping the floor, spreading the piss of her son which was shining and then drying as fast as the sun shone into the room.

The last thing I want to say is about her hunger. That first night when I slept on the stairs outside the room, she told Manish a long story about falling off a tree when she was little in some village in Bihar. The story went on and on about how few fruits there were in trees and how high she would climb to get to a last guava or hard green peach. At the end of the story we, all three of us, were sleepy. She spoke in her sorrowful voice, 'When I was little, I never knew what food I liked.' I woke up when I heard this and strained to catch the rest of her words. She said them to herself, full of the wonder I was feeling inside me, 'Never knew what tasted good. I just ate food when I got it. I never knew.' This is the last thing I can say about this girl. I mostly remember her as words, and her teeth, never as a full picture of her, of how she looked, just the words I used then to talk about her, and still use to talk about her.

III

The construction of the house is now at a point where Dhruv is anxious that he shouldn't miss a single detail. Where before there had been a deep pit, its mud walls squared by hands and shovels, now there are machines obstructing his view, and the handful of workers have multiplied to scores. In between their scurrying bodies Dhruv glimpses a meshwork of steel knitting itself under their feet. He cannot grasp the miracle in all its minute parts: the workers, their tireless multiplicity, the pebbles that are ground in a steel drum to the tune of an ocean's roar, the intricate dance of baskets loaded with two sets of shovels scooping twice each from the wet mound regurgitated by the drum, and the heft to transfer the heap, a basket at a time, out to the site where the floor is emerging. Times he knows the miracle is anything but a miracle: at the mouth of the cement mixer the man rising with the load to his head is sometimes old and breaks his motion to tremble briefly on bent knee before the final swing up. Then Dhruv sees the same man reach the end of his plank-walk to throw the cement with a motion so precise he is convinced again that this work is easy because each of its parts are minute, and only the whole must hurt.

If he could choose, Dhruv would like to be one of those men who smoothes the cement with the flat piece of wood with its fixed handle. The lumpy glistening cement under the hands that hold this tool achieves a milky quality as it spreads so flat and so real that Dhruv sees the picture from a magazine of a floor laid with rugs and furniture. Other workers appear ruthless in their swift motions, as if they would tear down rather than build. The women, he cannot see in the same way; something in the roll of their hips and the glimpse of their bellies will not permit him to see them as cruel. They are, some of them, carrying head-loads, as the men are. But most of them are stacking bricks in counts of five, and what he sees is their indifference. He would not be indifferent, he thinks. He would, if he could choose, be the man who, caressing the building with the wooden tool, shapes it. The merest fragment of what shape would emerge from his trowel—the shape of his mother's shoulders—disappears in the slipstream of larger plans but not without first shaping those plans; the thought of his mother has him dreaming of mastering the magic to build her a house.

He misses the bus he is waiting for. He forces himself to begin the wait for the next one without once crossing the road to get closer to the construction site. But within minutes he is convincing himself that the next one will not come for another ten minutes, and that he will do a better job this time of calculating what ten minutes might actually be. So he runs back and forth between the stop and the site, and when he misses yet another bus simply decides to give up and heads to the field near his home where he can find enough numbers of other children in similar predicament with whom to begin a day-long game of cricket. The bus, once missed, then twice missed, is no longer real to him. The destination he will now fail to arrive at, was never real. Although the ocean roar of the cement mixer had almost made it vivid in his mind.

Midway through the day his four friends on the field abandon the game and head to a meal they will buy and share with the bits and pieces of currency in their four pockets. Dhruv still has the money he was meant to use for the bus ride to his Dada-Dadi's home. Though hunger calls him, he keeps his hands stuffed in his pockets, jiggling the change and pivoting on his heels in an attitude of indifference as his friends drift away on the long, dusty road. When they are out of sight he crawls into the shade of a tree and tries to nap his hunger away. To go with the other children to the market would be to risk getting caught by his father who waits daily for work at the very tea shop his friends will buy bread-pakoras from. This time his father's hand will rise against him. This is the third time he has missed the bus to his grandparents. This is the third time he has failed the charge of collecting his grandparents' trunk from their old home. This is the third time he has pulled away from the unreality of their disappearance from his life. Lying under the shade of the tree he remembers the sound of the cement mixer and again his fingertips tense with the need to build— something real. The sound of the building he knows he can build— hasn't he studied the building of it in all its parts—would be the sound of the ocean, which is the sound his Dadaji had held to his ear in the shape of a shell, larger than any he, or anyone else in Delhi has ever seen. Could his Dada-Dadi be in the ocean now, he wonders, swimming as fish? Wherever they are now, he thinks, they are together. But he dismisses that thought as having no basis in reality. The reality is they lived together, were killed together; what happens after death is unknown.

The need to divide the real from the unreal is the obsession of Dhruv's childhood and has marked him, at least in his own eyes, as different, better perhaps, than all those around him. He is fierce in his loyalty to the real. As young as two or three he refused to play with toys, and would only swing a real hammer and pound the real nails that were scattered everywhere in his Dadaji's home. Now, it is real that Dada-Dadi are no more. It is real that Dadi's old body when uncovered in front of him was smaller than his own. It is real that they were both laid out and washed clean on the same piece of wood, an old door they had once laid flat on top of bricks to create a platform on which to display their hammers and other tools for sale. It is real that he saw the deep brown of their blood diluting in the wash water to stream down their sides, to flow from there ever more diluted down the gutters of the impassive street. He feels sleepy and comforted by the real. He sleeps till the sun is nearly setting. When he wakes he is lonely. Many new games are now underway in the field. His old friends have not come back. He has nowhere to go but home. What is unreal is the plan he had carried with him, since before his grandparents' death, to leave home, to leave especially his father, to go live with them.

When he had complained about his father to her, his grandmother had said, 'Manish was such a good boy when he was little. But I should have known. The least little thing he did wrong he thought marked him as bad. After that, he would only do wrong. The child could never see all the space there is between black and white, good and bad.' All of this had not mattered to Dhruv. He had laid his head on his grandmother's lap and said that she should keep him. She would not have that. 'You have to forgive your father,' she said. 'He cannot forgive himself.'

Thinking about this now makes him angry at his grandmother. Briefly he allows himself to believe that she died taking his grandfather with her so they wouldn't have to take him in. Now he is stuck with his father who won't let him touch one thing in the house without shouting at him. 'Take your hands off that bag. You will drop that bag. Then who will pay for the materials tomorrow on the job?' And the hard hand, gripping him by the back of his neck to shake him, to buffet his head, to push him away, reaches to touch his mother's beautiful shoulders. 'See this,' the voice grumbles, 'this son of yours is back again. Fourteen years old. Won't do a simple job. I have collected all the trunks and he only has the little one to bring and he won't do that simple thing. How many times have I to go all the distance to Chirag Dilli? Maybe he thinks his job playing cricket is more important. Maybe he thinks that's how we eat roti in this house, on his cricket-hero earnings.' His mother turns to his father, not to him. His mother looks with anxious love at his father, not at him. And then his father says in his loudest just-got-a-job voice, 'Listen, I've just got a job. Tomorrow. In Amar Colony. A big three-storey place. Brand new construction. I convinced them I have the men to do the whole thing.' His mother looks with gratitude at his father, not at him.

Dhruv wants to tell his mother that he can do more than plaster of Paris. That someday he will build her a house. A house in the shape of . . . But he can't remember what shape he had wanted the house to take. His brow furrowed, he bends over the homework spread on the bed and tries not to listen to his parents whispering by the stove. Plans, they are making. Plans that are not real. Plans to send him to school, where he does not want to go, and from where in the past he ran away to his Dada-Dadi's on a regular basis. Now where will he run to? This conversation of his parents is a familiar one. It follows a rutted path, dug bumpy but deep in their relationship. 'He is like your brother—a dreamer,' she whispers. 'What makes you think my brother was a dreamer?' Manish whispers back. 'How does a dreamer know to calculate the cost of plaster of Paris so there's always a kick-back in it for him?' She subsides. Manish continues, 'Why do you take his side? After all these years why must you take his side?'

Dhruv had met his Uncle Ajay at the funeral. Ajay had stayed away these many years from the family, removing himself from the family as far as he could get—to the Kashmiri Gate side of Delhi. Dhruv had been struck by the height of his uncle and by the calm with which he conducted himself as he performed all the duties falling to him as the elder son. His own father had talked big, cried handsome tears, talked even bigger about his willingness to undertake the full cost of the funeral. Dhruv scorned this talk, trying instead to emulate his newfound uncle's calm. From the bed Dhruv calls out to his parents who are across the room, still whispering by the stove, 'Ajay Chacha is real.' His father takes the stick from the corner and waves it threateningly, but is in fact laughing. 'Is there a day that goes by,' he says, 'where I don't have to show you some of this love?' Again he waves the stick, brandishing it close to Dhruv's legs.

Dhruv ignores his father. What is real he thinks are the long nails on the hands of the man who looks beseechingly into his eyes when spreading his hand flat and light on Dhruv's arm. Twice now this same man has stood in the market close to him and brought his hand to rest there. Dhruv wants to ask his grandfather what this means. How does it compare to the times when he has had his crotch grabbed by boys at his school? He wonders about telling his grandfather that he too has done his share of yanking and twisting the crotches of smaller boys. Then he remembers his grandfather is no more and wonders how he can find his way to Kashmiri Gate and whether his uncle will be anything like Dadaji? I can go live with Ajay Chacha, he thinks.

The roof is unbearably cold at night. He sits on the stairs, unwilling to go into the room. Later, he thinks, when they are done in there. He begins mentally packing what he will take when he leaves. A gift for Ajay Chacha, but what gift? He knows so little about his uncle. He will first have to collect his Dadaji's trunk. The shell is in that trunk. It will make a fine gift for Ajay Chacha. If when he gets to his Dada-Dadi's home, if somehow his Dadaji would come to him and allow him to ask one last question, he knows what he will ask: Why am I afraid of the trunk? Unbidden, the answer comes. He has been afraid that without his grandfather the shell will no longer yield the ocean. He is too old to cry, so he concentrates on separating his ideas— the real ones from the unreal ones. Then he thinks of one more question. If Dadaji were to come one last time, he would like to ask him about the men at the construction site who, laughing and pushing each other, had lined up that morning by the bus stop to receive leaf-bowls of a yellow mush. I wonder what that was, he thinks. They kept getting their bowls filled again, and again. After them came the women. They, like the men, and after them the children, had all laughed. I wonder what they were eating, and if it was sweet.

Jeans

RIPPED

The son of a bitch. I gotta wonder, you know, if the cops are going to call. Gotta sit here wondering. And Kareena's still not talking to me.

Of course she's not, you Bachchan. Get that headband off your head. You confused or something? Girls don't dig that homosexual metrosexual thing.

Cut it out. You're messing it up.

Cut eet out. You're messeeeng eet up.

Shut up, yaar. I'm trying to tell you. I'm so stressed right now. I gotta wonder, yaar, if the cops are going to call me, or if they're going to just show up, or what. What do you think? Will they just go over to my place? Dad's not home all day. So, that way, I'm saved. But it would freak my mom out. She would just freak out.

Nothing's going to happen. So some asshole wrote your licence plate down. So, what the fuck? You think those assholes know anything about getting the cops involved? Tell me, huh, how you let some asshole take your number.

He didn't get my number. My licence plate, yaar. I told you we were on the way to catch the Bond movie at Priya. I was just going by, you know that corner where the road curves just before the roundabout, the one with all the little huts; right damn in the middle of the street they go build that crap. Kareena, the bitch, was sitting there back of me, giggling and poking at me, in those hot jeans of hers—Hilfigers. Poking at me, you know, with her skinny little butt. There was like this metal thing sticking out in the road. I think that's what happened. This metal thing. And I was thinking, gotta avoid that. Can't jolt the bitch queen in the back. Her Royal Highness, Queen Kareena.

Leave it, yaar. Tell me what they said after you hit the guy.

I didn't hit the guy. Get it straight, okay? I just ran over his foot. And get it, okay, his uncles and stuff came out from these huts and said not to worry, that he is an idiot. He is always standing out there on the street waiting to be run over. It's not like I was drunk or anything, okay? I just fricking ran over some idiot's foot, okay? Some idiot who just hangs out waiting to get run over, okay?

Why're you so worried? Listen, his uncles said that. Then everything's cool. Just chill.

Yeah, his uncles were cool. But then some brother of his comes out and stands there in front of my bike and gets out this notebook and starts to write my licence. I'm not believing this. Where does someone like that get a notebook from?

It's all show.

I should have stepped off the bike and kicked him once. Right there. But Kareena, the bitch, is moaning away. Its then I see she's landed on the street and these guys are looking at her. I'm thinking, shit I don't want to play the hero. Not for Kareena. Not me. So I got off and hauled her up and all these uncles are saying, like, it's all right son. You didn't do anything wrong. And I'm like, no shit. The idiot's out there trying to get run over. It's not like I tried to run him over. It's not like I was drinking or anything. I just got Kareena on the bike and we got out of there. And the whole time this brother guy is standing in front of my bike with the notebook in his hand, blocking my way and everything; I had to turn the front wheel so I could steer around him.

You should have given him one hard kick. That would have set him straight.

How could I? I had Kareena behind me moaning away about how her Hilfigers are ripped. Not a scratch on her, but she has to moan because her frickin Hilfigers are ripped.

STITCHED

Today, this pile of jeans. Yesterday also it was jeans. Jeans every day. Doesn't the Boss ever get an order for anything other than jeans these days? All these hems are ruined. Make them new again he says. How do you take old clothes and make them new again? Well, that's the work of magic, isn't it? But how to work magic when this needle won't push through this cloth? Cut the torn hem and re-stitch with orange thread. Why orange? This one will be too short when I am done. Better make this one into capris.

Money? Always check the pockets for money. People forget all kinds of things. Children forget the most.

Playing card. A cheater probably.

Marbles. Kala's boy will be happy. Kala.

Rubber bands.

Hairpin. Only thing a woman will forget.

सवाल का जवाब दीजिए: मातृभाषा कौन सा हैं? (a) English (b) तमिल (c) बंगाली (d) हिन्दी

Must be an exam paper. Cheaters everywhere getting ahead. An honest man suffers.

Ah! Ten rupees. This is mine. Last week there was that lucky kabaadiwallah on TV—found a packet. Lakhs and lakhs. My luck's never worth more than ten.

Now look at this stupidity:

K I love you
Do you
love
*   me?*

Stupid! Stupid! I will never have luck. Only love. Always only the thick wads of love, never any money. Love is for people who have money and wear jeans to show off their money. And it's their women who come here and tell me to take in the legs and make everything tighter. I say, stand them in a row, with their legs apart and pinch the cloth up their legs. 'This much tight you want?' 'Higher', they say, 'higher'.

Look here. Look at this pile of garbage—more love. Must be someone with more time than he knows what to do with. Time enough to write a love poem:

Love is beautiful.
Like my girl in her jeans.

that hug her thighs.
She sways like the grass she lies on,
does the switch side butt slide,
to un-peel—a tether for her ankles.

Now she is the climber.
Now she is the coconut limb
and the fruit swilled
fermented in blue denim.

Filth and nonsense! They go to school to learn such filth? That's what's wrong with these fools who have so much money they sit around thinking up filth and garbage. Garbage!

You wouldn't have called it garbage. Nothing was garbage to you, Chacha. I'll sew this scrap of paper into this placket—a placket in memory of you. This is as good a memorial as you'll get. Some of your love to serve the public. I'll sew it in your name. It will fall apart in someone's wash, seep into the water, stain everything; bits of it will cling to everything in the wash, spreading the love you believed in.

Why not? Elsewhere love is expensive stuff and here I can give it away. I'm rich in it. It piles up here for free. It comes here in every other pocket I check—there it is: crumpled, ripped and stained love. Love, I don't need. Chacha, you would have disagreed. You said, 'Believe in love.' Now where are you, Chacha?

Money is what I believe in. You always said that's what was wrong with me. If I wasn't thinking about money all the time I could be happy working here. How to want to be happy working bent over the needle, high up on this shelf where the ceiling presses on my back, needle puncturing my fingers—'Be careful, don't get blood on the cloth'? Dogs live better than this. They roam free the whole day and still get their feed. Unfold my body in the evening, go down the ladder to dry roti and sleep at night between the machines. Get up in the morning and pay for a toilet to shit the same roti. Then bent over, earn the next one. You figured out how to be happy doing that. Good or bad, I won't. I'll pay with my anger, pay for this unhappiness. I'll kill before I live on this shelf and be happy.

Why didn't you teach me something other than this misery? Something to make me money. Think—if I had money I would have love and happiness. Money can buy love. But it never works the other way around, does it? So which is more powerful—money or love? People are so easily careless with their love—leave it to rot in their pockets. There now, I have sewn that bit of love tight into the cloth. Someone with money—so much money that he is careless with it, leaves it to rot in his pocket, someone with money must change my destiny. You. You died, folded in two, like some yogi, and hunched up like a camel. And dead. No money and no love for you.

I am young and I stand straight. I'll find love. Kala. Just need a clean piece of paper and a pencil in this pile of garbage.

K I love you
Do you
love
    me?

SOLD

The problem with your jeans is the way they separate your behind—each behind shows separately. Each one, its own separate thing for everyone to see.

You didn't have a problem with that when you wanted to marry me.

I'm not talking about then. These jeans are new. You said you wouldn't buy anymore, and you got another pair.

Only because you disappeared my old ones from the clothesline. I know it was you who took them. And anyway these are not new. They're seconds.

Old, new—you are too fat for them. The old ones were tight to begin with, and ever since we got married you are fatter and they got even tighter. You should see yourself from the back. Each of your behinds is separate and your underwear cuts each one into half again. See—like this orange—you're full of sections. Your behind jiggles in four different sections. Disgusting!

You never think twice about what you say!. I am not fat. I look good in jeans. You are saying that because you just want to control me. You think you married me and you can now control everything I say and do. You won't even let me cross a street on my own. When I check to see if cars are coming you say, 'What are you looking at? I am here, aren't I?' Well, how do you think I crossed before you got here, huh? When I ask the autowallah what he will charge to go to Lajpat Nagar you have to speak in between: 'Why are you asking? I'm here to ask, aren't I?' You are. You are. You are. And the more you are here, the worse it is for me. Is this what being married is supposed to be?

I never liked you in jeans. I said so then, before we married. I say so now. And you betray me—every single time you wear those trashy things.

You didn't. You didn't say that then. And you are not even going to answer me about how you control everything I say and do?

The way men look at you. You betray me. You are a traitor.

How dare you call me that? How dare you? For the last—how many days, how many times—you've been saying that to me. I've suffered you saying that. I have been putting up with this suffering. I won't let you. Don't come near me. Don't ever touch me again if I'm so dirty to you.

Dirty is this room. Like a ragpicker's room. You clean other people's houses but you won't clean your own. I must do all the cleaning. If I don't wash the dishes they lie there. The dog shits by the front door of the house and three days I step over it wondering when you will clean it. Then I can't bear it anymore. I must clean it. I come home and you can't boil a cup of water to give me tea. Touch you? Who betrays me every day, in every way? Hah!

That's right, take the phone. Go ahead, call your mother. Tell her she was right. Tell her you made a mistake. Tell her I don't make tea when you come home from work. Tell her I wear jeans. I never promised. You hear? I never promised to stop wearing jeans. I said I would give it up only for those times when we go to the village. You want to poison me to your mother—call her, tell her. Why not? Then I can wear jeans even there in the village.

Never! I'll, I'll—

What will you do, huh? You will stop lying with me? You couldn't stop when we went to the village. Didn't bring condoms, so you had to take the chance without a condom. You couldn't stop even with your mother in the next room. You couldn't stop even for the pain it caused me afterwards. 'Don't worry I'll pull out. Nothing will happen.' Nothing happened at the Clinic, right? Now you will stop—now?

Starting tomorrow I never want to see you wearing jeans again. I'll get rid of these ones also, if I have to.

I know you. All night you will lie as if my body is rotten and you cannot bear the touch of it. In the middle of the night you will put your arm on me and pretend it's in your sleep. You think I'm fooled? Call your mother. I'll be the one to tell her. You sleep with a dirty girl—one who wears jeans that separate her behind. So tight. You like it at night.

PROMOTED

I'll pretend to write. When they're seated I'll ask them if they'll fill out the form. This is hard. This is hard. Wait, he looks good. He's looking at me. I bet I could get him to fill it out. This is hard. This is hard. Count them. Filled: one, two, three, four, five, six, seven, eight. Whole day and only eight so far. At least they could have given me a pair of jeans to wear. Crazy orange blouse. What a revealing, horrible, have to keep hiding the strap, ugly colour, horrible, horrible, blouse. Can't breathe. If anyone sees me. I wish they had given me jeans to wear with this blouse. I would happily wear the blouse, if only I had a real pair of Hilfigers to wear with them. The Ganguly servant girl is always wearing jeans. A servant wearing jeans! I don't know who she thinks she is. She wears them so tight. I saw the label when she hung them to dry—Hilfiger. Of course, not original.

Take home the grand prize—an LCD TV—by filling in this simple form. Also win iPods, digicams and other exciting prizes.

Everyday. You are many people. One jeans.

Wear it and Love it. Hilfiger for all the many moods of your life.

Good afternoon, Sir. I'm with Hilfigers jeans company.

Uh. No. No, thank you.

Sir, it's a promotion like a lottery. Your name will be drawn—

No , I have to take this call. Please.

Sir, I can—Sir, for the many moods of your life. *This is hard. This is hard.*

Good afternoon, Ma'am. I see you are looking at my promotion.

Your promotion?

Ma'am if you will fill out this form you can win the grand prize—an LCD TV. And also many other cool prizes like iPods, digicams, and other exciting prizes.

I don't think so.

Yes, Ma'am, it is true. You would be winning.

No, listen, I don't give my information out.

I understand, Ma'am. Ma'am, if you tick mark the box here then no one will get your information. We won't be sharing the information with other companies.

You'll have my phone number? My address?

Yes, Ma'am.

I don't think so.

Yes, Ma'am.

All you need to do is fill in this form and hand it over to the Hilfiger promoter to win prizes galore. Winners will be announced on www.hilfigerbharat.com between 1st March and 15th March.

Conditions apply. Refer contest leaflet for detailed terms and conditions. Product prizes shown here may differ from the actual ones rewarded. Accessories shown may not be part of standard equipment.

Hilfiger 420s offer you:
   a)   personal fit and flair
   b)   style in a variety of shades of your choice
   c)   details like topstitching and riveting
   d)   all of the above

Which jean company has personified freedom and style since 1992?

The contemporary style and international cool of Hilfiger is best represented by Bollywood heartthrob
   a)   Saif Ali Khan
   b)   John Abraham
   c)   Hrithik Roshan
   d)   all of the above

I don't like any of them. If I had a choice to meet one person it would be Salman Khan. He's like my Kushal. So mischievous and smiling all the time. Even when he is sad Kushal is smiling. Two days since he called. If I could just leave everything and be with him I would surely run away. Nothing can stop me from loving him. Three o'clock. When will this end? If Kushal's people ever find out that I am doing this. If Amma ever finds out. This is hard.

Good afternoon Ma'am. I am representing Hilfiger company with a promotion which can win you many exciting prizes.

I already filled one of those out at the other Barista.

Yes, Ma'am. Thank you, Ma'am. *Heeeelp me. Somebody heeelp me.*

OGLED

The way the land whizzes by, I know I am in a big country, a great country. Outside the train window the land whizzes by fast. I belong to this great country, not to a small village.

You want to eat?

No, I'm not hungry.

Beautiful, isn't it?

Yes.

Eat. You can't eat beauty. It won't fill you. Ha ha. Joke.

When? I'm not hungry. No, no, you go ahead. Actually, my stomach hurts.

So eat anyway. When it hurts it is usually hurting for food.

Now. Now my mother is lifting the cover. Now she sees the bundle of sticks I kept there. Now she knows I'm gone. Now she weeps. When? When will we reach? Tell me how it will be?

Arre yaar, what's to tell? All this beauty will vanish. Then there will be the city. It will be dirty. And you will be hungrier. But here is the good part. You will make money. Stick with me, friend. I will show you where to spend the money you make. Movies. Brilliant. Such action. Such tamasha. Jokes that will tear up your insides. You'll laugh so hard, Coca-Cola will vomit from your nose. Heroines with such big melons you get to see, big as can be. How do I know? You've seen Madhuri Dixit in that movie? Yes, you know the one. What a singer you are, yaar! You stand to make money in more ways than one. Well, let me tell you. She's gone skinny now, getting ready for a comeback. But the way she looked in that choli back then. Every girl in the city will give you a free show as good as that one, if not better.

You don't have to talk like that about her.

Who? Madhuri Dixit? You're joking. You have a thing for her?

No, about any woman. You don't have to talk like that about

any woman. How would you feel if somebody talked like that about your sister?

What? This is a joke, right? You're going to the city—to Delhi—and you're going to look at all the melons on show and you're going to be thinking about your sister. Why, you sister-fucker, what a dirty little mind you have, you little fucker.

You leave my sister alone. *Now she shakes Ameena awake. Now Ameena cannot hide the truth anymore. Now Ameena tells her I'm gone. Now Ameena cries and my mother throws herself on the ground. Now my mother will rise and push the pot from the fire. Now the food will spill into the fire. Now they will not eat all day. My mother! My mother!*

Listen, you little fucker. You've seen the melons on the movie heroines. I got a big surprise for you in the city. The city sisters, you see, they wear these pants—jeans. You ever heard of jeans? You get to see a whole second set of melons. You gotta hold yourself just thinking about those.

SOLD AGAIN

They were my favourite pair. I looked so good in them. I thought I would wear them at the party. But I wasn't sure. If everyone else turned out to be wearing saris or suits then I would be the fool. Took them in a bag and wore the green lehenga instead. The one that I bought to wear to that dance competition.

The dance competition—that was another fiasco. All that money I spent and I never got to wear the lehenga. The stupid ma'am made me wear a sari, Bengali style. Who the hell dances to 'Dola Re Dola' wearing a sari, and Bengali style at that? No wonder I didn't get a prize. Aishwariya Rai wasn't wearing a sari when she danced to 'Dola Re Dola'. I just ended up looking like a big fat pot. She had to go and starch the sari. Like wearing cardboard. What's the point of moving your hips when you're moving them inside a cardboard box? Certainly, the judges couldn't see. If they had gotten one look at me in my lehenga, like I had planned. Oh, what's the point? The judges would have looked and looked, the bastards. In the end, no matter what, they only give prizes for Kathak and Bharatnatyam. Kathak and Bharatnatyam! *Taaa Taaa Taaa Thaii Thaii Thaii*. Prizes for all that *Taaa* and *Thaai*. Prizes for girls whose mummies and daddies buy them proper dance costumes and dance lessons and *Taaa Thaii*. Forget it. I'm never going into a competition like that again. At least I got to wear the lehenga to the party.

But my favourite jeans! Ohhhhh. I'm an idiot. They're gone. Left them in the auto, in the back, in that plastic bag. What made me think to take the jeans? Just in case. That's me. Always thinking, just in case. Why couldn't I have just worn the lehenga and left the jeans at home? Or worn the jeans from the start? In that whole lot, not one of those boys would have stood a chance against me in my jeans. One of them would have had to love me. Everyone was staring at me in the lehenga which doesn't show hardly anything. Even the little waiter-boy. What did he think—I didn't notice how much he was staring at me? Little fellow. Where do they come from, these village idiots? I should have worn the jeans. That would have given him something to look at. Now I've lost them.

They were blue. But almost black. If there's anything wrong with my figure, it's only that I am short. Those jeans made me look tall. The trick is you have to be willing to wear tight jeans. Tighter than tight. And low. That makes you tall, no matter how short you start out. They were blue-black and tight and there was a braid of the same blue-black material, running down the middle of the front, from the top of my legs, not the waist, just the top of the legs where the body ends, where the legs come together, from that top to the bottom, down the front with little white glittery stones. I always wear loose hair with jeans. My figure is good. But my hair is really the best part of me. It's black. But it has a blue shine, and it's really thick. Long and loose.

Oh, I'm an idiot. What's the point? Hair. Figure. What's the point? I've lost my jeans. What's the chance the autowallah will drive all the way back here to return them? He'll know for sure they are mine. But he'll give my jeans to someone else. Or sell them. The way he kept looking at me in the mirror, he should return my jeans to me. They were the best jeans—with faded blue stripes running down all over and with a flare at the bottom and they fit so well. They were low, but not too low.

RETURNED

Bhaiya, you said you would take them back if they didn't fit.

What's the matter with them? You keep them. They will look so beautiful on you. They will suit you so nicely.

Bhaiya, how do you know what suits me? I have to return them. They don't fit.

They don't fit? How can that be? I myself remember measuring them and only then you took them. They will fit you well, Madam.

Listen, it's not my fault you don't have a trial room.

Trial room? You think you can get such a good price in a shop with a trial room?

You said I could return them if they didn't fit. Look, I don't want my money back. I just want you to give me a different pair, okay? Just give me another pair in exchange.

Madam, I can give you a different pair. But no pair will look as good on you.

Listen, can I just see what else you have?

Madam, you come back in ten-fifteen minutes. I haven't made my first sale yet. My bohni time hasn't come yet. You come back in fifteen minutes. Maybe half-hour. I will make my first sale and you can have another pair in exchange.

What bohni time? What nonsense? You said if they didn't fit, I could come back for another pair. You give me another pair in exchange and I will leave. Here, you keep these. Show me some other pair that fits.

Fifteen minutes only, Madam. I will make my first sale.

Look, I came to the market just for this. What am I supposed to do for the next fifteen minutes while I wait for your bohni, whatever? And you say fifteen minutes, ten minutes, half-hour; which is it? It takes half-an-hour to get here. I had to get my brother to drive me here. He is waiting in the car right now. It will take half-an-hour to get back. You've wasted more than an hour of my time already today. You give me an exchange right now. If I come back in ten minutes or half-an-hour how do I know if you will exchange then? How come you didn't mention all this bohni time nonsense yesterday when you sold them to me? I want my jeans now.

Nobody is saying you cannot have your jeans. Take them. Here. They are beautiful jeans. Anybody will be happy to have them. They are perfect fit jeans. I don't know why you want to return them.

What nonsense. Look I'm going to stand here till you give me another pair. You want to know the truth about why I'm returning these jeans? They are stained. You sold me old, stained jeans. And the stain—so terrible—in such a place. You think I am going away? I'll stand here and show anyone who comes by these stained jeans and then see if you make your bohni.

Madam, the jeans are new. How can you say they are not new? This is not a used clothes store. All these clothes are 100 per cent new, export quality, branded, Hilfiger brand. If they are so cheap it's because sometimes the order for export is too big and there is extra stock. Export surplus, Madam.

Give me my exchange jeans.

Madam, come back in fifteen minutes.

Give me the jeans now, or else.

If there is a stain madam . . . maybe when you tried it on. Sometimes that can happen. Even I have two daughters, Madam. I know these things. Not to say anything bad, you understand. But in God's name, Madam, I cannot give you an exchange right now. No, no don't throw it down like that. Come back. Okay, okay, you take a different pair. I'll give you different jeans.

The Large Girl

She watches *Devdas*, remote in hand, so the magic of instant access to any moment in its 184 minutes of sequined shimmer is hers. She is a large girl. I knew her in school. She was there in school as early as Standard II, she tells me. But I didn't see her till maybe VII or VIII. Overnight, she came to our attention because she grew boobs and kept popping her buttons. Then she did the long jump on Sports Day and her skirt did that thing cheap umbrellas do, spine buckling and bowl upturning to heaven. Then she landed, and she was so pink, I thought: tulip.

Everyone else was laughing. But there were some things I knew even then, maybe about the world, maybe about me. In any case, the last thing I wanted to do was laugh. What I wanted was to slip my hands down those trunk-like legs. My own were so inadequate. What must it be like, I thought, to have so much?

In VIII she brought in a biography of Marilyn Monroe. Held between desk and knee it circulated down the row, across the aisle, down row two, and so on through the class: girls in one half, boys in the other. We flipped to the marked 'hot' pages, to the forty or so pictures in black and white, there to give some meat to the printed word, which in any case we ignored. Unlike the black-market quality paper with their bleed-through words elsewhere in the book, these thicker glossy pages in the middle were adequate to the task of delineating each angled thigh's unsubtle and tight press to hide—what? Nipples pulled oblong by raised arms floated free in what was already let loose—levitating fruit—front and centre of head thrown back and wide arched smile inviting—what?

Pushpa, the idiot-mouse of our class, burst into tears. She was needed comic relief; the sacrificial victim of our collective misgivings. What had we seen and how would this act now mark us? There was a sense of class VIII's free period having been turned, in Sridevi Nair teacher's absence and with the aid of Janet's wicked pinkness, into a communal orgy. 'Quick, let's forget.'

She was there till XII, and I knew her as the nun's charity-case, the unclothed girl to steer clear of. The nuns would punish girls whose hems rode above their knees. How they allowed hers to creep up and up and stay there so that we were, I was, forced to obviate her—well, that's a question between the nuns and their gods. Obviate her, I did. There are no other incidents to recount till we reached XII—just the buttons, the jump that tuliped her, and Marilyn Monroe.

✳

Our last day in school, the girls wore saris, the boys wore suits, and we prepared to dance—girls with girls and boys with boys. The school's Annual Day that year had revolved around a historical play, set in the colonial period, written by a team of nuns and credited to the Head Boy and Girl. For the play we had rehearsed a waltz fifty times in a day: boys in suits were paired with girls whose mothers cut saris into some understanding of ball gowns. On the strength of this earlier experience, the nuns urged us, the evening we danced our goodbyes, to pair up: boys with girls. The Head Boy and Girl to their, and everyone else's, discomfort led the line-up and the rest of us, in one of those stray acts of shame-faced rebellion, refused to follow suit. And so it was I found myself in Janet's embrace, and for the five minutes our feet described a dip-rise-dip square on the floor, I examined anew the corkscrew self, the twisting slumbering worm of me that had longed for this. Her hands on my shoulders and mine at her waist, and before or during that last dip, hers travelled as did mine from there to here, and then very quickly there were samosas and autographs and true and false expressions of sorrow across the throng of a 120-odd crying-smiling-unfeeling-anxious-about-to-die youngsters.

In school she was presented, whether by herself or by the nuns or somehow—as an orphan. But here's the story she tells me now: her father arranged her mother's death—murdered her. He was an electrician—stripped the insulation off the wire and lined it up so her mother would be the one to turn on the washing machine. He basically, as Janet puts it, 'fried her'. I read a short story, Hitchcock's, once—same plot. Maybe her father read it too. But in his case the ending was different. Where Hitchcock's man kept his mouth shut and got away with it, Janet's father told his brother who turned him in. I have a brother and cannot imagine doing that—turning him in—no matter what the crime. Her father has been out of jail for some time. He's written her, and she wants me to go with her to meet him. What kind of man would write his daughter thirty years after murdering her mother and expect that she would want to meet him?

Her favourite story—she reads it out loud to me, in her favourite reading position, lying full length on top of me, her belly smashed into mine, book propped on pillow above my head—is 'Kabuliwallah'. She is addicted to my stomach. She likes that I am the one who has given birth and worked my way back to flat, whereas she ... Well, I like her large and soft. She weeps in the reading. Every time. But how am I to weep when this is the fifteenth reading, and with every turn of the page, she must shift her weight and belly must renew acquaintance with belly with that sweaty, burp-cheer sound I find so funny. She weeps some more. Then she gets angry and says: 'You don't understand me.'

And even on those occasions when I accept this as truth, and there are more of these occasions than not—she still pushes to the inevitable: 'How can you understand me? You are the little Miss Richie Rich who ignored me all through school.'

Here's what I tell her. Here's what I say that mollifies her: 'God, give me another life so that I can do it right next time. Another life, so I can appreciate you and love you as you deserve to be.' I deliver this without rolling my eyes. I don't shrug my shoulders or in any other way temper the fact that I mean this with all my heart. This life has not been enough and will continue to not be enough to love Janet. And it's not because her hunger is so beyond the pale. It just is the case that the love she wants is not in my means to give.

✳

Here's another story from the past that Janet's father's recent resurrection has laid to rest. For the longest time there was a rumour in school that she was not a complete orphan; that her father was alive, even if her mother was dead; that he was alive and—get this—sailing the seas, an Australian Sea Captain.

Why Australian? Don't ask me. She likes her stories sequinned. She likes them to shimmer. So she embroiders. Some of us embroider, and others of us will briefly hold in our hands a particularly fine piece of embroidery, so we can admire the journey the needle has taken.

We did not believe this story in school, although it would have accounted for Janet's name, her fairness, the breadth of her shoulders, her large bones. But she was not the first Anglo-Indian the rest of us had encountered, and her Australian-Captain-father only made the class titter. I know now where she got the story from. My daughter is eight and addicted to a character in a book series—Pippi Longstocking—an enormously self-sufficient orphan girl whose missing Sea captain father she claims is still alive—a Cannibal King marooned on an island.

My own father, mother, brother, daughter and husband are alive and well. My marriage has been a good one for nearly fourteen years. It was an early marriage. I agreed to marriage because I lacked the imagination then to see how else a girl might make a life. My imagination, Janet believes, has continued to be lacklustre, and so she attempts obligingly to fill in where she senses inadequacy.

When I loan her money for the one-plus-one in the Shahpur Jat area, she immediately has us moving in, not just my bed and dresser set which she admires, the cut crystal in the dining room display which is a wedding present from Mohan's parents, but also my daughter Rohini, and even Mohan's newest pup, Chetan. The thing about Janet's claim to the gift of imagination is that this imagination of hers too conveniently, it seems to me, skirts the truth.

We go through a phase where she questions me endlessly about Mohan—his likes, dislikes. Yes, the likes and dislikes of our lovemaking are uppermost in her thinking. I never feel it necessary to answer these questions. But I have told her what I thought of him when I first saw him. We met at my house with the parents around, his and mine. I don't count that as a first meeting. I never really saw him that day. No, the first time it was just the two of us was at the club near his parents' home in Anand Niketan. He had more or less grown up in that area, and he met me at the club entrance with this certain assurance, and we went inside this room and talked. We passed through the topic of exes quickly, and I teased him some and asked him what qualities in him had attracted these other girls. He looked so terribly pleased as he said, 'You'll have to ask them.'

✳

Then there was some fumbling when the waiter came, and he ordered club sandwiches for both of us. He apologised to me for not doing better with the waiter and told me then that this was his first time in The Room. The Room, being the room we were in, a room in which children were not permitted, a room meant For Adults Only. He had celebrated Diwali in childhood at this club and spent summers swimming in the pool and I suppose had become an adult and moved away before he could take advantage of adult privileges. He was feeling grown-up that day and so was I. So in the end I married, I think, because it was the grown-up thing to do and right that I should do it with this grown-up that I was becoming fond of.

Janet refuses to understand this story. 'Yeah, so you are fond of him. But tell me you have the hots for him and I promise I will believe you.' She doesn't really want my answer. 'You can't say it, can you? Yes to hots? No? No hots.' She thinks she is taunting me.

Or lying next to me, when I turn inviting her to spoon me, she will peel back instead and run her hand from my shoulder to my butt and slap me there and ask, 'What's his favourite part?' If I remain silent she will pinch me. 'Is it here, your butt? Men always like a woman's ass. They never think to like her elbows or her toes. Or maybe he has a foot fetish? Does he? Maybe he sucks your toes, heh princess?' It's no good keeping my back turned. She will move on from favourite body parts to favourite positions. I turn to her and busy myself nibbling her front.

She keeps a picture of Rohini, and one of Chetan with Rohini, along with the many others of me in her room. She would no doubt have a perfectly imaginative tale with which to dress up the addition of Mohan's picture to this tableau. I can't imagine what this would be. In any case, I tell her, 'No, it will make me uncomfortable', and refuse her the picture when she asks. With

Janet, the truth, if inconvenient, is something to be ignored. I can't live that way.

*

Janet and I first run into each other in the parking lot outside my gym. She is coming out of a shop in the same complex. It turns out to be a beauty parlour, and she turns out to be working there. We light up, standing between the cars, breaking my big rule about public smoking. It would take any busybody in that gym, to whom Mohan is known, seeing me smoking, for me to get into a lot of trouble. For all that Mohan is a chain smoker, I am not permitted to smoke. On the rare occasion, say if we are good and soused, on an anniversary, at Buzz, or better still at The Imperial, and if I beg and nag, then, maybe then, he'll light me one and hand it over.

But my girlfriends and I always smoke when we get together. We do it on the roof. I keep a mat rolled up on the stairs. We take it up with us when we go. Ours is a rented place, and I have done nothing by way of plants and things to beautify the roof. The mat serves to soften the crumbling concrete on which we crouch to prevent nearby tenants from invading our privacy. The mat is where Janet and I first kiss.

The first time we kiss, she lights a cigarette and passes it to me, and then she lights another one. We are talking, but not easily. After the cigarette in the parking lot, and the exchange of phone numbers, a month passes before I realise she will not be the one to call. I call. She comes over. There is the awkwardness of her taking in the toys scattered throughout the house—most of them Mohan's, I explain to her. I am not the gadget freak, and the endless updating is his way of flexing his muscles.

She is subdued downstairs, but loud enough on the roof, so I am relieved when finally we sit quietly, leaning back against the short wall. I wish for time to get the clothes cleared from the line before they get infected with our smoke. But it is also strangely peaceful as they stir, combing their shade-fingers of coolness over us with each breeze. My shoulder is touching hers and she slides down and rests her head on my lap and from there squints up at me. She is still as she was in school—large hands and long legs. I am still as I was—content to keep within myself; my inner curve yearning in its own circular fashion, itself. So then why am I unfurling as she reaches for my face, her one hand doing the bidding and the other still locked on to the cigarette? A second passes, her hand is on my cheek, and I follow her example, my free hand cradling her cheek, so we are both leading and following together into that first kiss.

It is not a kiss to get lost in—we are each of us balancing, one half engaged in not accidentally burning the other. She flicks her cigarette away and with both hands pulls my head to hers. But I don't have her sophistication or just plain old ease. I am still balancing as she searches my mouth—her tongue acrid, like Mohan's.

I take to leaving her. After the first, second, third, fourth time, she stops mourning and starts instead to throw me out. I leave and the leaving is unbearable to me. For a day or two I remain gone from her. My last memory of her is of a graceless shrug of dismissal, the slam of her eyes shutting me out.

I leave her for many reasons. The first time—when Rohini comes up the stairs to the roof one afternoon, and the metal stairs, instead of clattering as I had expected, absorb her keds' tread silently, and suddenly she is there—looking at us. 'Mummy', she says. She is wearing a stricken smile. She is saying with her eyes, 'I don't see you with a cigarette in your hand.' She is saying, 'I don't see the pack placed square between you and aunty.' 'Mummy,' she says, breathless from the run up the stairs, shamefaced from the discovery she has made. 'Nina threw the frisbee hard at Indrani, and now Indrani's nose is cut, and, and . . .' she says, riveted by the competing drama of the story she has come to share and the story she has just discovered, 'Indrani's nose has sooo much blood coming out of it. It's everywhere.'

For the next two days, I try to tell Janet we shouldn't smoke together. I even tell Mohan the truth: 'Janet and I were on the roof, and you know she smokes. Well, she lit me one, and the next thing Rohini was up there, and I think she saw us.' Mohan does not get angry. 'Let's see if Ro says something. There is no need to bring it up if she doesn't.' After two days he and I agree Rohini has forgotten. But I remain frantic that Janet should understand why we can't smoke up on the roof. The more she shuts her ears, the more determined I become that I will not only stop our little smoking ritual, but also that I will never smoke anywhere, for any reason, ever again.

I am supposed to go to her place some days later. I don't. A week passes, and she texts me: 'Talk?' I can't help myself. She greets me at the door, pulls me to her and kisses me on her side of the length of fabric she has hung in the doorway. My one hand automatically searches behind me for the wood beyond this cloth, till she imprisons my hand in hers, pulls it between us and slips something into it. Our foreheads are touching and we both look down to what our hands are doing—transferring fruit—light green and translucent, from hers to mine. Then, she looks straight into my eyes and hers are smiling. 'Amla,' she says. 'It will be the oral fix you need to quit cigarettes.' My mouth is already puckering. The fruit is sour and tense in taste, but leaves the mouth sweet and wet as if washed with rain.

We kiss, and I forget about the door. She shuts it in the end, pushes me ahead of her into bed. But the amla is really only for me, and afterwards she lights up as always, ashing her sheets, pillows, my hair.

The fighting continues. It becomes about her father. She insists she needs me with her when she goes to see him for the first time. I tell her, 'Faridabad is too far away. How will I account for a whole morning, afternoon, and evening?' She is stiff in anger: 'You spend the whole afternoon here. No problem.'

'But', I say 'I am always there to pick Rohini up at 3:30'.

'Tell your husband to get her this once.'

'No, I can't. He doesn't like to interrupt his work like that.'

'This is important to me,' she says.

I don't believe her. Her neighbour has told me that her father has already been by to see Janet. I wonder if perhaps they have met more often than this once.

I don't say to Janet: 'You're a liar.' I wonder why she wants me to see him. She has not repaid me the loan which I wheedled out of Mohan. I wonder if she is going to ask for more money; if, perhaps, her father needs money. I don't say: 'You're a liar.' Instead I say: 'No'. Then, 'The truth is I am a married woman. And a mother.'

She says, 'That's never been a problem. What's there in that?'

We are silent. I think about her father in her room. I wonder if he wondered what we—Rohini, I, and not to forget Chetan—are doing on Janet's walls. I wonder what story Janet concocted to explain us to him.

'Why do I have to meet your father?'

She regards me seriously. 'I just want him to know that I have a good life. And you are part of what makes my life good.'

But I feel stubborn. 'No', I say. Mostly I am thinking, 'Why do I like her? She is so vulgar.'

I cautiously tell friends from school that I have run into Janet, and their reactions are uniformly similar. I think it is Shilpa who says, 'She must have had a hard life,' and I concur.

The last time we are together at her place, she meets me first at the bottom of the stairs leading up to her flat. She is four floors up, and the walls all along the climb are repulsive, stained with the spit-splat of paan. On the second floor landing someone has lined up some potted plants on either side of their front door, and taped to the wall is a sign pencilled in Hindi: 'Spitting on Plants is Not Permitted.' On the flight up from the third floor landing she turns to me and says, 'You're having your period.' I nod, and she adds, 'I can hear your pad rustling.'

The very last time we are together, she kisses me under my stairs. She has thrown me out the week before when once again I refuse to accompany her to her father's. She says that he is asking to meet me. I am adamant in my refusal. At the end of a week's silence, she shows up and gestures to me from the service lane that fronts my place. I wave back to her from the upstairs balcony, more to reassure the flower-seller who is studying the proceedings, than to indicate any sort of welcome. But then she crosses the lane, comes in the gate to the front door, and I pull her in from there. She takes her hand out of her pocket and, glistening in her cupped palm, are two amlas. I rest a fingertip on one and gently rock it in her palm where it bumps repeatedly its sister-self. And again Janet and I are facing each other. She is my height, I realise: her largeness is all in her breadth. There is a way we line up—eye to eye—that feels like pleasure.

'Take it,' she indicates the amla with her chin. I take one, and she folds her hand shut over the other. 'You don't want us to continue?' she asks.

'No.' I am wooden. 'Janet, I don't want to be destructive in any way. In my life or yours. You have to understand that.'

'Tomorrow?' she asks, 'You won't change your mind?'

'No, Janet. Tomorrow, I won't change my mind.'

She kisses me before she leaves. This, our last kiss, is quick. It is a kiss of dismissal, but also sweet. In the lean of her face, I feel her eyelashes brushing mine, and her tongue has no anger to it; nor any persuasion.

A time will come—a time that is starting now—when I will no longer know her. I will attend the Jahan-e-Khusrau festival and, sitting in the last rows, I will be surprised to see Anju seated two seats away from me. We will press hands across people's laps, and I will be embarrassed as I tell her that I will come soon to pick up the tailoring I have left at her boutique some months before. She will laugh and say, 'I have kept it all together for you. It is ready.' Rohini will place her head in my lap and ease the mobile from my purse and proceed to play a game on silent mode. I will be irritated and will want to scold her to enjoy the music. Mohan will put a hand on my knee and will still me. We will whisper together and wonder who it is that owns the splendid house with lit banks of windows overlooking Humayun's tomb and the festival. 'They are so lucky, dining there on the roof top,' we will think. The next day, I will meet at a party one of the diners from the night before. And I will exclaim: 'This is such a small city. I never thought . . .'

At Café Turtle, I will overhear a man talking about Jhumpa Lahiri's *Interpreter of Maladies*, and the next day the same man will be at Confluence, with another woman this time. He will turn out to be an authority on steel sculpture. I will meet him, and he will talk shyly about his expertise. It will be on the tip of my tongue to say to him, 'What a small world we live in. Just yesterday . . .' But he will break in and say much the same words to me.

I will stand one evening, in line, at the PVR in Saket, and Mohan's attentiveness will leave me feeling cherished. He will agree to watch *Memoirs of a Geisha* not because it is the only movie showing at 5:15, but because he will know how much I will enjoy this movie. In the next line, we will see our old neighbours quarrelling and we will happily embrace them. It will have been years since they vacated from above us.

I will begin soon to live all the days ahead of me. In the afternoons, I will think: Do you miss me? Do you miss me? A thousand and one chances will come and go in this small city, in this small world. I will never see you again.

Companion

She turned sixty-two that May, celebrating her birthday privately, receiving only a handful of good wishes, in one case announced by the rusty ringing of her cordless. It was then she became abruptly aware that she was cut off from the world. It was the companion's idea—brought on by his observation that it was becoming nigh impossible to keep her stitched together—to make Bhutan their destination.

At first, she did not believe that they could carry on being themselves outside the intimacy of her flat. She refused the adventure. But the companion argued otherwise and conducted himself so ably in making the arrangements for the trip that in the end she relented.

He rented out the woman's flat to a visiting professor at the Indian Management Institute. This was easy to do, as the woman's husband when alive had been on the faculty there. It entailed a few phone calls, signing and mailing a corporate lease agreement and transfer of keys by third party courier.

Then he called her son and was quite clever in making certain that the phone, when it rang at the son's home in Pune, where he held a position with a well-known American Aeronautic Firm, would do so in the afternoon hours when his wife alone would be at home. The companion let it be known to the young woman that her mother-in-law was leaving for a retreat. This, the companion knew, would be an easy story to sell because when new to the excitement of her widowhood, the elder woman had made a half-dozen such pilgrimages to ashrams, and dispensed there sums of money that had in at least one ashram, situated on the winding road to Gangotri, purchased for her the title of Maji.

✳

When Maji had written to them from this particular ashram, the son and daughter-in-law had thought their mother had finally found her abode of peace. They visited her there with the hope that this place of rest would be one to which they could endorse their mother committing her funds.

Once there, they had been impressed by the energy and labour of the Italian devotees who had built the ashram by hand; the light wood ceiling of the meditation room soared from walls of glass, forming a vault studded with more glass. On the morning of their visit, this room perched high in the mountain was wrapped all around in blue sky. The Italian, who met them at the gate and toured them within, said of the room, 'Guruji requires the sky. See, he doesn't speak. This sky around us is his speech.' The daughter-in-law was appalled by this conceit but had to concede the bathrooms at the ashram were cleaner than those at the four-star hotel, down the hill and forty-five minutes away by car, at which they had spent the previous night. And in the end the couple was quite happy when taken to their mother's room to see her wrapped in cotton sari and seated on the floor dispensing wisdom to the young and the wealthy gathered around her.

But the hope of an active widowhood, preceding a quiet, cared-for end, was brought to an abrupt end. Nature intervened, shifting the river below the hill a quarter kilometre off its course, flooding the hem of the spread-skirt mountain, eroding the soft-frilled base, and as its centre of gravity shifted, pulling to itself in lover's clasp all of the mountain's top-heavy, haughty beauty. At mid-level on the mountain, little hamlets vacated with great speed, and rock, tree and earth melted in a liquid pour down the mountainside. The glass cage perched up top, which had purported to capture the sky through the miracle of pajama-clad, Italian craftsmanship was smashed some thirty-nine seconds later onto the rocks below.

While chocolatetortebaking, engaginglocalsinartisansoap making, GayatriMantramchanting, Bollywood filmwatching Italians wrote home for more lire devoted to pickling Himalayan purity in glass, reinforced this time by steel girders, Maji, opting for financial solvency, withdrew from hurt Italian reproach, and returned post-haste to Delhi.

This return was fortunate for the companion who might have easily spent the rest of his daily-shortening life crouched on the back of a black metal bicycle under a blistering sky, forced forever to grin a monkey grimace while quailing inside. The companion's bicycle-pedalling employer had for some time been frequenting the colony where the erstwhile Maji maintained her flat. But in Maji's absence, companion and Maji were yet unknown to each other. On her return this unfortunate reality was quickly remedied. Hastening to the balcony when the dug-dug sound of the dhumroo reached her, Maji said no, she did not want to purchase a see-monkey-dance or a hear-monkey-screech or even a do-monkey-saas-bahu-drama. No, she had already seen enough of the drama to hear in the monkey's screech a favourite speech—'Maaa, Maaa, Maaa'—an entreaty she would not ignore. What she wanted to purchase was the whole monkey; and this she, in fact, did.

Did she know then the many talents of this monkey? Did she know that it would prove to be more than a singer, dancer, actor; that it possessed not only limbs of comical length, light-catching and light-hued fur, red-brown-stained, oddly pleasing eyes, but also a soul yearning for expression and greatest talent of all, for the right audience, expression itself?

Yes, this talented monkey could talk. And talking and talking and talking and talking, he became—her companion. This monkey could talk to keep loneliness at safe distance not only for its own purpose but also in service of any employer with such a need. This was, *he* was, for male he was, a talking monkey. And singular grace of Maji that she should discover this. The monkey as companion, endowing his new owner with grace, fell in love with her and a perfect loop of grace engendering love was his return. Forever more Maji absolved him from those tricks hateful to him of frantic tail chasing, or somersaulting with crushed ribs creaking, or most odious of all, the trick of sleeping with stomach rumbling, hunger continuing to live in dreams.

A life of love between human and monkey is not easy. Perhaps Maji was already coming apart, her own glass topped structure a bit shaken by the landslides, earthquakes and course-shifting rivers accumulated over sixty-two years of life. Perhaps adopting a monkey—however talented this monkey—as companion was just the first sign of the great unhinging which would require the monkey's talents to extend to stitchery. But perhaps the monkey, so capable and clever, was the cause and not just the symptom; in which case there was at least the redemption that he was a package—disease and cure all wrapped in one. In any case, good chap that he was, he strove daily to fulfil the task of ministering to Maji's shaky sanity.

He woke her mornings with tea and paper. And the many mornings she moved sluggishly, his nimble fingers sorted through her bones, rearranging them, so she could hang herself on a fresh frame. His inclination to groom found great satisfaction in her tangled morning hair. She was balding and had dealt with her vanity during her late-life search for meaning by shaving her head clean. Now, in the mornings of her life with her companion, her hair sprouted—richly curling and grey. The companion stretched kinky hair smooth over pearly pate and watched with delight the hair squirrel back, then grinning and sighing tragically, stretched it again and pinned it in place. He knelt at her feet with slippers ready when she, patting her head and nodding her pleasure at him, laid aside her morning newspaper and swung her feet over the edge of the bed.

All this the companion did after waking at five in the morning to sweep, mop and dust, crack eggs and beat to light froth for her preferred breakfast, of what he served with a wink and wolfish whistle, egg bhujri and ghee-smeared parantha. The joke between them being that he was cooking to kill. True, that in his eighteen months of serving her—bhujri and parantha, poha, sharp and citrusy, sprinkled with chopped cashews and chillies, or thinnest of bread, white and smeared with malai as thick as bread was thin, crusty with a crackling of sugar crystals, these just the breakfast options, lunch as easily veering to biryani chunk-full of fish, and dinner never failing to include syrupy hot jalebi from the market—she acquired hardened arteries necessitating two stents in her upper right thigh, and an alarmed understanding that the tightness she felt in her chest could well be the beginning of her end.

Nights, she was at her most fearful; she would bid him to keep awake till she slept. Nights, she woke from disturbed dreams, salt in the crevices of her face, he made reply to her pleading, promising her he would not go before she went, promising her she would never again alone-suffer nights. Nights, when even this failed, when she sat up gasping for breath, when aged arm refused to unbend to unhook blouse, to spill free paper-soft chest, on those nights he pattered from the kitchen with a fistful of sugar and, grain by trickled grain, soothed her.

As for hardening arteries—the companion's ministrations simply failed to account for them. He was busy feeding her body in order to feed her undernourished soul, to plump up and cohere from within her scattering senses.

A life of love between human and monkey is not easy. It was, for the companion, who was sensitive as even humans perhaps are not, most difficult. It was the companion who found the hard eyes of the neighbouring women, their 'Hello, hello, tell us we can stay for tea,' unbearable. It was the companion who suffered their wrinkled noses, their 'It must be so hard with your son so far away? You must be careful to not let this one handle the keys. They so easily get ideas, no?' But perhaps Maji suffered as well, if not on her own account, then on her companion's, the hard eyes, wrinkled nose and raised brows of the once-uninterested neighbour women.

What Maji did (after all this was the Maji of mountain-climbing-to-dispense-wisdom-up-top steel) was throw the bitches out on their elephantine behinds. She acquired belligerence in dealing with any and all. In the market, she quarrelled when the fruit vendor enquired how it was that Madam alone was consuming this many mangoes? Was her son or perhaps 'some other' guest visiting her? She need only tell him and—the mangos being so sweet this season and having a tendency to sell quickly—at her word he would be too happy to put aside a supply just for her guest, whoever that guest might be.

✳

On her sixty-second birthday—despite the companion's credible efforts to recreate the chocolate-torte of her Italian memories; shortly after taking delivery of a tangled mess of gladioli and roses (order placed online from Pune), shortly after placing the phone receiver on its hand rest, grandson's 'I don't want to talk to her' still smarting (but he's only three and he doesn't know what he is saying and if only they lived closer he would know her, and a job in an American Aeronautics Firm is nothing to be sneezed at)—

Maji left the flat, armed with squeegee mop, handle divested of rubber head. The companion frantically tugged at her to hold her back. Maji, in very like and very unlike Maji ferocity, took mop handle to a dozen car windows on the street outside her flat.

As her fist dove to follow mop handle through glass, stray shards embedded themselves in Maji's hands, arms and face. Like sprinkled sugar other shards took showered flight to pavement. The companion screeched and hopped. His fur tingling to the danger he pulled at her to leave. But now that the job was done and her anger expressed, Maji was busy nursing her shoulders, which had not exerted themselves thus in many years. The ache there was not only the ache of this new exertion but also an ache pinpointed to coin-shaped impressions multiply scattered on her skin, from where mop handle had been powered into glass by the weight of the torso thrown behind it.

When the show was done, the crowd gathered in awe found nervous relief in picking, from among the shards, small pebbles and loose gravel and, in the beginning rather humorously chucking these at Maji. Her companion danced to protect her, his thin limbs flailing in inadequate expression of terror. He knew; he knew what was coming. Had he not once seen a man and two and three moving blindly from within themselves to form a mob of four and five and more? He had.

Once, in New Delhi Railway Station, where he had arrived on the train from Calcutta, having earlier taken the train to Calcutta from Murshidabad and, having arrived in Murshidabad from Siliguri, and before that from the Bhutan border town of Phuntsholing by jeep to Siliguri, he had sat chained to a blue metal bunk inside the train and peered through a scratched plastic window at a boy shoving another out of the way to snatch a packet of rotis. The fallen boy had rolled on the ground, clutching his stomach, howling in a show of agony and a man had intervened and slapped from the hand of the snatcher the roti packet. The rotis jumped to the platform floor and from there to the tracks under the train. The boy jumped the man, and another man entering the melee made two, and then there were three and four, and fists flew to pummel the snatcher to the floor.

The companion, positioning himself as shield to Maji, knew to be afraid and his fear showed. The laughing men saw that everything they had ever suspected they should hate was founded on truth. They saw the monkey crooning over the hunched form of Maji and the horror of his tail lifting and thinner than tail, his member, wet-red and alert, a flag waving. One of the men snatched from the ground the stick which had been Maji's weapon of choice and swung it in the air. Another tackled him, perhaps reason possessing him, perhaps only for the pleasure of swinging the stick himself. Maji and companion made haste to leave.

A life of love between human and monkey is not easy. At least, in Delhi it is not. It was on her birthday, the day of the stoning as the companion referred to it, that he began his campaign to convince her to leave Delhi. 'We should go to Bhutan. All my family live there. They will love you,' he coaxed. He described to her the beauty of the hills, rivers and sky of his childhood home. She shuddered. Nearly two years since her adventure with the attempting-at-sky-catching, but to-earth-tumbling Italians, she was still waking to the receding roar of a crumbling mountain. The doctor in Delhi had said on her return, 'Post Traumatic Stress Disorder', and prescribed sleeping pills and ongoing visits. She had taken the pills and foregone the waste of doctor's visits, which she was convinced were prescribed only to cure the doctor's own malaise of American bills for acquiring an American degree.

Maji told her companion, 'No.' She preferred flat brown lawns to lush green slopes. The companion beseeched her; even tried growing angry at her. When all else failed he told her his story, relying on her to understand him as she always had.

✳

'I lived in the garden outside a house in Phuntsholing. I knew I lived in Phuntsholing because after I made friends with the children in the house, they and I stole money from the windowsill jar, and bought orange bars at Bhutan Gate, where the guard said to the ice cream-vendor, 'You get out of here. You don't have a license for Phuntsholing".'

'You made friends with the children? You mean you talked to them?'

'Yes, it happened like this. I had a favourite place I hid in. In the garden. At the bottom of the bougainvillea, which grew over the iron gate, there was a tap that dripped. In the heat of the afternoon no place was cooler than the damp earth there. One day, while napping there, I woke to the sound of a boy crying. I thought he was crying from fear of me. To comfort him I told him my name, and he was astonished.'

'The boy wouldn't have cried, he would have run and gotten his parents, if he was any sort of normal boy. And they would have kept you tied up after that.'

'Yes, you are right. He should have done that. And I was wrong. The boy was not crying because he had seen me, he was crying because his teacher wanted him to draw a portrait of Nehru.'

'A portrait of Nehru? In Bhutan?'

'The little boy, Aman, went to Central School in Hasimara on the India side of the border. He was an Indian. The family were all Indians. The father, an engineer, went there to build a dam. One of those joint ventures—an Indo-Bhutanese hydroelectric project.'

'Well, everyone loved Nehru. Must be the Bhutanese did too.'

'Yes,' the companion agreed. 'There was a lot of love in the air then, and afterwards for a certain time, there was love also. I drew the portrait for Aman. I was a good artist. When they were first setting up the project, hiring for it, my father had sent me to ask for a job in the draftsman's office. He thought I would impress the draftsman with my drawing skills, and maybe get trained. But I hadn't been to any real school, had never been inside an office and I got tired of standing at the office door hoping to be noticed. I never really wanted that kind of work. Thought if my parents just left me alone, I would eventually show them, produce some art of my own.'

Maji was not in the least impressed. 'You are a good cook,' she assented. 'As good as those Italians. But an artist?'

The companion stitched while he talked. He picked out eight stitches on the brittle skin of her hands and arms, the needle rupturing dried flakes to warm flesh within. Her face he dared not touch. The thin nostril was severed at its edge from the face, but so slightly, he thought he could hold it in place till the blood congealed. She was too scattered, caught both in his story and caught in the tumult of all that was coursing through her, to feel the needle's deft pinch.

'So what happened—did they love the drawing and decide to take you into the family?'

'Yes, they did. They took me in. They took me in and I lived with them. Aman rode on my shoulders to school everyday. I went on doing his homework for him. It was a long time ago. Aman is a man now, I am sure.'

'And then?'

'Then? Then they left me.'

'But why? Or how?' she grieved for him. You must have been so good to those children. Why would the engineer do that?'

'I don't believe he meant to. When the time came for the family to leave Phuntsholing, the kids clamoured for me to go with them. I didn't want to go. But I was young and it was a chance to travel. Engineer Uncle convinced me—'Don't worry. We will take care of you.' And I believed him. I think he was telling me the truth then. But on the train people stared. When we ate, all sharing from the same tiffin, people looked disgusted. When Engineer Uncle passed biscuits around to the children across the aisle from us, their mother pushed the plate away. Then when I went to the toilet, I saw people entering our compartment and whispering with Engineer Uncle. I think he meant to keep me with him in Delhi but along the way, on the journey, he must have realised that there would be difficulties.'

Maji saw the companion cry for the first time. He remembered the trunk being unchained and then unloaded onto the platform, and then the same chain binding him to the blue metal bunk. He remembered the scratched plastic of the train window, and through that window and now through his tears he watched the family distributing a journey's-end packet of rotis. He remembered the child who was dragged away wailing for the love of his companion, and the other child who wailed rolling on the floor for the packet of food snatched from him.

Maji snorted at the past, at Engineer Uncle, at her companion's pained efforts to believe in Engineer Uncle. Then she softened, 'Love is difficult, but never impossible.' The companion's only reply to this—more tears addressed to her back. And she: 'I would have kept you with me.'

The companion seized on this eagerly. 'Then you will come with me.'

This bit of manipulation Maji, shaking her head free from the companion's grasp, forgave, and stitched whole, she allowed him that they would adventure forth to Bhutan.

✳

At Bhutan Gate, the companion stretches, discards his erect bearing, and the windbreaker in which he had encased it. Maji waits inside the car while he prances off and soon returns. He is quite gallant as he offers her the mango bar he has just purchased. He has tried for orange but to no avail. Maji is very tired; the ride has left her sore. But she is forced to lick miserably at the dripping stick he thrusts in her hand.

All the while he bustles about. He has made enquiries and found out that the green house in which the engineer once stayed is empty. The offices of the hydro-electric project have been turned into a school and the houses nearby serve as boarding for the little scholars who come from too great a distance to return home nightly. The green house is empty, temporarily, because the principal, a Bengali, who occupies it, has rushed off in the middle of exam season to attend to a family matter on the other side of the border. 'Just yesterday,' the companion is gleeful; his tail swishes and its tip curls to lovingly lift the latch of the house gate. 'Left just yesterday. The whole place is ours.'

'But, you don't know when he will be back.' She is once again full of doubt.

'Look, you are hobbling, Maji. You should rest.'

'It's the spurs in my heel. I should have submitted to the operation when they told me to.'

He can hear the tears trembling in her voice. He turns back to the car, fetches her scarf and wraps it around her neck. The undergrowth at the gate is in need of a pruning. He can only glimpse through leaves the metal tap, still there. Certainly, Maji would not be able to crawl under there. There is no space for someone her size. A monkey or a boy might manage, but not a hulking old woman. And it is clear the tap no longer drips. Where there used to be vapour in the air of that bottom gate hollow, now there is only dry sunshine sparkling the drifting dust. 'It will have to wait,' the companion consoles himself. And seating Maji in the shadeless open he starts off on a lope through the mix of old and new that surrounds him.

Fifteen years gone by and the dove cote still stands. He wants to run back and tell Maji about keeping pigeons. How stupid they were—allowing themselves to be killed so easily, never making a sound, not a coo, as they were slaughtered in the dark by a marauding wild cat. How on acquiring four fantailed dancers, the engineer made the decision to haul the dove cote and its expensive inhabitants higher off the ground, onto an eight-foot pole. The children had cried that they would now be denied watching their new pets dance. And how dim-witted the new birds had been as well, lining their little dark cubbies with twigs so thorny, their chicks had hatched to be impaled.

He remembers the snakes the mali caught with a pronged stick and cooked with wide flat noodles in a broth gilded with oil—a smoky dish, and not to his taste. But what the companion remembers truly abhorring was a different meat. When the children had clamoured for more than vegetables, bread and Sunday chicken, and when the engineer's wife had spoken mournfully of winter's onset and the importance of nourishment such that staves off its chills and aches, then the engineer had sent Rattan the cook to the market for cow's meat. The companion had assisted in carrying the moist packages home, tenderly unwrapping them on the kitchen's cement counter where Rattan, with brute haste, rinsed, chopped, rolled in flour and cooked to crisp the meat within. This, the smokiest of all dishes, was eaten by children and parents with stinging eyes.

The engineer, his wife, the children, Mali and Rattan the cook—all Indian imports—could choose to remain oblivious, as the companion couldn't, to the local practice of evading the injunction against cow slaughter by pushing off the top of boulder-strewn mountains cows that bumpity-bump landed transformed (accidentally?) into meat at bottom.

The companion wanders further. He sees now that the chicken coop is no more. But the gutter from kitchen stoop to where the coop had stood is still there—where Rattan had plucked chicken heads off chicken bodies, where the children had pranced around while the chickens, drunk on burbling death, wove a blind dance. Rattan had caught the bodies swiftly as, one by domino one, they tumbled. He had held them over the gutter, with a knife jerked them open, dipped them—eviscerated and drained —in boiling water, then plucked them clean. Chicken curry, brown with fried onions, and creamy with curd. The smell had been good. But the notion of consuming it had held little appeal.

The memories—the memories are everywhere. In the compost heap, still situated in the same back ditch, tomato plants picked clean, yet retaining their green, lie strewn on top of older blackened matter. He marvels that tomato plants are still grown in the vegetable patch, which is at present cleared earth awaiting next season's seed. Perhaps a day or two earlier and he might have eaten the golden tart fruit. But then, he muses, if he had come earlier the Bengali principal would have still been here. He would not have wanted to come here as an intruder to pluck at the season's last tomatoes in the dark.

The companion skirts the very edge of the property, searching for more of what may have remained intact. The rock garden has been dismantled. Where then do the mongoose and snake now battle? He returns to the centre, to the green house. The rose bushes outlining the house's front parapet are there, but they are anaemic and appear no longer to produce. The path from the parapet to the back fence gate, on which he had once pulled the children in their wagon, is heaved up in places as if to wrest itself free and follow the roses in flight to wherever they may be. He turns again to the house. It is no longer any particular colour, its green paint having faded all over and peeled in long strips to expose greyed wood.

Abruptly, the companion turns from the house and returns to the front gate, where Maji lies in a stupor. Entering the house must wait, he decides. Despite the chill, the skin above Maji's upper lip is glassed with wet. He wipes concernedly at the moisture. He tells her about the winter the engineer had taken the whole household on tour to Thimphu. 'It doesn't snow here so that was the first time we, any of us, saw that white magic. In Thimphu it snows. But oh, so wet, so cold!' and he shivers dramatically.

She smiles, but it is a thin effort, murmurs, 'I would have dressed you properly. Snow is to enjoy.'

'Come,' he begs her and leads her past the dove cote, the kitchen stoop, the gutter by the old chicken coop, the compost heap. Back, he leads her, to the very edge of behind. There, where the mountain top crumbles and ends, he presents her with his gift. Hanging from the great muscular branches of a tree arrested in downhill stride is the old swing. He had looped it up among the branches and left it tucked away there that day, fifteen years earlier, when he had exited the green house and its grounds to leave with the engineer and family. In his exploration he has found it and unwound it and tested its strength.

The monkey had once taught the engineer's children that if unafraid was their talent then hanging over nothing would be his gift. And he had demonstrated: swinging from branches, punching at the air, stopping the children's hearts, and landing with a flip securely on ground. Then he had hung for them the swing and pushed them off the edge so they swung out from the tree, following its arrested trajectory; they had swung to sky, passed over nothing and returned to his push, once again. 'Unafraid, unafraid,' they had screamed, each one in turn.

Maji's large body is cumbersome on the old wood seat. But her companion's nimbleness compensates for her. He seats her. He admonishes her to hold on with both hands and he pushes her dead weight. She won't swing, won't pump with her legs as the children in the past would. She is limp and his cheer is hoarse.

He pushes again and again the broad back that does not want to leave earth, each push building momentum; she reluctantly soars. The sky enters her head and clouds clean her from inside one ear and on and out through the other. And she hears her companion behind her, calling urgently, 'You can let go now.' She feels no urgency. The stitches he had lovingly picked into her skin, black as ants now from the dirt of the journey, begin marching within the scheme his needle had outlined, but then scatter as if at the approach of a giant foot. She feels her arms come undone from her shoulders and drop to her lap. She looks at them with affection. So inert now, when once they accomplished so much. The sky calls again, and with relief she lets loose her legs, which have been dragging so from the bulk of spurs, stents and tortes. Now she is a neat little torso, teetering a bit on her wooden seat, but the companion is still there to steady and push. She turns her head and smiles at him over her shoulders and soars again to answer the sky.

'How do you like to go up in a swing,
Up in the air so blue?
Oh, I do think it the pleasantest thing
Ever a child can do!'

She remembers more absurdity: her husband's penis emerging at dawn to elephant-trunk-salute her thighs. She feels herself next lose a trickle from within, a trickle that swells voluptuously. A memory now of this same voluptuous vacating of her bowels preceding the birth of her son. 'That ungrateful idiot.' She smiles, pushing alone now; old muscles no longer aching. 'Hello, hello.'

And she hears the river rushing in her ears. A deafening sparkle and ears closed and eyes open wide she rushes down, a banner thought trailing her:

> 'Up in the air I go flying again
> Up in the air and down!'

*

The companion is at the kitchen door. This one will be open, he knows. Inside there will be sugar in a plastic canister and he will fill his fist and walk back out and curl himself into the garden gate hollow and lick till he gets to the last stray sweetness in his palms. Then he will turn the metal tap and wash.

Today Is the Day

PEACOCKS IN THE PARK
Monday 12 noon

I can see what other people don't see. And I am small. These are
the two things which make me different.

Yesterday when I took Reggae for his morning walk in the
jungle-park I saw peacocks. When I returned home, as usual,
Chachiji wanted to know what I had seen. I told her about the
peacocks dancing. Even though I sometimes add things I haven't
really seen, telling her the peacocks were dancing when they really
weren't, I mostly tell the truth. Then Adhitya's mother walked in,
and in a soft voice called me a liar. I call Adhitya's mother Didi. But
I always think of her as Adhitya's mother. She doesn't like me. She
might even hate me. She said, 'There are no peacocks in the park.
And there haven't been any in twenty years.'

I kept quiet and made tea and gave everyone a cup. I left Didi's
cup on the dresser in her bedroom and went to hang up the wash.
Ever since she caught me that morning in the kitchen when I
thought she would still be asleep, she hasn't drunk the tea I make.
These days when she leaves the bucket full of clothes for me to
hang I notice there are no brassieres and underwear in it. She has
washed and hung them in the bathroom since that morning in the
kitchen. So then she is still angry at me.

Chachiji believes everything I say. She follows me around the
house. She always wants me to tell her everything that is happening
outside the house. Today, she wants to know if the peacocks are
still there in the jungle-park. I go to the balcony to hang clothes

and feel the sun. She follows me there. I tell her today the peacocks were not dancing. They were running. She nods, and as usual her head is so loose on her neck, I wait for it to fall. It doesn't. I am still thinking about how to catch it if it falls and she says:

birds on the run don't fly

She follows me around all day, while the waiting for Adhitya's bus occupies every chair in the house. I tell Chachiji, 'Every room in this house is a waiting room.' She says, 'Suraj, you're on your way to poetry.' Then she nods and nods and her head does fall forward, but not completely off. She catches it by the little bit of hair on top and pulls it back and her head settles deep into the hole between her shoulders. The voice that comes from there sounds to me like the voice in the well.

inevitably hurrying to wait
peacock running, crown slipping

I am supposed to tell Adhitya's mother when Chachiji's voice goes into the well. But I am not going to.

SPECIAL
Thursday 10 a.m.

The voice is very pleased. I tell the voice some more truths. I tell the voice about Rajveer who lives in my village. This boy is deaf. My mother says being deaf makes his eyes sharp. I think being deaf gives him extra eyes inside his empty ears. I think this because when I lived in the village I used to hide myself in bushes and grass and follow behind to catch him. Just as I would get ready to jump he would spin around and scream, chase and catch me. When he caught me he always thrashed me good. His thrashings were always mighty. After he was done thrashing me we would talk. One more special thing about Rajveer is that he talks with his hands. His mother said she noticed his restless fingers right when he was born. Later when he became deaf his mother said now she understood the use of such fingers. His mother said that Rajveer was born ready to become deaf. My mother used to say that Rajveer's mother made too much of Rajveer's specialness. My mother used to say we are all special. This is what the voice says about being special:

today is the day

This is the voice's favourite thing in the world to say. The voice says it over and over, all day, everyday. But I am not listening. I am thinking about how I am small, and how that makes me special, and about Rajveer and how God gave Rajveer extra eyes to make up for the stuff that oozed out of his ears when he was a baby, and then I have a thought that makes me stop dusting the same spot over and over. I think about what I did to Adhitya in the jungle-park earlier today when we went there instead of to the bus stop. I start to worry because I remember his ear was sliced and how when Adhitya comes home from school his mother will yell when she sees her son is hurt. I dust really hard, swatting the music player with the cloth and the god on top almost falls off. I catch it just in time. I feel very worried. I try to change my thinking back to how I am special because I am small. I try to think of what God has given me that is extra instead of letting me grow up the same size as everyone else. Then I remember, I know—even though I am not able to see someone sneaking up behind me like Rajveer can, still I can see things that others don't see. I see more.

Last week in the jungle-park there were dead butterflies littered on the path. When I bent close to pick them I found that some were not dead yet. When I touched them they flapped in the dust and ruined their yellow wings. Some were so dead they lay still in my hand. Soon I had four in one hand. One was the colour of a leaf. My other hand was the lid shutting them in. Reggae was jumping around my legs, pulling my hand which was tied to his neck with a long rope. The rope got shorter with each jumping run he took around my legs. I waited for someone to notice me holding the butterflies. I waited for someone to tell me what to do. No one saw. No one stopped.

Then I felt the butterflies in my hand do the same dance as the ones on the ground, and when I removed my lid-hand they jumped around like Reggae until they fell to the ground. Reggae jumped more and I fell to the ground with the rope tight around my legs. A lady screamed because she was walking by right as I was falling. I think I might have bumped her. She didn't fall. She left quickly.

I picked up more dead butterflies as I walked. Some of them had wings so thin I could see through them. The ones that came alive in my hand I left sprinkled in flower bushes and the dead ones I tried to feed to Reggae but he didn't want them. In the end, all the morning walkers in the jungle-park, who walk everyday on the red paths, walked right on top of the butterflies. The walkers went home and removed their shoes and never searched the undersides where butterfly bits stuck.

Chachiji has a lot to say when I finish telling her about the butterflies:

they live so brief their lives
open pinned wings
in fluted pleats of the sun's spread skirt
flutter pressed between wooded thighs
till swish rustle
withdraw the bustle
leaving a dainty mince of merciless feet
winter
again I round this bend

BROTHERS
Monday 9 a.m.

When I was eight Adhitya was six. Now Adhitya is twelve but I never got past eight.

When I was eight I was Adhitya's birthday present. He wanted a brother. Adhitya's mother said, 'You will take care of Adhitya. You will be like a brother to him.' I thought of all the things I would do as Adhitya's brother and I liked the idea of going to Delhi so I left my village. The last time I walked on the path from my village, down the mountain to Maneri, to take the bus to Uttarkashi, to meet Adhitya's parents there, I was thinking an awful thought. I thought when I am Adhitya's big brother a fire might break out in their house and I will have to save him. I was thinking about whether to save myself or save Adhitya when my best friend Rajveer jumped from the tree where he was hiding and landed on the path in front of me and thrashed me so hard I fell on the mountain which came up and smashed my teeth into my tongue.

That day Rajveer said to me with his hands, 'Tomorrow I will remember you here.' Then he made the sign for laddoo. He thought in the city I would get to eat laddoo every day. Rajveer is stupid. The truth is, though I am getting pretty smart, back then I was stupid too. Then, I too thought people ate only good food in the city. That was the last time I saw Rajveer. When I see him again I will tell him people in the city eat everything, even cockroaches.

One of the first things Adhitya showed me when I came to Delhi was how to make a fire on the old foundation stone in the back where no one could see us. He made a little fire. I pictured it getting bigger and spreading. I started worrying again about saving him. He took two broomsticks and made a cockroach kebab out of one for me and a cockroach kebab out of the other for himself. I vomited it all right up. Bits of legs were floating in the green snot made by my crying. I was scared Adhitya would make me eat that too so I kicked mud over it and then kicked the pile of mud into the fire. Then I cried harder because I remembered my family's Chhani where we stayed three times every year when it was time to do the planting. When we stayed in the Chhani we slept on the ground because our beds were left in our house in the village. We slept on the ground which was warmed by the fire built right in the middle and if we felt like drinking tea we could reach for the pot and put it on the fire without ever getting up from our sleep. My mother mixed sugar with poppy seeds and fed it to us with our tea. When we left the Chhani my father always let me kick the mud on the fire to put it out.

I don't remember how I left Uttarkashi and came to Delhi. I came with Adhitya and his mother and father. I remember I cried the first night and said I want to go home. From Uttarkashi I know the way back to my home which is in Syaba. But from Delhi I don't know the way. I told Adhitya to tell his mother to send me home. Then she made her eyes sad in front of me and Adhitya and said, when you are a little bit bigger you can return. She said, how can we put such a small boy on a train by himself. I was small and scared to go alone on a train so I agreed to stay. I think I made a mistake. I didn't know then that I was going to stop growing.

The reason I cried to go home the first night in Delhi was because they told me to sleep alone on the drawing room floor. In my whole life I never slept alone in a room before then. In the night I heard many sounds. I made my eyes sharp and thin and pretended to be asleep behind them. I saw clearly that many people were in the room. I could see their dark shapes, which were darker than the dark of the room, bumping and colliding as they circled the room. Adhitya's father came and stood over me. He put his legs wide over my face. Far away inside his lungi I saw the biggest tota of any man in the world—it was hanging like a jackfruit, like a snake, like a broken leg between his two good ones. A long time later he went out of the room and all the huddled dark shapes left one by one.

When I became eight I became Adhitya's brother. His father and mother did not become my father and mother. In Syaba I have a father and mother. I know this very well. But Adhitya's father's brother's wife is my Chachiji. I met her for the first time when I came from my village to their house in Delhi. She was waiting inside the house for me. She said to me on that day:

a person can have many relations.

CHACHIJI
Saturday 3 p.m.

Chachiji's husband, I never met. I was not allowed to go inside his room where he lived in bed till he died. I smelled him from outside the door when I passed by, and sometimes through the door, when it was open, I saw the sheets on his bed moving. Then one day they put a big piece of ice the size of a bed on the drawing room floor and pushed all the furniture away and put Chachiji's husband on the ice.

Adhitya says before they put him on the ice, when Chachiji's husband was still alive, they cut both his legs off. When he had his business to do, they balanced him on the big wooden box they built over the toilet. There they wedged his tota and his bumpy, there into the hole in the box. Chachiji still keeps the box in her room. And sometimes she sits on it and nods her head. When she sits on the box she likes to say:

> *today is the day*
> *I fall into the hole*

People say Chachiji became crazy after her husband died. Adhitya's mother always says, 'Poor Chachiji is crazy from sorrow.' Only I remember that even before her husband died Chachiji's head was already always nodding and dropping.

When Adhitya's father and mother catch Chachiji nodding on the wooden box they call the ambulance right away. Men come and chase her around the drawing room. Her legs get caught among table legs as she tries to run to the front door. She tells me later that if she could only get away to the house of the aunty across the street, Adhitya's father would never dare to send the ambulance men there. I think, next time I should block the men's way so she can escape. But I know next time I will do the same thing I do every time. When she gets her legs caught in the table legs I leave the drawing room and sit under the kitchen sink till I hear the sound of the front door closing. I tell myself I cannot help her. Everyone knows Chachiji hasn't left the house in all the years since she came here as a bride, not even to go across the street to the neighbour-aunty's. The times she tried to leave, they caught her, so the only place she ever ended up was the hospital.

So far Chachiji has always come back from the hospital. She comes back with wet clothes that smell bad. When she comes back her head is shinier and it looks like the doctor has done a good job of attaching it to her neck. But it might be too good a job—so tight she only looks straight ahead. To talk to her I have to come from around and face her. If she is in bed she won't turn to the door from where I call her. I go to her bedside and put my face above her face till I am looking right at her. I can see she has something to say. I bring my ear close to her mouth. She whispers:

today is the day
I fall into the hole

On Chachiji's bedroom wall there is a picture of her taken soon after her wedding. In the picture I see that the wire the doctor used to attach her head is too tight. Her head in the picture sits on her neck as hard as stone, hard enough to keep from falling out of the picture.

PIECES OF GLASS
Wednesday 7.25 a.m.

I always take Adhitya in the morning to the bus stop. I carry his schoolbag which is big and heavy. I pretend the bag is so heavy that I cannot stand straight under it. I hang my arms and, bent over like a monkey, I let my fingers touch the ground. Adhitya and I laugh and laugh.

Adhitya says, 'Let's keep going today and go to the park.' The jungle-park is behind the bus stop. The jungle-park is the same park where I shit and pee; it is the same park where I walk Reggae after putting Adhitya on the school bus, and where Reggae sniffs till he finds where my shit is so he can add his shit to the pile. I have Reggae ready, tied to my wrist. I have Adhitya's school bag. Adhitya keeps walking and Reggae pulls me to follow. Behind another bus I see the D bus coming. Adhitya starts to run and I run because Reggae is running. I keep hoping the bus driver will see us and stop for us. From behind the wall Adhitya and I watch the bus waiting for us. After a long time the bus driver starts the engine and leaves. I am so upset I say, 'You have missed your bus. Your mother is going to be so angry at you for going to the park.'

He says, 'I'll tell her you made me.'

I hit him on the head. His ear cuts open and something oozes out. I say, 'You are bigger than me. How can I make you do anything?' I kneel on Adhitya's back. I think my hand is going to fix his ear. I rub Adhitya's hair. Then I take the back of Adhitya's head the way Chachiji takes her head by the hand to fix it and I crush his head into the wall. Over the wall the road crawls. I am surprised at how strong the back of Adhitya's head is. It has extra muscles in it that push my hand. I push the head back and each time more pieces come away and spread the sound of wet leaves all along the sharp bits of glass stuck to the top of the wall. If I walk back home with Adhitya now that the bus is gone, will people see the way his face is missing pieces? Reggae pulls the rope and I whip him with it. I kick piles of mud on top of Adhitya. Reggae and I leave.

If after we left, Adhitya got up and got on the bus and went to school, then he will come home on the bus today. At 2.30 I will go to the bus stop to get him. When we come up the stairs, Adhitya's mother will be waiting at the top. It is so dark on the stairs. At first she won't see us very easily. When she notices his horrible face she will make an expression like she is eating something too salty. Then she will make her eyes big like she is going to cry, then like she is thinking about something that took place a long time ago, or about something she wants to clean in another room. She will say, Suraj child, have you seen what you have done to Adhitya's face? Go clean it for him right now. She will put her hand out as if to pick out a piece of glass. But her hand will go back to her waist.

I will have to take Adhitya to the bathroom and sit on him and pick out of his face each tiny ground-in sliver that is hard to see.

MORNINGS
Everyday 5.15 a.m.

The first time I used the toilet in Delhi I didn't know you had to sit on it. I used it like a latrine. Afterwards the cook from the kitchen came and forced my head close to the hole and said 'clean your dirt'. I learned to use the toilet. But as soon as I found the jungle-park I started to go there instead. Early in the morning I get up quietly and leave the house. Only Chachiji sees me leave.

This early in the morning it is dark. That is good because I don't have to see anyone and no one has to see me. But when I first came to Delhi the dark frightened me. I used to go in the open on the red path. The jungle on both sides of the path was full of noises. It is all right for small children to use the middle of the path. Everyone is careful where they walk afterwards. I am small and even now I could use the path but I am braver than before. I balance on the stones that line the edge of the path. My bottom, high off the ground, stays clean and my shit falls away from me. When I was still shitting in the middle of the path my legs hurt because the shit piled up higher and higher, and I had to climb with it, rising and balancing.

When I grow bigger I will need to start using the bushes where the men go. But by then I will return to my village. I don't know which will happen first—if I will get bigger and start using the bushes before I am sent back to Syaba or if Adhitya's mother will notice me growing and send me back before I begin to use the bushes.

Squatting on the stone edge of the path I have seen that I am growing. My tota is long and I have to hold it up if I don't want to dangle it in the dirt. Maybe it is not as long as the one I saw inside Adhitya's father's lungi. But it is long. Probably Adhitya's mother does not like to see me grow. When she came into the kitchen and saw me with my tota in my hand that morning when I thought everyone was still in bed she hit me. I went ahead and finished making the tea like I do every morning. Then I took it to everyone and only Adhitya's mother didn't drink tea.

GAMES
Thursday 1 a.m.

The games we played were 'Island-Island' and 'Ship Attack', which is where a frisbee must be thrown below the knee. In the park we also played 'Dust' in which teams formed and we threw dust at each other. There were other games—pittu and badminton and cricket. The games we played were a long time ago. Adhitya no longer plays with me. The afternoons go on and on and never stopping, stop. I still go to the park sometimes and watch. The faces of children look up and see me and they point to the place in their game where I must stand. And I play again. In their middle I see Adhitya and Adhitya sees me.

Once I followed him to the house of another boy. I waited outside for him to come out. When many minutes passed I got tired of standing. My legs ached. I went inside the gate and sat in the garden and watched the ants that came in a long line from under the front door, over the floor of the verandah and into the garden. They were each carrying tiny specks of white in their mouths. I closed my eyes and slept and dreamt. In my dream I saw the house of sugar the ants were building under the ground. I woke up and saw the walls of shining white.

I went and knocked at the door and said to the aunty who answered, 'Please, can Adhitya come home. His mother is calling him.' I was so frightened to be telling a lie. I felt ice tumbling down from my brain to my feet. My face started shivering. I could not stop my eyes from staring at everything in the house. I searched behind the aunty standing at the door to see what Adhitya was doing in this house. I saw him with two other boys. Adhitya was standing by a chair. Another boy was also standing, but on that chair. And another boy was sitting in the front part of that same chair. I recognised the other two boys. They were brothers. I recognised the game they were playing. The same game was back at the house in Adhitya's computer.

I saw Adhitya saying something to the aunty. I saw the aunty move away from the front door. I heard her voice say, 'You work at Adhitya's house, don't you?' Then she returned to shut the door behind me and went to the phone. Soon she was talking to Adhitya's mother. Her voice said, 'Yes yes yes no no no yes yes yes'. All this time she looked at me and nodded and looked at me and nodded. I knew she knew that I had told a lie. She put the phone down. She did not scold me. She told me to stay and I stood by the computer and watched the game for a long time. The ice stopped tumbling, melted and trickled water inside me. My face grew hot and I touched the front of my pants to make sure they weren't wet.

The phone rang again and the aunty told Adhitya it was time to go home. She nodded at me standing by the computer. I walked home behind Adhitya and he joked with me. After that we walked with our arms locked around each other. I noticed Adhitya was getting fatter and taller. Adhitya's mother was waiting at the top of the stairs for us. In the dark I saw her face opening and smiling at us. I stopped being afraid. She said, 'Hurry and dress. Daddy is coming home early to take us to a movie.'

I again didn't know what to do. I could put my green pants on. But then she would know that I thought I was going to the movie with them. She might laugh at me and Adhitya might say, 'You thought Daddy was taking you. He is only taking us.'

But, I wondered, if I don't dress nicely then Adhitya's father could come home and say, 'Suraj, you stay home since you are not dressed.' I went to the front of the house to see if he had come. Then I went back inside. I did this again. I was still not sure whether I should dress or not. Then I decided I would dress in my green pants and hide in the bathroom till they called me when it was time to go. If they called me and said, 'We are leaving. You go to bed,' then I would say, 'Yes, okay,' from inside the bathroom. But if they said, 'Suraj, come let us go,' then I would run out, dressed and ready. I went into the bathroom and waited for a long time and then I couldn't wait anymore. I left the bathroom and went and waited in front of the house. I thought, if they see me dressed up they will know I want to go with them to see the movie. Even if they laugh at me they will have to take me.

Adhitya's father came soon after that and said, 'Quick, everyone, get in.' I got in.

I don't sleep in the drawing room anymore. I sleep on the floor by Chachiji's bed. Sometimes in the night we talk before sleeping. I ask her, 'If there is a fire in the house and I can save only one person, whom should I save?' Chachiji says, 'Save yourself.' I think about asking the question more clearly, 'What if it's Adhitya or me?' But then I am afraid to ask the question like that. What if the answer changes?

Tonight I tell Chachiji about the day I saw ants crawling under the door, across the verandah, carrying sugar into the garden. She asks me, 'What did you think, Suraj?' I tell her, that day I thought about what was underneath the earth, waiting to be discovered. I tell her, if only Adhitya and I were still playing together, we would make a new game called 'Digging' and we would find out everything about the inside of the earth.

I tell Chachiji about lying to Adhitya's friends' mother, about standing by the computer waiting for punishment. I tell her about waiting in the bathroom, wondering if I was going to be taken to see the movie. When I finish telling her everything, she is asleep. I can hear her loud breathing. I keep talking. I tell her how long the days are, how hard it is to keep dusting and making tea and walking Reggae. I tell her I think time is finished. I am not growing. She keeps sleeping. Soon, I fall asleep.

In the middle of the night Chachiji shakes me to turn the light on for her. She returns from the bathroom and I get up again to turn off the light. In the dark, she hangs her hand over the side of the bed and pat-pats me. In her pat-patting I hear her say, 'You are growing so big, Suraj son.' Then she sings:

> I have seen such things
> the orderly return to earth
> of stolen sweetness.

She sings it over and over and her hands become heavy and spread over me like a blanket.

Intimations of a Greater Truth

In 1978 when Pope Paul VI dies, she is almost nine years old. There is a holiday, and the propriety of celebrating his death is not something she knows to question. She assumes it is a celebration. All school holidays are for celebration. In fact, during the mourning period, when scores of the unwilling—those disabled from declining by the failure of mothers to disallow it—are dragged off to chapel, Hindu and Muslim alike, to pray for the repose of his soul; she, the sole Christian and a Catholic at that, joins in the fervent prayer that the new Pope die as well. And without further ado, when die he does, it is with such haste that there is little break for her in the celebration.

That long week of holidaying is marked by her failure to remember to study for the exams that she has just escaped. Instead she roams the convent garden with her friend and fellow boarder, the delinquent Miriam of indeterminate age and ferocious will. To prove herself worthy of this friendship, she drinks with kettle upended, one-two-three kettlesful of the newly-installed pump-well's draw. Her stomach bloats unbearably. With each step, the water, clear and sweet, sloshes in her throat, lapping at the root of her tongue. Having duly impressed a vague crowd of onlookers, she sets off to discover what else there might be in the world to know, please herself with, and fear.

This is also the year she launches her career as a reader. From *Lamb's Abridged Shakespeare* she moves to *Mandingo*. What she can understand— living as she does on the Indian subcontinent, in a different century, and at her age—of quadroons, mulattos and miscegenation is irrelevant. The fact of having come upon this book in the nuns' private store, and the titillation this lends her intimacy with Miriam, spurs her to risk discovery and hide it under her mattress. Dipped into again and again, the book yields a relevant wealth—the ritual caresses she and Miriam administer one to the other (fair is fair and mutual is must). The tastes and smells they sample in the solemn dark have little to do with the games of daytime girlhood. Thus, come day, she can stand to the side, not unmoved, but nevertheless removed from the pain, as the nuns bid the gardener to bare Miriam's back and beat her with bundled twigs from the pomegranate tree that grows in the central courtyard.

At breakfast she slides toward Miriam her plate with the extra rations of double-yolked eggs, paid for with the boarding fees her parents continue to remember to send. There is nothing she can abide in her stomach save endless cups of water.

The fear that she has been left behind permanently fogs her mind so that she begins the lifelong habit of accidentally or otherwise misplacing all of the titles and authors of the books she reads. She comes to know in these books what she should not know and so she edits for herself the best she can. When she emerges, eyes glassed to the world, there is little she can tell Miriam of the story, and so their play loses some of its juice.

In her after-school music class, she is sent daily to fetch water for the music master. His thirst appears unquenchable, although his exertions with the harmonium can little tire even the old man that he is. It is a creaky instrument, and his only students—she and Miriam—don't warrant effort. She is definitely tone deaf, and Miriam, who has no parents to cover their trail with money, is as usual on the periphery, is there only to consume what crumbs of musical wisdom may be slid in her direction. But it is Miriam who is made to remain in the room when Masterji sends her on the long walk from the music room, through the courtyard, past the statue of Saint Joseph and into the kitchen for glass after glass of water. What is left for her to do on these walks but to fall into a trance as she moves through a hallway of endless classroom windows? Motes of dust swirl in precise shafts of light bequeathed by the late afternoon sun. Shadows cast by metal bars punctuate this watery warmth. She is in light. Then in shadow. Light, then dark.

On this day, she removes the school scarf from around her neck. From somewhere she equips herself with matches, sets the scarf on fire and slides it into the dark of a classroom cupboard. Whether she does this on the way to the kitchen or on the way from the kitchen is a truth that eludes her for all the years to come. Among the surfeit of truths her life is invested with that year, a new truth is intimated in Masterji's unquenchable thirst. She walks back to the music room, glass carefully balanced in hand, sure in her belief that this will be the last glass for a long time to come.

The package from her mother that brings news of the year in exile drawing to its close contains barrettes for distributions to the orphans of the convent. There is a doll for her, and a pink and white nightdress—nylon, shirred and smocked at the yoke—which the nuns declare pretty enough for Sunday church. Miriam informs her that her mother's handwriting in the accompanying letter is sophisticated. She knows this is envy speaking and holds back her fear at this new layer—sophistication—she must add to the faltering image she carries of her mother. There is much arguing over who gets the silver and who the gold barrettes, and it is understood that when she leaves, the doll will be Miriam's to keep.

When the Child Was
a Child

From one Thanksgiving to the next, a father, a mother, a child and her siblings lived together under one roof. Their home was an apartment and the 'roof' was really a ceiling coated in drips of stucco. The real roof punched up eight floors above their heads, and contained under it sixty units to house the residents of 1609 N. Normandie, between Sunset and Hollywood. And although the child thought of these other residents as families, even as an extension of her own family, they were really the left-over bits of what were once families—families fragmented by any number of great upheavals that had torn them apart and sent them from all parts, long distances, to 1609.

They were not the amputees but rather the amputated parts from surgery on a scale that required a 1609-sized waste dump. It is said that the amputee experiences the ghost presence of what is removed, even scratching at the space vacated by a severed limb. But neither is the absent limb immune to the twitching of sundered nerves. So there was old Mrs Markham who woke the building, her terror spasmodic in nature, only on certain nights, to check that the building's electric stoves were not doing the impossible by gassing them all in their sleep. And directly above the child lived Short Hair who, when he wasn't vacuuming the floor side of her ceiling, wept into the nylon fur he cleaned—wept the loss of girlfriends, wept the coming-down-from-speed-sound, which the child listening below thought the sound of the vacuum bag now filling with pins. There was the childless couple—the Mudiamus—whom the child's mother told her to be nice to—*poor things they realised too late that all the years they day-and-night-managed the Dairy*

Queen should have been years they were making a child instead. Being nice to the Mudiamus was not an unpleasant task; as easy as agreeing to bags of M&Ms, excursions to Griffith Park and Castaic Lake.

On Thanksgiving Day, in 1979, inside the apartment with its built-in bar with a Formica top curving out from a mirrored wall, the child swivelled on a chrome and brown vinyl bar-stool and studied the comings and goings of her family members in the mirror she faced. The child's name was Emma. That was the day her father came from far away where he had been living in a place called a Correctional Facility, which she knew from the enemies at school was also the place called Jail. He came home that day with boxes of Twinkies and Dingdongs, and a lap into which he pulled the children's mother. The children, exultant and uncomfortable, ringed the tussling parents, and in the mirror Emma observed the great satisfaction of the whole.

Emma remembers it as the year they ate fish every night. But she is corrected when she brings up the memory to her mother who says, 'No, we might have eaten fish once or twice, but we were too poor to cook like that very often.' Emma, grown-up, won't allow corrections. She murmurs her memories the better to savour them alone. 'We ate fish and you fed us like we were still too little to feed ourselves. When we had fish you always fed us. You made balls mixing the rice and the fish and the yoghurt, and we all saw you had to hurry to make more in between putting the balls into our mouths. When you couldn't keep up, we were mean. We would each yell "Mine" and confuse the order of your feeding. When you had a ball in your hand again we would each say, "Give me." Then you would scold us, you would, yelling and saying, "I made it for you; who else am I going to feed it to?" We laughed at you then. You called us names in Malayalam—"fisherwomen", "Tamilians", you called us, and "starvelings". We never understood then how bad those words were in your mind. But the way you said those words, we knew you were angry, and we stopped laughing.'

That year, Emma remembers, they ate vindaloo pork patted into flour: soft fat thick on stringy meat, and the rind of each piece that started out tough between her teeth crackling to release oil so rich she wanted nothing more than to live in her mouth. There was a dry preparation of beef, fried dark, to which slivers of coconut clung; and chicken in creamy gravy with bones good for crunching open and sucking the marrow from, till the sharp breaks in the crenulations within grated fine the surface of her greedy tongue.

Her mother does not answer with memories of her own. Emma continues: 'Ribbon cake, like French crepes. Do they really make ribbon cake in Kerala—some kind of Malayali dish, right? Or did you make it up yourself? We had that for tea a lot. Why did you call it cake? We kept wishing for real cake. I wanted Duncan Hines yellow cake with the pudding in the mix. We didn't know then how good the ribbon cake was.'

'We ate bread,' her mother says.

Emma smiles, untroubled. 'Weber's bread in a blue and white plastic wrap. Snoopy on the wrap. A cartoon of Woodstock saying something to Snoopy. They kept changing the cartoon but Woodstock's words were always just scribbles. You think I'd forget something from that year?'

Emma had been a skinny child that year, and fast on the playground and street. Mostly people saw a blur, or if they paid attention they saw a blur of chapped cheeks-lips, and grey knees-elbows. That year Emma's sunken eyes had bled black under her lower lids. Her teachers, who noticed, worried that she reminded them of something worrisome. But they could not pin a finger on what it was they were worried by till, flipping through old issues of *National Geographic*, seeing there similar eyes paired with swollen bellies, they made a mental note to check on her home situation, a note promptly peeled loose and lost to them till the next day, seeing her eyes, they again began worrying.

'I don't remember anything called ribbon cake,' her mother says. 'Maybe somebody else made it.'

'Once at school when the counsellor asked me what we ate I told her that we ate bread. Dr King, that was her name; she kept trying to find out what we ate with the bread, and finally I said, "Nothing". Then she stopped asking and stared. That's how I knew that I had given her the wrong answer. I knew she was going to call you. Kids always know what adults are going to do. I always knew. I knew I was going to be in trouble at home that day. See,' says Emma brightly, 'I remember everything'.

'We were never hungry,' her mother says. 'Day-old bread was dirt cheap and much older than that, it was even free.'

'I used to roll the bread into balls. It was such soft bread, so full of air. I would eat the outside first—the brown part. Then I would roll up the middle and make balls and dip it into the fish curry. That was good.'

Her mother stares blankly at Emma. 'I don't remember making fish. Maybe once for your birthday.'

Emma had been taught that year—*turned ten is time to learn responsibility*—to do the bread-run to the corner of Normandie and Hollywood. This same corner she encounters at twenty-three in screen images and newsprint words minting history, making her corner the corner where somebody else's story is unfolding. She leans forward to show her mother the pictures in the newspaper she holds out. 'That was a wonderful year,' Emma says. Emma is itching to read out loud the words in the paper but stops herself because she doesn't want to be mean to this old woman, whose hands are scuttling sideways over the front of her gown, plucking at the cloth for buttons that are not there. She covers her mother's hands with one of hers to stop their spider-legged run.

Her mother does not want to see the pictures. She loosens her hands from Emma's and turns away with difficulty; then defeated, turns back. Emma knows this is because the gown they have given her mother to wear must be unbearable to her with its gaping back and the strings she cannot reach to tie.

Her mother closes her eyes and tucks her chin deep into her chest. Some moments of silence follow. Then, not satisfied that she has effected a retreat, she again attempts the turn away from Emma, leaving behind just one arm to endure the struggle to pull up the bed sheet over her back. Emma gets up from her seat to offer assistance but is halted as the searching arm panics and thrashes blindly for the sheet end. She remembers the same hand, when younger, motioning to reach the sari end, to draw it from the back to the front. Then, it had been a gesture to admire, a gesture of elegance. Emma covers her mother, though she longs instead to slap her.

Free to do so now that her mother has turned away, Emma makes hideous faces at the great white-sheeted mountain her mother makes laid on her side. Not satisfied with that, she makes karate-chop motions above the figure and jumps softly with each chop. The carpet underfoot absorbs the sound as it does the sound of the woman who enters from behind Emma. Emma pretends to be leaning over her mother, adjusting the sheets, but gives up when she realises neither she nor the nurse really care what they each think of the other. This is the night-nurse coming to say her shift has ended. Before leaving she picks up the remote and switches off the screen which is endlessly replaying the images of Los Angeles burning that her mother had turned away from.

Emma is not sure if her mother is asleep or pretending to be. She talks to her mother's back: 'The time when Daddy came home on Thanksgiving you didn't know that he was coming, right? You didn't prepare. But the next year, I remember watching you cook.'

That second Thanksgiving, the meal her father sprang from the table when he flipped the table onto her mother's lap—springing the legs from under her mother's chair, springing a fleck out of the youngest sibling's right cornea, springing 1979 free from the whole— had also sprung Emma's father from the family. 'You didn't want to make turkey. You thought maybe Daddy wouldn't like it to be so American. You made whole boiled eggs fried first so the skin was bubbled up the way I like it. I should get a recipe book for Indian cooking and try it for myself.'

Soon after her father left, Emma's oldest sister followed, to keep house for her father. Then another sister left, to continue to keep to herself, but to do so even more convincingly by making her location unknown. The first sister came home to care for Emma and the younger siblings the one week—every three weeks—her mother worked the graveyard shift. When Emma asked her sister if she liked living with her father, her sister held to silence; moments passed and Emma, coming to know and feel her own stupidity, giggled. She was grateful when her sister giggled back with her. Her sister said, 'I will teach you to cook.' And once Emma learned, her sister no longer came; she was taken along when her father moved away.

For a long spell after Emma learned to cook she concentrated on perfecting the one recipe for which ingredients were usually available. She made what the younger siblings called 'Emma Pizza' by taking slices of Weber's bread, opening a can of tomato sauce, slathering the one with the other and by laying smooth over the whole a freshly-freed-from-plastic slice of cheese. These steps reminded her of nothing so much as making her bed. She was especially convinced of the similarity when the bread slices emerged from the checkered bag indented on two and sometimes all four sides, so that collapsed from the original square a bread slice was inadequate to the task of mating a whole cheese sheet. Her sister had advised cutting the extraneous bits of cheese and re-piecing them on another slice of bread to increase the count of 'Emma Pizza' at dinner. Emma discarded this economy, preferring to tuck all around, and folding down just on one side the extra cheese, as she folded down just on one side the top sheet of her bed. And when there was hotdog in the fridge she sliced it round and slipped a slice for a peeking-out face under this fold. Then she toasted her creation. Her cooking was good and her siblings told her so.

But the days there was no cheese and no sauce the siblings hated her, and to win them back Emma made tea and taught them to eat dipped-in-tea bread which they called 'Emma Tea Cake'. While they dipped, she talked about the great meals they had eaten when their father had come to live with them. She talked about fish curry and rice, and chicken curry and rice, and beef curry and rice, and pork curry and rice. The siblings were too young to disbelieve her, although they could no longer remember who and what she was talking about. The nights they complained they were still hungry, she reminded them there would be eggs and hash browns at the school breakfast and spaghetti with taco meat for school lunch.

When all else failed, she launched them in a search for quarters under the washing machines lined up in the building basement. The search was suspended only when the furnace, asleep within a swirl of tentacled funnels, roared itself awake, reminding them of the dead babies roasting within. Emma congratulated herself, as they fled upstairs, for having lucked into the perfect mix of hope and fear necessary to combat the boredom of their empty stomachs. On the occasion a stray quarter or two or three were found, the siblings headed to the bread corner, first racing past the dangers of the 'Mesican yard' filled with 'Mesican kids', then crossing the street, dodging the late evening Chevies, Buicks and Caddies exiting

Sunset and turning the corner from Normandie to re-enter the parade cruising Hollywood.

Armed with found quarters, the bread corner became the Hubba Bubba corner. And when the younger siblings prevailed, their whining and moaning forcing her will to bend to theirs, then the Hubba Bubba Corner transformed itself into the Bubblicious corner. Down the street the younger ones swung, imitating the bounce-bounce of the agitated cars and trucks, too young to blow the proper bubbles that Emma, who hung back, strained her cheeks blowing.

Nights their mother came hurrying down the street toward them, home early from the late shift, gleaming white under the street lights, even from a distance shooing them inside, Emma pushed the younger ones in and stayed to witness the car windows rolling down to release the hooting and hollering heat within. Lingering, Emma saw the men in the cars push their heavy elbows out from the now open-to-the-dark interior and heard the drivers gunning and lurching and stopping their cars to mock her mother's gunning and lurching and stopping anger at them. Then Emma scooted herself in before her mother reached home.

The day in December Emma's mother reached the 1609 street door and found Emma still standing there blowing Hubba Bubba in her mother's face, she grabbed Emma by the ear and dragged her in, all the while moaning, 'I don't care about the Fire Marshals. I'm locking you all in tomorrow when I leave. What kind of example are you to your sisters, Emma? Standing here in the doorway like some Mexican; teaching your sisters to be out on the street like the Mexicans.'

In the kitchen her mother brought out a bag of pink lentils and another of yellow and another of a different yellow and another of green. She settled distractedly on one of the colours, reached above the stove in the spice shelf and began quickly-tumbling to the counter bottles of whole chillies and mustard seeds.

'Did you cut and keep the onions and ginger and garlic like I asked you to?' Her mother washed her hands and started to wipe them on the front of her uniform, and then stopping herself, stripped in the kitchen; wiped her hands on the folds of her belly and turned to Emma, 'Did you put the rice to soak?'

'I fed them,' Emma said. And the siblings, their hunger chewed into the gum they were not supposed to, but had swallowed, nodded. 'We're not hungry. Emma fed us.' Then her mother cried and, sobbing, threw the cooking pots, clean and dry, into the sink and the younger ones went to bed.

That night her mother chopped onions, stirred and cooked in her pot something Emma, watching the simmer of anger, feared to eat. In the middle of the drama of siblings woken from sleep and dragged, heavy-eyed, to the table, Mrs Markham set up her alarm. 'We're all going to die,' she wailed from the eighth floor, and wailing, swept down the stairs. At each floor she circled, pounding on the doors near the stairs. 'A conflagration,' she screamed, pointing her bony fingers up. Emma ran to the stairway, and peering up the steps spindled together and turning free from the ground, she saw clear to the glowing roof, and looking down, she saw a too-bright light in the lobby below. With her head wedged in the fourth sharp turn of the banister Emma called to her mother, 'Amma, Mrs Markham's doing her crazy stuff again.' Through the open front door Emma heard in response the quiet misery of spoons moving in plates. Up and down the dim hallway, doors opened and emitted, 'Shut up', and closed against Mrs Markham's continued keening, which descended and descended till she was squatted with her nose pressed to Emma's, the smell from her mouth as she whimpered into Emma's face: foul. Emma heard, as if in a brief interlude, the licking sound of Mrs Markham's long gown dissolving in small flames.

Then, from above Emma, people poured and poured out of

their apartments, past her, down the stairs. And in the pouring of people and smoke she saw her mother—strange sight out of the house in her bra and slip—and sisters; she saw the youngest one turning her head hard around the one blind eye, searching for Emma. 'Emma,' her sister screamed and they swept past Emma who held still and heard the scratch in the voice of the man pulling at his wife, 'Honey, let's go back. There's still time for me to throw some stuff together. The fire's only on the eighth floor.' From below, the voice of the building manager shouted into the din, 'Go back. Fire in the lobby. Head to the fire escapes.' And the crowd turned back up the stairs, and turned again on the sound of 'Locked'.

It was Short Hair who took the keys from the manager and raced heroically from floor to floor unlocking the fire escapes on each of the eight floors. Emma moved in a line of people that stepped over the ledge of the fourth floor's hallway window onto the black metal fire-stairs that crawled down the side of the building. She climbed down to the ground. There she found her mother and sisters and was forced with them across the street as they and the rest of the gathering crowd watched the fire-fighters go about their business.

Later that night, they were issued vouchers allowing them housing in the nearby motels. The stories circulated there were delicious. It was said that before the arrival of the fire-fighters, a mother in desperation had thrown her baby down from the eighth floor. But no one recalled a mother and baby living on the eighth floor. Emma played a bit-part in the storytelling; she described Mrs Markham's nose crisping up right in front of her. After the fifth telling, even her sisters refused to hear more. It was known that the fire-fighters had transferred Mrs Markham and Short Hair to County General. The speculation was that they would receive some sort of reward from the insurance company.

The fire-fighters made the decision, once all the residents were accounted for, to cease the effort to put out the fire. Instead, a limited team worked to contain it. It took eleven hours for the fire to burn itself out. By that time the crowd outside the building had melted into the dark of their own homes where they repeatedly woke in the night to check for faulty wiring and stoves left on. And the exhausted residents of 1609 were sprawled atop scratchy coverlets, asleep in strange beds, breathing in, in ragged rhythm, sooty sweat.

It took the fire-fighters five more days to move through the building and, floor by floor, clear the debris and declare each floor ready for the salvage crew; safe for eventual occupation. The haunted sleep of the building's residents and neighbours continued during those five days. Not until the fire-fighters came to a halt in the basement, where they discovered two charred bodies pressed into the twisted metal and puddled plastic embrace of the once-alive washing machines, did the area-dwellers rest, their rent sleep healed.

The morning after the fire, calls to the hospital had found in stable condition not only Short Hair who had suffered the graver injury of second-degree burns, but also Mrs Markham who, though the burns she suffered were minor and confined to her legs, had because of the fragility of her age been considered in some danger. The bleary-eyed gathered around motel lobby payphones had hidden the anxiety that pierced through them on hearing this good news. They voiced pieties: 'What matters is not things. It's people. That's what matters.'

'Amen,' echoed Bernard Mudiamu, who spent his Saturdays pastoring the 'New Voice in the Desert Fellowship of Christ Church,' and added his own: 'Praise the Lord from whom all good things come.' When Emma's mother bristled at this he amended his prayer: 'Sister, bow your head and praise Him who is merciful.'

But neither Bernard Mudiamu nor Emma's mother were relieved of the conviction that somewhere an account remained to be settled. Unspoken, the collective wisdom held: attendant escape from a conflagrant wind, as had just blown through their lives, was surely a price. What price, they wondered, the wholeness of 252 lives spared? What price, they wondered when they woke untouched the morning after and filled their lungs to capacity? What price, they wondered for each of the ensuing five days as, aware of breath and air, they exulted in the rise and fall of the breast? And at night, resting their heads on one another's chests—husbands and wives, mothers, children, siblings, friends and suddenly-sprung lovers— thrilling to the sonority of the pumping heart, wondered in the dark: what price?

Only very young children were immune to this wonder. They occupied motel closets for hide-and-seek and invited one another to bathtub parties. In the afternoons they slept with their eyes open in front of *Loony Tunes* and woke with bologna sandwiches squashed to their necks. For five days, under Emma's leadership, the littlest children did battle with fires in motel stairs and howled louder when asked to turn their fire engine siren sound down. On the fifth day after the fire, when the story of the bodies in the basement first made the rounds, the children who had played at discovering these bodies many times over, simply blinked in astonishment at the adults joining in their game. And in their discussion the adults were animated, smiling and giggling as the children did when dead bodies made appearance in their play. The adults were relieved. This once in their lives, they found the price paid for escape from further fragmentation cheap—as cheap as the lives of two strangers, perhaps bums who had found their way in to the building basement to sleep off the drink.

Emma alone was distraught. Once she understood the bodies were real, she decided they were the bodies of her father and sister who had come back to the building to live as a family again. At times she thought they had remained in the building all along, never leaving it, hiding there and watching over her. Other times she thought they had heard of the fire and come to rescue the family, got there before the fire-fighters, entered the building, and remained trapped there once the doors were sealed.

In the worst moments, she tore at her mother: 'You shouldn't have let them leave. You were mean to Daddy. You never even gave him a glass of water when he asked. You didn't love him. He'd have stayed if you'd loved him. It's your fault.'

Unexpressed was the calculation in her mind of the many sins she had committed: the times she had wished for a father who wasn't a dark cloud suffocating her from the corners he hovered in; the times she had woken from dreams of herself pinned under his legs and thrashed her own legs in twisted sheets to feel them hers again; the times she had muttered when he, home in the middle of the afternoon, roused himself from the couch moments after chuckling at the show on TV and, cursing disapproval at the trash his children watched, turned the set off; the times he had asked her to bring him a glass of water and she had pretended to not hear.

The clean-up of the building took three weeks. Emma no longer led the children in play in the motel's hallways, and, absent their leader, the children lost their confidence in themselves as a gang. They were sent to school again during the day and come evening they ate using more county-issued vouchers in splintered groups in the parking lots of fast food restaurants. During that time Emma's mother told her that the coroner had found the bodies were of two men, both of them too old to be that of her father. Months after her mother moved them, at first back into the old apartment and then to another neighbourhood, Emma's father called from her grandparents' house in Delhi. The line crackled alarmingly. Emma held the phone away from her ear, and heard her father shouting to confirm for her that he was alive. Her mother said to her then, 'I had to call a lot of people to find him and get him to call here.' Emma only said, 'You just always try to look good.'

✻

'You know what I really liked about your cooking back then?' Emma asks her mother. Her mother's body gives a jump on the narrow bed. Emma knows she is now truly asleep. It's good, she thinks, for her to sleep. And somewhere below the surface ease of that thought lurk less purposeful thoughts: I wish I had some coffee, or even some tea. Yes, tea would be good right now. She says aloud to her mother's back, 'You used to give us tea on school mornings.' Her mother twitches again. Emma walks the length of the bed, rounds the foot and walks to the head. She studies her mother's face. Absent teeth, the mouth is a collapsed tent, but the brow is concentrated in watchful ridges; as if, Emma thinks, she is afraid her hold on life will loosen in sleep. 'Let go,' she whispers to her mother. And as quickly, growing afraid herself, she thinks, Only fifty-eight. She has another twenty years, at least.

-3-2-1, First Time

3. Dominic tells Kaavi about his first time. They are perspiring in the heat of a long afternoon spent hidden from the world, in the dark, under bleachers. The cricket game hangs, a steady hum, distant in their consciousness. She has trouble responding to what he is saying. She wants to spit out the gum in her mouth. There is nothing to spit it into. The napkins have been left where the rest of the picnic is spread, on the other side of the game, clear across the park.

'I don't know. Twelve. I just think it's not right.'

'You the one doing wrong. I see you sticking that gum on park property.'

'You were twelve?'

'You still have something in the corner of your mouth there. You want, I'll get it.'

'And she was?'

Dominic is enjoying himself. He hadn't expected to find himself here with her. Kaavi is, he decides, not the typical Indian princess all tits and tease. Not, he admits to himself, that he can claim first-hand knowledge of the existence of such a type. It's just what he's heard.

He grunts, annoyed that he has let his mind stray.

'What?' she asks.

It's her turn and he waves at her to indicate she should begin.

'I certainly wasn't twelve.'

He smiles so all his teeth crowd forward. She looks down and immediately tells herself it is not because she is embarrassed.

'It was by the lake where we have a cottage. This boy I've seen every summer. For years. Years of looking, and then it's almost inevitable. You know.'

'Older than you? Same age? Let me guess, you were the older woman.'

'It was back when I was in a place where I felt like a boy. Dressed like one all the time.'

'Juicy! A boy and an older woman. One package. And then another boy. That's a threesome.'

'Dressed like one all the time. But felt like one only some of the time. Tell you what—we weren't the same age but we were the same decade.'

She allows time for him to concentrate on her. Instead, he waves her on, indicating that he wants to hear more. She likes this about him—his need to talk with his hands, although in this case, it seems more the result of how busy he is keeping his mouth.

'Didn't you say yours was twenty-one?' *That's the exact other way around of twelve.*

He manages something inarticulate.

'How old was she?'

Dominic's smile threatens to swallow his face as he puts his finger into her mouth. She rolls her eyes and sucks obligingly.

'How old are you now, Dominic?'

'I'm hungry.'

A little later she shifts from above him and bangs her head on the wooden riser. She moans; he giggles and shushes her. Their heads cocked in the direction of the game, they listen—for the thump of the ball, for a cheer. It's quiet out there. Dominic cranes to see what is happening with the game.

'Looks like it's the Bajans,' Dominic crows. 'The Indians sure know how to take it lying down. Especially from us Bajans.'

His fingers haven't stopped their slide in the narrow space he has created for them; his knuckles, the pole that tents her panties.

'The game is over,' he urges her.

But this brings her to an abrupt halt. What she means as a light slap, a scolding with her hand, lands hard. He doesn't stop smiling. She yanks back, hits her head again and they roll apart. The sun comes in from where her head had blocked it, shining striped through the slats. He kisses her methodically wherever he sees shadow. He knows there is little hope she will stay here another five minutes. She will want out on the field with her pitcher of iced tea, and the smile, and the pour-pour as she moves down the line of players. He doesn't mind. It was in the line-up, sucking on a lemon from her tray that they met earlier in the day. It will be a long week but the weekend will come again and, he thinks with gladness, he will meet her here again. Saturday and Saturday and Saturday. He sees himself under the bleachers many more Saturdays.

One of these Saturdays. And he doesn't believe her. Not for one bit. Not the cottage. Not the boy she saw growing up. Not, he thinks, especially not the part about her as a boy.

'You know what she taught me?'

'Your older woman?' she says with some sourness. 'Twenty-one, under the palm trees?'

'She taught me to tell.'

'Tell what?'

'She taught me to tell when a woman comes.'

'Tell what?'

'I can tell.'

'Tell what?'

'I can tell when a woman comes.'

Kaavi laughs hard as she crawls away. It is a troops-in-the-jungle crawl, belly to the ground. Where the wooden seat under which she is crawling ends, she veers to the left and, rising, follows the edge of the stacked seats as they rise above her, till she is high enough off the ground to come to her knees and, still helpless with laughter, zip and button before pulling out into the open.

A quarter of the field away, men so gleamingly beautiful they halt her, are separating—two tides of white parting the green. Women on both shores are rising from the midst of foil-covered casseroles scattered amidst toys, bags, children. The women bear in their arms trays of drinks, bowls filled with ice and lemons. Kaavi runs to grab a tray, a pitcher. Running, she can feel her hair rising, haloing her, then dropping. She can feel the men, the two tides of men, pause. *Their turn to stop and stare.* Dominic is watching. She can feel that too. She slows for him. The unwavering light of the California sun shatters against her silhouette, setting it ablaze.

*

2. Driving to the Greyhound Station he cannot stop talking about his mother. She listens, half-distracted from her worrying by the unsuppressed note of wonder in his voice. Now he's saying something about kitchens, and again the wonder in his voice.

'See, whenever we moved to a new place, the first thing Mom did was pull curtains down, remove the doors from all the kitchen cabinets. She'd pull up a corner of the carpet to see if there was wood underneath. If there was, she would pull it all up. She'd tell me to knock on walls, listen for a hollow sound.'

'Why's that?' Kaavi is amused. 'Calling out the ghosts?' She can see a little boy Dominic knocking on walls.

'Seriously, my mom believes in obeah. That voodoo stuff. Serious. But actually, the knocking on walls was because I used to read this dumb stuff about secret rooms and castles. You know kids' adventure stuff. The walls—she was just going along with me. Playing with me.'

He steers the car hard into the lot. Then resting his hand on the wheel, eye darting to the clock display, there's still time, knee bumping up then down, keeping time to the music in his head, he speaks and the note of wonder in his voice is magnified by the quiet in the car. 'Just tore these places apart and wouldn't pay the landlord afterwards for damage. Would force them to give over the whole deposit. She'd say, 'It's an improvement.'

Kaavi's mind jumps to the house in South Central where Dominic lives with his father and stepmother, June. The bare front-yard—not a bush, no grass—is a mask the house wears. Inside is all of a fuss: curtains and cushions in the bathroom, a rug-skirted toilet, the matched rug on the lid, the doily under the porcelain toothbrush holder, the wallpaper coordinated to the rug. *This is the bathroom?* June had beamed at her, had even touched Kaavi's hair, lifting a lock of it an inch by its tips and then dropping it.

'You look like one of those island girls,' June had said. Kaavi wasn't sure if she meant the girls in Barbados or some other girls on some other island. Kaavi wonders idly what this mother, who from Dominic's account sounds nothing like June, will have to say about her.

'You think she will like me?'

Kaavi's question emerges unguarded—the newness of the tone, a match for Dominic's breathless adoration.

'She's always liked everyone I ever liked.'

'Everyone?'

'Yeah, well. I like my mother to meet everyone I like.'

'So how many?' she teases.

'Many. Every-many-one.'

Kaavi turns her ears off and plays in her head the previous weekend at Dominic's—her first time at the dinner table, her first time staying overnight: Dominic had been particularly adamant that an overnight stay was not a problem. His hands had reached up to slice the air above his head into 'X-es' as he persuaded her. This had mystified her. Was he 'X-ing' anticipated problems with Richard and June? Or was he indicating that there were no problems in need of 'X-ing'?

Dominic turned to his parents early during dinner and said, 'Kaavi and I are going upstairs after dinner.' For a moment Kaavi pictured an X shimmering in the air above his head. But then it dissolved. It was as Dominic said. His father's chin remained glued to his chest, which was the position in which he seemed to do everything—read the paper, eat a meal, carry on a conversation. Her stomach churned at the thought of having to walk past him to go upstairs and as abruptly it settled. June drew various serving dishes across the table in a circle around Kaavi's plate. Kaavi saw this as acceptance. She quailed at the idea of June knowing anything and everything about her when her own parents, her siblings, her grandmother who was teaching her to sing—none of them knew Dominic, certainly not by name, and perhaps only a little by sight.

Dominic took her hand under the dining table and she felt its strangeness next to the song now running in her head, one of her grandmother's songs.

But as if he was reading her thoughts Dominic said to his parents, 'She can sing in Indian. The other kind of Indian. Delhi, Bombay, Taj Mahal. You know, Tendulkar. She's going to teach me a song.'

In his room, she insisted on touching everything—running her fingers across bare walls and then without the intervening bump of frames onto posters, floating her fingers off the wall, rimming lightly the shade of his lamp, trailing them from the shoulder of one hung shirt to another till neatly pressed, flattened arms swayed gently in response and metal and plastic hangers tapped and clinked. He pushed her into the closet and they squeezed together on the floor. The bed had looked formidable. They knew each other in small tight spaces. Here was familiar, where space had to be made by lifting her bottom so he could pull out the shoes they were sitting on. Even so, she protested.

'I haven't finished looking at everything.'

He was agreeable, pushing open the door that had just been shut. From their side-by-side seat on the closet floor they looked out into the room, watched fish swim in a murky green glow. It took her a moment to adjust to the idea the fish were contained in glass and not just in that light.

'Do they have names?'

'Ya poppit.'

'Huh?'

'You crazy.'

'I like your language.'

'I like yours.'

She didn't know why, but they were whispering. She hung her head and he traced a fish, wet with his spit, on the back of her neck. She felt its chill shape expire and guessed, 'A heart? K? No, D?' The hand done tracing, circled her further shoulder and met his other hand at her chest, and together the hands unbuttoned the top two buttons of her blouse, traced cool and slithery fish on her breasts, paused to tap a message to her heart, which beat back harder. She raised her arms. He peeled the shirt from her, pulling it over her head. She unbuttoned him and imitating her he put his arms in the air from where she hadn't the height to pull the shirt free. It pooled around his neck and he wrestled with it. She pulled at his pants. They were clumsy in the dark, tugged at hair and skin and yelped when teeth and tongue snagged and toenails scratched.

Outside the closet, the paired windows on the opposite wall, two eyes, finished turning from orange fire to black. The only light in the room—the iridescence of the fish tank—rippled across the ceiling. Dominic and Kaavi studied their reflection in the glass of the windows. Their eyes met in study and sprang apart. Met again. This game played out in all its variations: she straddled his flexed thighs, they smacked their chests tight, brought tips of tongues together, and in the end he ran a careening lap of his room, with her piggyback. They cheered when they passed the image of their two bodies entering the frame of a window, locked together, a second later exiting it, locked together; the thrill repeated, entering and exiting the second eye of the second window. He wanted to do it again. She became aware that it was a window they were playing mirror with, that they might be staging a performance for the world outside. He promised her the windows opened to the backyard. She thought of her own backyard and felt sure that at this hour at least her sister and the dog and possibly her grandmother would be out there to allow the dog a last go at doing his business. She said no, they should stop. Dominic disagreed and forcibly ran with her while she pounded his back, half-crying, angry at the way her hair was getting in her face, angry at not being able to free her hands from the fists they had formed, fists unequal to the task of keeping hair from face. Chastened, Dominic stopped, set her down and grumbled.

'How long are you going to keep saying no to me?'

She lay down on his strange bed, on its furry top printed in something graphic, something suggesting some sport, patted the place next to her. 'Not yet,' she said, then traced fish down his belly and swam them with her tongue. He stopped his grumbling and turned attentive to her circling.

At the bus station they are somehow late picking up Marilyn Sampson. She is at the curb—a dainty eccentric in a man's felt hat with a satin band and crushed crown. The hat is costume and false, dusty, and stolen from a prop room. The woman under the hat has a tiny torso in a tiny little jacket, which when she turns to pick up her luggage sports tails—*like a ringmaster's*! Kaavi can believe this woman unscrews the hinges from all her cabinets to reveal their insides messy with cans of beans. She longs for a glimpse of her own mother, even if right here at the bus station, even if it would mean being found out a liar. She longs for a sense of decorum. It doesn't matter, she thinks, tries to be polite about helping lift the many suitcases, gives up and stands aside. The drive to South Central is filled with his mother's talk of the campus in Durham where she teaches. Kaavi fumes. *French literature!*

That afternoon in his room it is the noise from the large gathering downstairs that makes Kaavi nervous.

'Don't they wonder what we are doing up here?'

'Noooo.' He leaves the 'dummy' unsaid. 'What's to wonder? They know.'

'Doesn't June care about having Marilyn under the same roof?'

'What's to care?' Then: 'You mean like you care about my first time?'

'What first time?' He turns her and smacks her not-too-gently on her bottom. She screams.

'They'll hear us.'

'Nothing for them to hear.'

She is practised at not replying to this charge. They stand at the window and he keeps her pulled back so only the tips of her breasts enter the frame. All is light and bright outside the window. In the backyard, a tree stands tall and the glass of the window is green with the glory of its foliage. The sense from the previous visit, of being trapped in this house with nowhere else to go while her parents believed her at the school camp-out, the sense that wrongdoing of the magnitude she was engaged in would surely be punished, is no longer part of her. She breathes, watches the smudge of her nipples rise and fall against green. On a bed utterly familiar to her on this second visit she drifts into a light and secure afternoon sleep. He drifts, still mumbling into her neck.

'Now if you would only laugh. I've been with laughers before. Girls who laugh as soon as they're done. With them, you know.'

I don't believe him, Kaavi thinks. She dreams of island girls and palm trees festooned with felt hats.

✳

1. In the centre of a traffic island ringed with shrubs a horse rears and paws the sky. The figure astride it raises a sword. The sword, like the hooves, seeks sky. The two of them—horse and rider—are set to leap. The urgent whispers of two below leap ten feet up the pedestal and another fifteen seeking entry in gilded ears.

'We could hitch a ride back of her.'

'Behind Joan of Arc?'

'Yes. We could ride away from here.'

'You crazy. You know that?'

'No, you crazy.'

'I'm not the one heading out to the land of kitchen cabinets minus doors.'

Dominic looks away. Something tender and something angry contend in his face. He is not smiling.

'You don't want that I should live without cabinet doors.'

Kaavi turns away from the accusation in his voice, returning him to the showman in him: 'You could never climb that high, anyway.'

'You want, I'll show you.'

'You wouldn't go very far with Joan of Arc.'

'Yeah?'

'She was a maiden you know. That means a virgin.'

'You crazy.'

'You, the maiden.'

'You, the maiden.'

They strip as they talk, each concentrating on their own clothes, folding neatly, stacking against the possible need for quick retrieval. This late hour a lone headlight sweeps in an arc the intricate twig-work, last season's new growth, now dead underbrush, vaulting scant inches from their noses. The same headlight shows Kaavi's hair spread weblike and picked out in green and yellow leaves. It shows Dominic prone, strung in the length of time it takes an old Audi to half-circumscribe their island at thirty-five mph.

'This is my first last time.'

'Mine too.'

Their eyes are wet. They don't cry. They shake the leaves from her hair and don't hurry as they dress. Then she calls out, the sound stung from her.

'My payal. The anklets I always wear. One must have fallen in there.'

They search, turning over the stones, retracing their path to the figure on the pedestal, first on foot, then on hands and knees. They brush against each other, too sad and distracted now to turn the touch into play. She calls an end to the search.

'It's okay. I have a bunch more of them at home.' She is lying. This is not the goodbye she pictured. She doesn't want to ruin it further by telling him that these were her grandmother's, given to her on the promise she would take care of them.

'I'll stay and keep looking,' he says. 'You go home before they catch on.'

'What, then you'll mail it from wherever it is that you are going?'

Now they let the tears run, and she turns from him. Her retreating figure dwindles as the street lengthens, carrying her away. He doesn't have a word for this, doesn't search for one. He stands very still and jiggles the flattened strand of silver in his pocket.

Romancing the Koodawalla

It is winter, and the six or eight men jostling at the crossing wear their cotton sleeves long and buttoned at the wrist. Their shirts are in varying shades of pastel, and when the wind kicks up, they look like a bouquet of ruffle-petalled carnations. They are tall, every one of these men. If not for the fact that they are all so obviously of one age, it wouldn't be impossible to imagine them birthed from one womb—so alike are they. Perhaps some one person in the PERA office is possessed of a particular aesthetic bent and has brought this to bear in his hiring practice. When the fog lifts from chill streets with the thin shine of a tin box lid, it is to reveal these men, identically arrayed and capable, each one, of eliciting the same charge of opaque pleasure.

Mona swoons over these men, distinguishing them in her mind from other clusters of six and eight men—also encumbered with PERA handcarts and also beating off churning melees of stray dogs—by their penchant for pastel. And while these other groups can only look on enviously, the chosen vie daily amongst themselves for her undivided attention. But divided she remains, hurling abuse impartially on all comers.

The men, with abashed smiles, take it in turns to approach the sacred ground below the balcony on which she stands stroking the parted curtains of her hair. The exchange opens, as always, with a request for drinking water. At seven on a winter morning, this is slim pretext for the proximity sought. Her voice berating the supplicant rises to a crescendo before she descends from her height to hand him his glass, allowing his fingertips the succour of contact only with the warmth emanating from her body, never the salvation the twitching fingers seek, never the actual contact with the actual body, not even the compromised satisfaction of a fistful of the blue flowered polyester she covers herself in. While grins grow wider among the watching men, she expertly snatches the glass from the moustached mouth and whisks away breasts and buttocks, leaving no room for doubt as to who is mistress of this game.

Those in D-16 and surrounding homes who have managed to sleep through the clatter of wooden wheels and the jubilation of mongrels eager to feast, can no longer escape the inevitable. They rise, their grumbling a minor note in the triumphant aria Mona sings as she ascends the stairs to return to the lesser challenges of duties in the kitchen. The men scatter and ring—no, jangle—colony doorbells with impunity, and from within the rubbish of bathrooms and kitchens is bundled, and modest plastic bags of the same are presented to these men, who bear them off with such loud laughter as six or eight men may muster to embolden their claim to dignity.

I have been watching the men wooing Mona for some three months and have an understanding of the script they are playing out. Then one morning it is all changed. Mona is, as usual, leaning over the balcony railing, her fifteen-year-old girl hips bending easily so she can better flash what she wishes to flash. Held in abeyance in her hand is the glass. But Mona is not holding it in her usual ready stance of one just as capable of flinging its icy contents to douse too eager a fire as she is of quenching a respectfully expressed thirst. No, in this case she is cradling it. And what is this rising, evanescent, from the rim of steel—not Delhi fog, I don't think. No, it is something cloudy but pure—something possessed of delicacy. Rising from the glass, a veil of vapour announces that Mona's heart is no more indiscriminate. How long has this been going on? How long, I wonder, has she been giving some lucky koodawallah hot tea instead of water?

I am curious, but practise restraint. From where I am seated, far back in the dining room, I can see the street and the koodawallah crowd. But I cannot see which of the paramours has successfully netted his prey and disappeared with her somewhere outside the range of my view. The men hanging back on the street are, none of them, in a mood to grin today. I watch them shuffling uneasily. There is the sound of muffled laughter. In one accord, they turn their backs to my house and stand, still graceful; their shoulders touch briefly in defeat, and they separate.

Now commences the work of sorting the garbage gathering in the cart. Large plastic-coated canvas bags are opened and made to sit on the street. Smaller plastic bags are torn open and refuse from various households is rained into the mouths of the stiffly-seated bags. The mongrel bunch comes to heel rapidly. Their true nature— one of discipline—becomes apparent as they sit back and wait patiently. The men separate the paper from the cardboard, the plastic from the peels, and gather for the dogs the crusts still stuck to pizza boxes, the noodles in take-out cartons, the dal, the roti, the chawal and the occasional donation of gristle and bone from a non-veg meal. Newspaper is spread open on the empty street, and the dogs, for all the earlier frenzy of their hip-wagging tails, now proceed gingerly from one pile to the next, picking and choosing according to their taste the breakfast with the most appeal.

While the dogs eat, the men close off with string and load onto carts the neighbourhood's discard. They set aside for themselves the toy car with the missing wheel and the running shoes with the sole that gapes at the toe. And, tied to the cart fronts, they keep as talismans mangy, leaky bears and plastic dolls no longer beloved to their once owners. The fog has burnt itself out, and the air is filled with dust clouds raised by carts departing Panchsheel Enclave.

'What is she permitting him?' I am irritated and cannot

concentrate on the headline in the *Hindu*. Why do people keep trying to make sense of this nonsense? I, for one, am inclined to shut my paper, and I do. Tomorrow some dog will feast from it. Today, I am in desperate need of my tea.

'Mona,' I shout. I know there is no way my voice will carry past the thick cement walls, or through wooden doors and down the flight of stairs to wherever in the dark below she is permitting him his liberties. Does he stroke her cheeks? They are strangely slanted. When I first saw her, I was surprised by her obviously Dravidian appearance. They had promised me a north Indian girl. Mona was dark and, as she later told me, had been passed over because of her skin by many who came to the employment agency to interview girls. I do not have such prejudices. I am also not one to visit and pick over the girls in a seamy agency office. I prefer to work with whatever material they send me. If I stipulate 'north Indian' on the phone, it is only because I find it frustrating to deal with the south Indian girls' tendency to speak mangled English. Much better that I speak mangled Hindi than listen to them take apart English.

'Mona,' I call to her. 'Mona. Mona.'

He is touching her on the neck, on her breasts. Perhaps he knows he is chosen because her breasts strain in response. I have tried to explain to her my theory that her resemblance to the darker people of the south is because she is one of the stray remnants in the north of a civilisation that the Aryans pushed south some thousands of years in the past. 'So those you call Madrasis are really your kin.' Mona takes this seriously, as she seems to everything I say. She offers that because her father was in the army, she was in fact born somewhere in the south. 'In any case,' I say, 'Mona, you are here now'.

✳

At each step, she must pull not only the weight of herself, but also the weight of her heart. At each step, she carries the weight of years of unclaimed life. She has been fifteen for six years now. Her deception has been aided by her habit of picking at her food. The shopkeepers in the Jalpaiguri of her childhood had looked up with a start when the little girl they slipped toffees to suddenly eschewed interest in sweets, sliding her hand across the counter, collecting her change with such shyness they were made aware of their own middle years: a tightness in the throat and a tearing in the groin. Six years later, she retains the appeal of eyes newly opened to the world and of frame newly moulded to curve.

Dragging herself up the stairs and against the pull of her heart, she is clothed in the spent years of her youth. Her cheeks are ruined with tears, and her eyes swollen with the torrents still to be released. The toffee-catering shopkeepers of her past would have found her thus better suited to their waning years. The shy, the bold, the brass, the mistress of herself—are all gone now. And who is climbing these stairs is not known to anyone, not even to herself. Who is climbing these stairs knows only that in the corner of the kitchen cupboard, behind the jars of sugar and flour, she has a store of brown clay that she longs to melt in her mouth; she longs to slip the dry cool wrist of Hanumanji's arm, broken off in the haste of her dusting (or was it on purpose?), and melt it there into the tender mush of an old need.

Mona is fifteen when she first begins licking the clay sides of the doorjamb in her aunt's home. Mona is fifteen when her aunt finds her savouring this strange sweet. Mona is fifteen when her aunt drags the stunned child to the street and there whips and screams: 'Bitch, what are you carrying in your belly?'

Within weeks, perhaps even days, her aunt is catching her on the way to the outhouse and telling her that she must urinate away from the home this midday because there are guests seated in the front grounds of their home. Her aunt accompanies her, and when they both rise from the bed of jungle leaves, shaking last drops of gold to dusty earth, her aunt tells her she is to meet the guests, that one among them will wed her in a matter of weeks, perhaps even days. She thinks that it will be well to leave this aunt who grudges her her keep. But at night, in her sleep, Mona dreams there is a man whom she does not know how to feed. She balances herself between these twin poles, swinging in a circle around one, and reaching and swinging with other arm around the other: flight and fear. Her aunt's only advice the day she is prepared for her departure under the shade of night's stars is: 'Always, always do what he tells you to. Never deny him his due.' Her aunt looks with searching eyes at this girl who eats dirt and sits daily with legs spread wide under her skirt.

But Mona knows what is expected of her. She worked in her thirteenth year for a clinic in Siliguri. The hour-and-a-half trek to work and back had not decided her to quit, nor had the doctor's bloody work between the legs of village women. The doctor had employed her to hold the hands of these women. And with face averted, she had stood aproned; the comfort she afforded suffering sisters was a view of the plane of her cheek. No, she had not quit when the doctor pulled from women babies healthy and sick. All of this and more she had borne, but not the dishonesty of pills she was told to feed at a premium to women who came monthly to moan that the only stir in their innards was of gas bubbles looking for release. The doctor whispered: 'These girls think they need another child.' 'These girls don't know what they need.' 'These girls,' he whispered, a kind man who had offered to train her in his trade. But she heard his whisper take on sibilance, and she left, but not before she had come to clutch in herself the knowledge of every intricate turn of frilled and smooth tube and sac, and the possibility of beads of life deep within her.

She knows what she owes and to whom, and though she shies, she is confident that, from their bed, she and Gopal will rise friends. She is patient and waits to know him and to be known. But both of their lives are filled with long days spent apart—his in field and hers in factory. And in her mother-in-law's home, she is careful to keep between her husband and herself the space his mother needs. When the night comes after the long day, it is only then, when they curve to each other, knees (pulled up) touching knees (pulled up), that his hands play with hers childish games of clapping, and only then that he slips into her restless palms the clay she desires. In the dark, she sucks his gift of earth and he sucks the grainy slime of the land from her lips.

In a matter of weeks, or perhaps days (her life moves so quickly), she is filling the space between them with a new prominence. Her mother-in-law is pleased. Mona's skin stretches tight, and her husband admires in the dark the moonlit streaks of new silver there. She, in their first nights, had reminded him of nothing so much as the burnt curled leaves that clung to her skin after the day of sifting tea in factory bins. Now her pregnant beauty startles him like the fish that rustle and slip past his shins in the flooded fields of paddy he bends over to seed. He tries to tell her this, and she laughs at him. He is hurt and never knows that she traces his poetry on her skin after the belly withers and too quickly she is delivered of her dead babies: a boy and a girl, twins.

She is not shown the babies. They disappear. She is told only that there were two and that they were blue. The midwife corrects herself—'No, black. And not to worry,' she pats Mona, 'there will be more'. These are black or blue because they came too quick, and in delivery they burst their blood vessels. The midwife has seen this before. She theorises it has to do with the bending women do these days. 'In our day,' she says, 'we never let a woman work outside her home. We did not even let her pour the water for her own bath. Not in the last months.'

Gopal is not allowed to enter the room Mona now occupies. Their bed on the roof lies empty. She sleeps for weeks in her mother-in-law's bed, cradled in the old woman's arms. The old space that ached to be filled when first she and Gopal were wed heals or closes, she is not sure which. She tries, but she cannot recollect her husband's face, except as he had first appeared to her, screened by garlands and later filmed by the cloth she keeps peaked over her head. In time, too soon, they return to their bed, and there the business of their nights turns her stomach, and she snips herself free and wanders the night sky, far from his sharp elbows, the hairs on his calf, which she had marvelled once were finer than hers, and the sweet stench of his labour.

It becomes known to her mother-in-law that the children are no longer able to love. And it is she who urges them to try their luck anew, elsewhere. One year in Delhi will fill their pockets, as it has the pockets of the groups of six and eight who every year leave with this agency and that, some returning with 15,000 or more, and others not returning at all. This latter worry, the old woman keeps to herself.

It is a relief to Mona when the train pulls into Delhi, and the man from the agency, who has been a benevolent figure to this point, suddenly turns belligerent. 'You two will not find work together.' He tells Gopal, 'We will take her to a good family situation.' Seen through the lowered corner of her eyes, her husband is a semicircle of clothed chest, cuffs, belt and knees in new pants. She never looks at his face, only tells Gopal that she is willing to go but must have money for soap and paste. The agent's assurance—that a phone number answered in the drawing room of the good family situation will be provided to help them remain known to each other—is wasted.

Mona moves rapidly from one home to the next, discovering her calling: caring alternately for the feeble young and the feeble old. She assumes that her husband has, at the end of the year, returned to his mother.

For six years she lives in the self-made age of fifteen. And if at times this life is one of fleeting links with the fleeting lives of employers old and young, sixty-three and three, it is no more fleeting, she reasons, than what she has always known. The sunny terraces of paddy outside her husband's home, the cool dark of the factory where she had laughed with other young girls sprouting bumps in their middle, are anomalies in a life that she has come to understand on the train journey to Delhi as a series of way-stations too unimportant to register except by the merest slowing of speed and then quickly onward and screeching to the next unimportant destination.

The first time she sees Gopal standing among the men below her balcony at D-16, she knows him only by his shirt—a pale affair of distinct stripes. She has buttoned and unbuttoned its length in the past. That shirt, cotton, long-sleeved, and worn buttoned at the wrist, which was all that she had seen of him that first day of their life together, had been handsome, had stood in for his face and given her reason to hope that he would be handsome. She had grasped its presence, where a kurta would have been more the expected choice, as evidence of the lifelong friendship she was meant to hatch with him. It still looks new on him; preserved in some way, if not in fact, then in her memory. But Gopal, she does not remember.

'I am not the same person I was then,' he offers. 'I have changed. I made so many mistakes then.'

She can't think of what those mistakes might have been. But she knows change, feeling it within herself. The first day, she proffers the cup of tea she has hastily made with all the formality she had practised in the long ago days of their marriage. She reaches nervously for the head covering that isn't there and, when she does it again, he drains the cup, gasps as it scalds, places it between their feet and takes her hands in his. There he admires the smooth skin, the sun-caught-glint quality of it. His fingers trace and retrace the mystery of his ache, but it is beyond her to decipher this, and she pulls her hands away from his.

The second morning she meets him with tea, she looks at him. It is a conscious decision. She has spent the previous night preparing for this. She sees that he never went home, that he is aged by his life here. She sees he might be as old as forty—as old as the shopkeepers of her childhood. But his eyes are moist, and the brush of hair on his upper lip trembles so that she might as well laugh as weep at his frailty. She tells him, 'I am sad. I am always sad. But I know I shouldn't be, so I don't let myself be.' His eyes spill over. And this she wills herself to see.

He leaves her then with the photograph. It is late at night when, having finished her work, she sits and studies it. The image is indistinct. There is dirt to be seen and a corner of a half-sawed clay wall, intruding from the margins to the centre, drawing attention to a huddle of shapes there.

The dirt and the wall, she recognises—her mother-in-law's plot at the front of their home. He, too busy in the rice fields and she, responsible for bringing cash home—they had, neither of them, contributed much to this plot of cauliflower, peas, onions, green chillies, tomatoes and brinjal. But Mona had been the cook and had gathered the plenty for each meal. Her toes remember curling in the soft loam. She knows this piece of land. But the huddled shapes laid there are new to her.

What she has not known, was never allowed to see, and now tries to drink in with her eyes, in all their mangled beauty, are two blurred sets of darkened limbs, each positioned by her husband to cradle the other in infinity. Her children are surrounded in this fanciful portrait of his love and loss by the harvest of that summer season—dark red blobs of tomatoes, white clouds of cauliflower in green. She is surprised to smile, and her fingers stroke the grainy image—they look like little brinjals, neither black nor blue, her little violet babies.

✳

I wonder how much longer Mona will be with me, now that some lover makes his daily appearance. Mona has been crying, but I am sure, as that is natural with lovers, there is no use hoping for her to stay. The thought of her leaving has me irritated. But then I don't want to be one of those selfish old men whose needs are paramount. I have let my children go (to Amritsar, Canada and faraway Greater Kailash), so why would I grasp at the straw of her. I think I will tell her to leave and save her the trouble of lying about a sick relative who needs her wherever that she might be from.

It is reassuring now to see her here. She is squatting, cleaning the floor, the pocha in her hand; she pays more attention to such tasks than most. Today when she gave me my tea she held in her hand a second cup she took downstairs. I admire the honesty that has her acting so openly. I will tell Mona she can go.

'Mona,' I say.

She looks up. Her face is radiant. It is a sign of the weakness of my age that I cannot see the sun as I used to; I must shield my eyes from it. Her face must be catching and reflecting the light of the sun coming in through the balcony's glass doors. My chair seems to be moving under me.

'Mona.'

Her face is radiant, and the smile there is tender with such love—somewhere in the past, someone smiled at me thus.

Not Known

JANATA COPY BOOK

Name:
Subject:
School:

SHOP NO. 30; DARYAGUNJ; OLD DELHI

```
  400        My name is Shanta Dal.
  175        My father's name is Bhuvan Dal.
  100        I am studying in
  100
 +300
 ─────
 1175
 ─────
```

I want to be a singer. I can sing in three different voices. I can sing Asha Bhosle, Lata Mangeshkar and Kavita Krishnamurthy. Actually I can do Alka Yagnik also. But my favourites are Asha Bhosle, Lata Mangeshkar and Kavita Krishnamurthy. Once I worked in the house of Pooja Bedi's daughter and she heard me sing and said there was no difference between my voice and Lata Mangeshkar's. If only I could find out if I can be on the *Indian Idol* show. On Radio Mirchi they always say 'Dial 646' and you can enter to be on Indian Idol. But if a person doesn't have a mobile, then how can a person enter? I used Didi's mobile to call *Indian Idol* and I sang '*Hum Dil De Chuke Sanam*' in Kavita Krishnamurthy's voice. I shouldn't use Didi's mobile. But she'll never even notice. Only if they call to say I am in the show, then she will find out. But if that happens Didi will be happy for me. I know she will.

Competitions awards

Anju Dua is one of the ~~moust~~ *most* wel ~~non couchs~~ *known Coaches* in gymnastics in the ~~stat stet~~ *state* of Haryana and a no of her study studons are today wining aw*a*rds in many gymnastic ~~competions~~ in the ~~steds~~ and outside, And ~~exsllant gynast~~, Anju's ~~achievemans~~ are far ~~gred gretar~~ ~~seens~~ she ~~this~~ *is* a special ~~pson~~ Being Both ~~dufb~~ *deaf* and dumb

gymnast   excellent
greater   since
achievements person

When I first came to work here they said they wanted to help me. They wanted me to say what I want to be in my life. They wanted to help me become something better than a servant. I was very sad when they said this and cried because I couldn't think of anything to say or anything that I wanted to become. Didi asked me if I wanted to learn tailoring or if I wanted to work in a beauty parlour. I didn't think about singing then. Later I thought I should have asked them to give me tuition in singing. But if I had said that then they probably would have said no.

I said I wanted to go to school. First I had to tell the truth that I am not 8th pass. The agency people always tell us that if anyone asks in an interview we should always say 8th pass, but when I was living in Jalpaiguri I only studied up to half of 5. Didi did not know about Open School. I told her and then she found it on the Internet and I got admitted. Even then she came back to me and said in Open School they have tailoring classes and girls are learning tailoring and after the classes are over they will give you money to start your own shop.

I said to Didi I only want to go to school and become 10th pass and then I want to keep studying till I am 12th pass. I knew Didi would become very impressed if I said this. But still she kept asking me, 'Why, Shanta? Why do you want to do studies? You will have to join Open School in Class 10. How will you pass Class 10 when you have only studied up to Class 5?' I said to Didi that I will study hard and pass Class 10 and then I will be able to get a good job in a shop. Maybe in a shop that sells clothes, or I could sell jewellery, maybe in Shoppers' Stop, or if I can't do that then I want to work at Pizza Hut. I already know that to get those jobs you have to be 12th pass. Didi said she would help me with all my homework and studies. But actually she only did that in the beginning and now every time I ask her something about studies she says she is too busy.

I have to write about the Tsunami. She just looked for Tsunami on the Internet on the computer and she wants me to read about Tsunami from the computer. So far I am not understanding anything about the Tsunami.

I know you. I see you looking at me. You were at the wedding. You wore an orange sari and you were so fair the colour suited you. Everyone said you were the most beautiful girl there.

this is Shanta. I am 47 years old. I have two and a half cm white patches near the folds of my eyelids. They have grown in size over the period of two years. I am concerned about these patches.please recommend a cure for this asha NaimCochin

Cochin

I am 47 years old. I have two and a half cmwhite patches near the folds of my eye lids. They have many grown in size over about these patches. please please recoment to the mountane my name is Shanta Dal

I am 47 years old I have two and

gound

this is my name.

fun.

I am very beautiful. I have a boyfriend. He and I are going to be married soon. We are in school together. His name is Nadeem. I love him very much. He is very tall. He is fair. He is more fair than I am. People stare at us because of that. He has wavy hair. Sometimes he is silly and jokes and laughs at everything I say.

My friend Chinky is very jealous of me. When I wear anything nice she tells me I look bad in that. Then later she will ask me if she can borrow that same blouse. I know what she is doing. But I am not worried about anything. I let her borrow anything of mine she wants. But I just hate it when she borrows money. She never returns the money she borrows. Where does she think I get money from? I work to earn money.

When Kalyani's sister got married, Chinky said we have to wear saris to the wedding. I said, 'All right, but I don't have a good sari.' She said, 'No problem. You can borrow mine.' Then she saw me wear it one day when we were just trying on clothes to see how we would look for the wedding. She realised how good I look and said, 'You shouldn't wear a black sari. You look exactly like a witch. Let's not wear saris for the wedding.' Then she took back her sari which was dark blue net and had a border with white stones. But first I took a picture of me in it for Nadeem because I knew I looked very beautiful in it. Maybe this is the picture he can send his mother.

After Chinky took the sari back she said we can wear jeans for the wedding. I knew what she was doing but still I agreed. I wore jeans to the wedding. Then when I reached there she was wearing the same dark blue net sari I was going to wear. But I didn't care. When we started dancing everyone moved out of the way and only the two of us were left in the end. But I just kept dancing to the music, not paying attention to her and I knew she was trying to do all the steps I was doing but in the end she had to stop and only I was left dancing.

But later that night Nadeem really made me cry. He said 'Don't you see how people look at you. Why do you have to dance by yourself in front of everyone?'

When Nadeem and I sit together Chinky comes and sits closer to him than I do and takes his hand in her lap. I don't pay attention to her. It is her nature to act like that.

Nadeem's brother is telling him to not marry me. He told Nadeem last week that people say love is blind but your love is also black.

It's true. I am black.

When I leave home to walk to School,
Dad always says to me
March, keep your eyelids up and see
What you can see

My father gon to Jalpaiguri
But when I tell him where I've been
And what I think I've seen
He looks at me and sternly says
He looks at me and sternly says
And what I think

My name is Shanta Dal
this is my name
I am studying in N.B.S. Public School
My fathers name is Bhuvan Dal
My brothers name is Darshan Dal
I like to watch T.V.
I like to play with my Friend

My father's hand shakes all the time. He drinks all day and all night. He does not care about us. He left us and ever since then we have been alone.

When my mother left us I was three years old. I remember the day she left us because I burned my hand on that day. She was sitting on a cot outside our house with a man. I asked her to give me some food because I was hungry and she screamed at me and said 'Go get your own rice.' So I went to the stove and tried to put my hand inside the pot and I screamed because I got burnt. Then my grandfather heard me and came to help me. After that day my mother never was in our house again. She even left Darshan who was only a baby.

My father is an angry man. He used to say to us when we lived with him, 'If I ever catch sight of your mother, I will cut her into pieces.' He would sometimes say, 'I should have cut her throat when I had the chance.' My aunty told me when I lived with her that my mother was an evil woman who made my father take the operation that cut his manhood and after he did it she left him, going away with another man.

My father used to be in the army so he gets a pension. Even though I tell everyone my father and mother are dead, I know he is still alive because when Darshan went to Jalpaiguri last year he saw my father at the bank where he comes one day every month to get his pension money. If I want to see him I can go to the bank on the right day in Jalpaiguri and see him. Darshan saw him there and he said my father's hands and parts of his whole body were shaking. Even so my father was carrying his army sword and he pulled it out and told Darshan that if he catches our mother he will cut her and feed her to us.

My mother. No one knows for sure if she is alive but I can go to her village and ask. I haven't yet. I think about it. I can remember a lot of things from when I was so little. I remember when I was so little that I could not climb out of the bed. How old must I have been to be that little? I remember sitting on the bed and crying for someone to come and get me off the bed. I remember my mother's voice calling me and I can hear her coming. I wish I could remember her face.

I don't think I could ever wear any clothes that are orange. The time I did Nadeem said I looked like an orange ice cream bar. Then he said he wanted a lick but I was hurt because he was laughing at me. He got angry and said my blouse was too low and the material of the sari was too transparent. I said to him 'What kind of a boy from the tenth century are you?'

My name is Shanta Dal.
My name is Shanta Dal
Shanta Shanta Shanta

When I was little there was a teacher in our school who was Rosie Teacher Ma'am. She made her students smile and laugh and she taught me things I always remember. She said to me, 'Shanta, when you begin writing always write your name.' Ever since I always like to write and when I write I write my name.

My name is Shanta Dal
Shanta Shanta Shanta

Who are you? Who are you? Who? I see you sometimes. You have good handwriting. Not like mine. You look nice in your orange sari. Your boyfriend doesn't make fun of you and get angry at you. You have everything I don't have. How?

I will tell you who I am. First let me tell you the bad things. The bad thing that happened to me today is Nadeem came back from his home. He called me from the station to say he is back. It woke everyone up when the phone rang. He said, 'I am sorry but I cannot marry you.' I didn't know what to say so I said 'All right'. He said his mother wants him to marry someone else. He said his mother said, 'Don't make me repent the milk I fed you.' I said, 'It's all right, Nadeem.' He was acting all sad on the phone, speaking in a sad voice to me, when really I am the one who is sad. Now where will I go? All the beautiful things I was planning. The cup and saucer set Didi gave me for Diwali. I thought we would make a house together. Now where will I place all my beautiful things? You tell me.

My name is Shanta Dal I am studying in N.B.S. public school I like to Studying my ticher name is kumr Mam my ~~freid~~ *friend name is Suneeta*

I am working in panchsheel Enclave Police protect us
We have to skate ~~scary~~ ^(scared) *with*
~~on~~ *the God*
What are you doing there
I am ~~plaing~~ ^(playing)

When I had to register for school they asked me if I was a Dalit. I said, 'No, my name is Shanta Dal.' Still, Principal Ma'am kept asking me, 'Are you Dalit?' I said, 'My name is Shanta Dal.' Finally I said, 'No, I am not Dalit.' She was thinking I was black so I must be a low-caste. But I am not. She said, 'I am asking you so I can give you a special admission. It is good if you are a Dalit.' I said, 'No, I am not Dalit.' As if anyone who is Dalit will agree to tell her and get a special admission. Probably Principal Ma'am gets a special fee from the government for the special admission. She should at least offer to give a share of that money. Otherwise why should anyone say they are a Dalit?

When I had to register for school they asked me to bring a birth certificate. I said to them, 'My father has my birth certificate.' Then they said, 'Bring it from your father.' I said, 'He is dead.' Then they said, 'You must make an affidavit.'

I wanted to tell Principal Ma'am that our house in Jalpaiguri when I was little was a real house. It was a pukka house. I slept on a bed. It was a small house but it was beautiful.

I went to get the affidavit from Mehrauli. The Magistrate in Mehrauli is where the Principal Ma'am told me to go. All day I had to wait in queues and many people who gave bribes got ahead of me in line. I waited till a man said that I was in the wrong line and to come outside with him where he would give me the form and help me to fill it. I went with him like a stupid and he filled it for me. He held the form out to me after filling it and when I tried to take it from him he kept holding my hand and saying, 'You haven't paid for it yet.' Normally I yell at a person who touches me like that but I thought to myself, I need the form.

I paid for the form and went inside to give it to the Magistrate and again I had to wait in queues. In the end I was sitting in a chair and almost falling asleep when another man called from a window and said, 'Shanta Dal Shanta Dal Shanta Dal,' and all the people were laughing to hear my name. The man in the window started laughing and said, 'What kind of a name is Shanta Dal?' He started laughing again and saying to me, 'Your father and mother must like eating Dal.' Again people laughed at me.

The same thing that happened with the man who wouldn't let go of my hand happens all the time to me. It makes me so angry. By the time I got my affidavit done the office closed. They did mine last and when I went outside the evil man was gone. I wanted to follow him and go to his house and scream at him in front of his wife and children.

Whenever this happened before to me I had no one to tell. Then I had Nadeem. Now I again don't have anyone. But even with Nadeem often he said all the wrong things to me. He was always telling me to not wear jeans. When he saw some boys at school looking at me he would say, 'Why do you have to wear tight jeans?' He made me feel like I was the one who was dirty. 'Nadeem, the boys are the ones who are dirty by looking at me with dirty thoughts in their mind. Why are you punishing me by making me feel dirty when it is they who are dirty?'

When my father left my grandfather took care of us till he died. The day he died for three days people kept coming to my house and looking at us, at me and Darshan. At first I thought they were going to help us but they were only interested in looking at us. I started to worry because soon there would be no more food for Darshan and me. Then my aunty came and for a little while we stayed with her. But then my uncle started to act dirty around me and when I tried to tell her she slapped me and said 'You dirty girl'. But one night he really tried to with me when I was taking a bath and my aunty stood outside the door and kept knocking and knocking and all the while I kept screaming and screaming. I didn't let him do anything to me. After that my uncle told my aunty to send me away to Delhi to work.

I was alone on the bus and when night came the bus driver said some things to me about how I must be a runaway and he would take me back home if I didn't do what he said. It took me two days to come to Delhi and I had to keep finding people on the bus to sit with so the bus driver would leave me alone. I didn't go to the bathroom for two days and when I came to Delhi I couldn't wait anymore and I went right by the street behind a wall and it burned as it came out. It was dark yellow and as more and more came out it became pink. I knew I must be very sick then.

Even when the worst things ever happened to me I never thought about dying. I get so angry when I hear about people who take their own lives. I never ever think like that.

I have been here in Delhi since I was fifteen, working as a servant always, and I have never seen Jalpaiguri since I left from there. I don't know what happened to our house and except for Darshan who came to Delhi the next year after me I don't know any of the people I used to know. But when I was little and lived in Jalpaiguri we lived in a beautiful house.

Ve are sew there
Ve are dedan't hear ther any
Voices of bird aneny voices of Traffic.
Now is the places of amptinas

That plase smelling
of Ded body of human bing and smel
of animal. That plase smel like
a burial ground.
Ve hurt ve must helf
Them to are foutec.

   raiting H.W.
   Tsunami

When I heard about the Tsunami I wanted to send some money to help the people. On the radio I heard about people sending money. But nobody was asking people like me to send money so I never found out where I could send my money. I felt very sorry for all the people whose families were killed, whose houses were destroyed. Those people lost everything.

I dream all the time about people dying. I dreamt last night that Nadeem was being carried in a giant wave of water. When I was little I saw the pipe that comes over the bridge into our side of the mountain tear open. The water was spraying everywhere and my uncle with water spraying into his eyes and with his eyes closed had to work to repair the pipe. My dream was just like that. In my dream there was water in my eyes and I couldn't see Nadeem who was being carried away. Then the wave was over and Nadeem was lying on the road with his hands and legs cut off and with blood coming out of the places where his hands and legs used to be. He cried and called out to me. He was calling again and again but I couldn't go to him.

Can you call someone to you by wanting him to come? I did it to Nadeem. When he tried to leave me I called him to me and he came back to me. At night I called to him in my mind. Sunday morning at school I stopped allowing him to pretend he didn't know me. I went up to him and talked to him. You must be surprised that he came back to me. Now I don't know if I want him back. He made me suffer when he pretended not to know me at school. People at school said such things about me. Because of him people are insulting me.

Now Nadeem says his mother has agreed that he can marry me. But I have to change my name and become Farzana. That's what Muslims do when they get married. He chose my new name which is beautiful. He made me talk to his mother on the phone and she said when I come to see her she will give gifts and food to all the villagers and she will have a celebration for our wedding. Only she made me promise that I will not take Nadeem away from her. Then I heard her tell Nadeem's sister, 'Come talk to your Bhabi.' That was a moment of great happiness for me.

But I also know that most of the time just wanting something is a great way to not get it. Or you can get it and it turns out to not be a good thing. I am careful what I dream about. If I feel myself dreaming about something I really really want I stop my dream. If it is something not important that I want like new curtains that are so light they blow in the breeze then I let myself dream and my dream comes true. This year I don't sleep in the kitchen or drawing room. I have my own room and there is a curtain that is made of white and green cloth. Nadeem will move to my room after our wedding. I will become Farzana.

These days Nadeem fights with me all the time. He tells me what to wear. He tells me not to dance. If we are sitting with our friends and I take food in my hands to give it to him he yells at me and says, 'I already said "No". Why do you have to turn everything into a drama?' I fight with him. He asks me to change in too many ways. I don't know what will happen to me after we get married. But if anybody keeps pushing me down I can't help it I get angry. He asks me for too much.

I still see you in that sari you wore to Kalyani's wedding. You were so beautiful that day. Someone must have seen you that day and chosen you for his own. But the person who chooses you will never leave you. Will never want to change you.

These days are hot. At night even with the window open and the fan on the sweat pours from my body. I sit with very little clothes on. Sometimes I speak to Nadeem in my mind. I feel shy because I am not wearing much clothes. But soon we will be married and he will see me in this room just as I am today. So I tell myself not to mind. When I was sick last month he asked me why I looked the way I did with pain on my face. I told him at first it was because my stomach hurt then I said it was because my period had started then I told him the truth that something was happening that was making my period go for too long and it smelled bad and made me hurt more than before. I thought I have never told anyone something like this. He told me to talk to Didi and if she doesn't help me, he will take me to the doctor himself. I know I should marry Nadeem. Finally someone will take care of me.

These days at night I sit studying on my bed. I try to tell Nadeem what I am thinking. Then I think I hear from behind me footsteps and I hold still because when I don't turn to look a hand touches the back of my neck, so gently, and I almost hear your boyfriend's voice in my ears. What must he say to you? When Nadeem touches me on my wrist I wonder if you feel it. These days I feel such loneliness hurting me from inside.

> *This is me Shanta Dal speaking*
> *My name is Shanta Dal*
> *Speaking*
> *My th the this girl is speaking*
> *hapent*
> *raiting these those*
>
> *Now it happened that as they were going along*
> *they stumbled over a bush, and with the shaking*

the bit of poisoned apple flew out of her throat. It
was not long before she opened her eyes, threw up
the cover of the coffin, and sat up, alive and well.
'Oh dear, where am I?' cried she.

Raiting Practis

I burnt my hand last week when it touched the cooking pot. There is a shape like a thin piece of the moon on the inside of my wrist. A white part of me is showing from under the black skin everywhere else. Today I will ask the man when we put mehendi on my hand and arm to keep away from my thin white moon. I will put haldi on it instead. It will burn. Maybe then it will always stay like this. White.

Will you still be in a beautiful orange sari when I lose my name? I will always write my name and I will fold the paper. Shanta Dal. You must come to me then.

Stray Blades of Grass

The day Renu meets Suroma, she is not the least bit surprised to see this pressed-frock version of herself hunkered under the gardenia bush, waiting. There have been clues—a forgotten water bottle once and a grubby towel spread out to (now it's obvious) protect the frock. There has also been the anticipation building in Renu since her discovery of the park. And when Suroma—after some noises about Renu as intruder in Suroma's park, to which Renu replies with appropriately chastened trailing of toe in dirt and sucking of pigtails—deigns to share her name, the elusive trail Renu's mother had taken out of this world is once again visible to Renu.

'My mother's name,' Renu tells Suroma, 'is Suroma'. Suroma is disdainful, maybe even disbelieving, and shyly Renu adds, 'Also.'

'So what?' Suroma enquires. 'Your mother is the presswali. I know because my mother gives her my school uniform, and all my other clothes also, for pressing.'

'That's not my mother. That's my didi,' says Renu miserably. The promised happiness of friendship with her mother's namesake is not materialising. And the return of her mother's name to her is rapidly coalescing into something solid in her chest; something with sharp edges. Water swallowed too quickly has done this to Renu; stuck itself like a knife in her throat.

'No, that's not your didi, that's your mother now. Everyone knows your first mother is dead. And you are the presswali's new daughter.'

When this fails to elicit the earlier toe trailing, Suroma gives Renu a push, and an angry Renu bursts out with, 'Well your mother is an idiot who, who . . .' and Renu doesn't have the experience trading insults with children, of middle class or any other provenance, to know how to continue.

Suroma, the much worldlier Suroma, judiciously sums up this introduction to their new-found intimacy with, 'You don't know anything. My mother is at least alive and she doesn't even have to work. She is home right now. And anyway, you can play with me.'

Renu tries mightily, at first, to interest Suroma in the wonders of her world. She does not think names of birds important so introduces them to Suroma by their colours. On dun-coloured hillocks they ruffle their dun-coloured breasts. And then she points to where vivid green trees burst vivid sparks of green into the sky. 'That's just parrots,' says Suroma. 'If you want, you can come to my house and see one the cook keeps in a cage.' Renu tries again. Her birds are everywhere, in soft clumps of dust, in wet grass, perched on the tender tips of swaying branches, in bushes thorny to their breasts. 'But show me their eggs!' Suroma cries angrily. 'What's the good of just birds?' Renu despairs.

Suroma prefers to read, and has glasses to prove it. Because Renu cannot read, at least not well enough to understand what she is reading, Suroma reads to her. She reads from Tagore, and the two girls weep together to think of the Kabuliwallah who must seek his lost daughter's face in the face of another girl. She reads in English and tirelessly translates as she reads—the various adventures of Peter, Janet, and Jack, Barbara, Pam, Colin and George. 'I want to be a writer someday,' she tells Renu, 'you tell me all the stories you know.' But the only stories Renu can offer are the ones heard from her father's superior, the senior pundit; the ones she enjoys, about Krishna's childhood antics stealing butter or sucking the demoness Putana's breasts till he draws blood, leave Suroma disgusted. 'You don't understand. I want to hear all the true stories about your life. What is the temple like? What is your father like? Does he beat you? Is your new mother mean like Cinderella's stepmother? What do you eat?'

Renu hangs her head and their friendship becomes one in which Suroma talks and Renu listens. Suroma tells Renu about the time she had seen an accident and how a disembodied hand had flown through the air and landed on her lap. Secretly, Renu is sceptical of this tale but knows better than to express her doubts. Instead, she tells Suroma about the time she found an eagle's claw, the leg still attached to the claw, but chewed by rats. In truth, though Renu has seen this claw, its discovery had been made by the senior pundit and had left Renu's mother in a bad mood in the days prior to her death.

*

When her mother was alive, Renu's feet cycled in sleep, tangling themselves in the rope of the charpoy. If her mother failed to lay a hand on her and whisper, 'Sleep now, I will wake you in the morning,' Renu would thrash her legs, flinging them up from the waist till she woke. So when Renu's mother died giving birth to baby Jai, Renu's greatest fear was not that there would be no one to whisper to her at night, to keep her in sleep, but instead that, without her mother, God's bright hot mornings would come to the temple compound and she, locked in sleep, would miss the glory.

Her father brought home a new wife—too soon for anyone's taste. But no one dared openly criticise the temple's junior pundit. And everyone agreed that the baby, who appeared to want to follow his mother, would need one if he was to remain. This marriage had the added benefit of bringing to an end Renu's clenched hold on night-time wakefulness. What she heard in the dark from her father's bed frightened her. She wrestled herself into sleep with balled-up fists and screwed-up eyes, and with legs stilled—before her father could find his way to the giggles emanating from his new wife.

When her mother was still alive, Renu's days were spent in the tangled-manicured paradise of her jungle park, which radiated from her home in the temple compound, and was the known universe. The tangled-manicured grounds were so because malis numbering in the hundreds would have been necessary to impose order on this vast stretch of land. When its great trees dropped soaked limbs at the end of the monsoon season, the pundits gathered other men to discuss what it would take to push city authorities for more staff and maintenance. The conversation concluded, as all such conversations did, in a hopelessness alleviated only in small measure by the insults Renu's father heaped on the malis: 'Those lazy, worthless, third-rate jokers. Bloody bastards. Those Johnnies need a severe beating. That will cure them of sleeping the day away.'

Renu could not imagine anyone ever willingly sleeping during the day. Nor did she understand her father's low opinion of the malis. She revered them because her jungle park was perfect as it was. Its paths circled and circled and though hours of wandering led her endlessly onward, they had never failed to bring her home.

After her mother's death, these paths that meandered in brick dust through the jungle park offered new wonders; most of them involving some stage in dying. From these wonders Renu came to know the precise place where time creased and tore sharply to allow a dung beetle, eased of limbs and wings and cradled in palm, to pass from frantic motion of appeal to dry shell. Once, she built a shrine and returned for a period to the same spot under a gulmohar tree where a dog had left a turd longer than any in dog history. She watched its snake-like existence crumble softly at the edges and collapse to meet the furry earth, leaving behind a vague structure of fibres that, by remaining changeless, dissuaded her further interest.

In the morning, the ochre pathways were strewn with mehendi-green, casually dropped splats—some oblong and others perfectly circular—of cows making their way to forage in surrounding colony dumps. Crows pecked at these piles of what was still recognisable as chewed up grass, undigested grains. And what was pecked at in the early hours was, by midday, pocked with minute holes through which vapour steamed—a sign of life lingering? No, gone was gone. She was adamant on this point. And to confirm the absoluteness of endings, come evening, she checked: the mali had passed through and gathered the dung cakes to reconstitute with water and offer to the young plants grown in the nursery behind the temple compound. As far as Renu was concerned, once dead, always dead—no rebirth, no recycle, regardless of the claims made by her father's superior, the senior pundit.

But cow pats did convince her that life could extend itself past death. What convinced her was not the grains, the crows, or even the mali's trick of reconstitution. Seeing grass blades whole and intact in those soft piles, she was sure that some further search of the void where her mother used to be would yield, whole and intact, the stray-blade extensions of her mother's life. At night, lightning bugs flashing for mates left similar trails of their passing. With eyes squeezed into slits, she watched them blink and spin in a plastic bottle. A swift shake of the bottle and a single blink of light extended into a zigzagging trail, tracing eternity, before the stunned creature was extinguished.

Renu's only experience of desperation up to this point had been her need to wake up in advance of the sun. Her only experience of life had been within the jungle park that extended for kilometres from the temple centre—north to the back of Gargi College for Women, south to Soami Nagar, east to Panchsheel Enclave, and west even to Shahpur Jat. These neighbourhoods had been as distant to her as the people, mostly fat and old, who came after her mother's death to the temple and chucked her under the chin, harshly, she felt. With her mother's death, the neighbourhoods became real, and metal turnstiles (how had she missed their parameter presence?), that stuck and pushed her back at her bony chest, turned with additional pressure and tripped her out into this new world. She was given a job—working alongside her new mother as a runner in her new uncle's business, picking up crushed and crumpled clothes from Panchsheel Enclave's D-Block homes (D-16, D-18, D-33 . . . D-91), and returning them pressed and folded and neatly wrapped and—here was her part in it all—counted correctly or risk the swift blow to her head and the ringing it brought.

She was desperate now. Perhaps it was the ringing in her head, but her dead mother—and she has accepted the death, its irrevocability—had a name once, and she could no longer remember it. Jai had grown so he no longer lay feebly on his back. Now his little fists pumped the air, cheering, when really he shouldn't, she thought sourly. She remembered that her mother was Ammi to her but something else also—a name, a name, which one? She called her new mother Didi for she was just a few years older than Renu and not really old enough to be an ammi. She whispered 'Ammi' to Jai when Didi was not around. But despite her best efforts, when Didi stepped under the cloth-strung bamboo poles that sheltered their little enterprise from the scorching heat blasted from sky above and radiated from tarmac below, Jai pumped that fist and cheered, making 'mi-mi-mi' noises as Didi scooped him up and fondled him. 'Yes,' she crooned, 'I am your Ammi. Say it, my sweet, say Ammi.' Renu was angry; angry enough to want to imagine taking the heavy, charcoal-filled, monster of an iron that glowed in the hands of her uncle and using it to press shut Jai's baby face.

Instead, she stalked out to continue her running from D-13 to D-16 to wherever there might be a glimpse of the continuity she had divined for herself in slim blades of grass.

The first she saw of it was when, walking past the morning haggling of grandmothers, conducted over mounds of fruit, walking along the side of a green metal fence, low-built, trailing her waist, she stumbled (how had she not known of this entrance, having walked this very route morning after morning?) through a gap in the fence, through a turnstile, also stiff and unyielding, and then yielding, into a miniature of the world she had once inhabited. There was no tarmac here intruding into the oblong, almost circular, green of grass, only a soft path of red circling the grass—and trees, shrubs, and flowers, arranged high to low, from back to front, shielding D-Block Park's handkerchief breadth, the green map of a connection to her past.

In this park she found herself a space suitable for observing wonders familiar and new. She spread someone's cast-off towel under the boughs of the gardenia, lay back and watched a bird perched above, not on a branch, but actually on a leaf. Her heart sped as the bird twisted and cocked its head at her. And the bird in turn, aware of her regard, hung in the air to stare, and its heart slowed. That afternoon in the park she renewed her faith in: birds, trees, cow dung. The discovery of the park was proof that time possessed the ability to intersect itself. And when time broke apart, with a flutter and a flash of red heretofore hidden beneath wings and now revealed throbbing in flight, Renu was done crying and ready for this portent to reveal its meaning.

Jai progressed from crowing to rolling and was now crawling. But his antics didn't hold her, and daily she came to D-Block Park, resting between running her loads, sometimes below the heavy perfume of gardenia, and sometime between hedges of scentless star jasmine. She was mesmerised by the birds of this diminutive park. In the jungle-park surrounding her home, the scale of her life and the scale of the trees were similarly large and unknowable. What she had concentrated on were the poisonous caterpillars, frogs and fire-ants marching across the paths. Then, her eyes had seen the ground below, and now she concentrated on the expanse above—and flight.

✳

It is late evening on the last day of June. Renu's knees wink slyly at her as she pumps them higher and higher. She holds in her a secret pride that if she lets herself she can outrace Suroma any day of the year. But today the race is not against Suroma—it is against time, and to Suroma.

Earlier that day, Suroma informed Renu that only five more days of summer holidays remain, and soon she will go daily from her home to school, will wear daily her school uniform and not her play clothes, and the park will be a stop on her new schedule only in the evenings, and not even some evenings, since Tuesday and Thursday evenings she has to go to tennis lessons, and Mummy is also arranging for her Kathak lessons on other evenings.

It is evening on the last day of June, and Renu has been absorbing the idea that time will move forward and soon she will lose her friend. Already morning and afternoon have passed, and Suroma, who has taken to accompanying Renu on her rounds dropping off pressed clothes, has long since fulfilled this daily ritual and returned home. Renu is in the twilit park, hidden in the lower branches of their secret-club tree, absently searching for stray crumbs of gur and coconut, a treat which they keep hidden, and which provides them with an agenda—eating—for their secret-club meetings. A noise in the distance is growing nearer, and fearing its entry into her sanctuary, Renu scrambles down.

She eases herself through the turnstile and sees the tail end of a group of eight or ten men, marching in the direction of A-Block. The men carry lanterns and sticks which they pump above their heads. What are they shouting? Not words that Renu can hear, just elated sounds of anger. Bystanders gather: colony sweepers, and servant girls with thin hair and thin faces. Above, in the balconies, screen doors slide open to allow housewives to lean over railings and witness the commotion. Chowkidars in their khaki uniforms lounge at the gates separating these housewives from the suddenly turbulent colony street. They look at one another—finally some excitement to break the monotony of their vigil.

Renu slides behind the gathering knots of people and hurries toward the press stand. She is likely to be scolded, but at least she will avoid getting slapped for lingering over this piece of street tamasha. Among the many lessons her uncle has imparted to her is the importance of keeping clear of trouble—especially the kind generated in the late hours by young men.

In the market, the lights have been lit against the approaching dark, and there is more noise—loud wailing of women. The women are outside the press stand's burlap awning. They take turns to enter and exit the structure, and with each circling, the wailing increases in tempo to subside again. Renu is scared because she sees no one she knows. Jai, Didi and Uncle are not among the circling women. Her feet tell her to fly back home to the temple compound where her father, she thinks, must be conducting the evening puja. But she has never made the trip home on her own and so late. She frightens herself imagining the temple empty, her father vanished as Jai, Didi and Uncle have.

Reluctantly, she draws closer and spotting her, the women pulse around her. 'You poor, poor thing. God has spared this girl. Oh merciful God, you have spared this girl!' The women register in Renu's mind as a circle of crows. She mistakes for wings the arms they use to push her forcibly into their circle, and having hemmed her in, then to transport her into the shack. Inside, among the bundles of pressed and crumpled clothes, her Didi is a bundle as well, an abject bundle, a bundle with a baby, a baby in her lap, a baby that lies still, as still as Didi holds her tear-washed face. Renu understands how important it is to be still when all around crows are flapping their beastly wings and cawing and cawing. But in their caws, she hears what propels her from their midst.

She flees, her knees pumping and winking. Baby Jai is dead. He is dead, her chotu bhai, her little brother. He crawled because he is now able to crawl. And a driver, an employee of an A-Block family, backed his jeep without checking for the presence of crawling babies.

She has never been to Suroma's home before. She is not as familiar with A-Block, where Suroma lives, as she is with D-Block. Nevertheless she flies, she is sure, to Suroma's house. The driver who backed the jeep is from A-Block, and the marching men were headed for A-Block, and that is where Suroma was headed when she had tidily closed the door to summer and left Renu in the park. Renu flies, knowing that if she can head the men off and reach Suroma, she will be a heroine. She will save Suroma, whose mother will be grateful because Suroma's father, as Suroma has boasted time and again, has a jeep and employs a driver who drives Suroma in it everywhere.

A-Block is the neighbourhood Renu circumvents each morning on her way to her job. The streets are quieter than those of D-Block. There is no market here and the 100-150-odd homes are smaller and tightly packed. All, however, have the same overhanging balconies as homes in D-Block, and today the balconies are filled with women and children. There are no chowkidars guarding these smaller homes; the husbands are not back and the housewives must defend themselves from the rude, young men who are shouting up at them and whose ranks have swelled considerably. Renu no longer races, but squeezes around and among the men as she tries to find Suroma's home.

The men demand that the driver be brought out. The consensus is that he is hiding behind the women and children. The women are silent, and only occasionally does one or another ask the men to leave, reassuring them that no one in A-Block drives a jeep, that they are mistaken about the identity of the driver they seek. The men scan the numerous vehicles parked in front of these homes; among them are any number of jeeps. But already, there is an air of something stale in the confrontation. Neither the men nor the women are convinced that there is a crisis here. Only one woman, who the other women identify as a troublemaker-type, attempts from her balcony post to inject some heat into the standoff. 'You people,' she says, 'think nothing of putting your babies on the street to get run over. Then you come and make demands. Is that not wrong?'

Renu hears it all, but really she is only concerned with finding Suroma. It is hard to read the house numbers inscribed on slate slabs and embedded in house walls because there are so many men in the way, and ducking between their hips and searching, she stumbles over the exchanged words of men and women, over their excitement and boredom, and it is with relief she finds herself once again tumbled through the turnstile and into the dark of her jungle-park.

Again she runs, but the old familiar paths turn and twist under her and with great cunning steer her to the area beyond the nursery where the mali makes compost in a shallow pit. Here the path bumps up and gives her a push that sends her sliding under the barbed wire and into the pit, and there she stays for the night. There, her legs continue to run under her, pinned though they are between brambly branches—their motion fuelled even in the death-sleep she sleeps by the slow heat of all that moulders at the malis' behest. She runs there, in the pit, with all her might, and runs so fast, she runs right past Suroma staring back at her from behind the broad back of the troublemaker-woman, and keeps on running past the little bier on which Jai is being carried ('Ram nam satya hai'), and past the old men counselling her father to make offerings to appease his first wife, past her loss and into the clear future of the morning sun, which rises and bathes her in light so she can be found.

Jane Eyre

Mr R touches Jane on the shoulder. She doesn't know then that this is the moment. She continues with her unknowing mouse-like existence or, as Mr R sees it, her pale, elfin, mustard seed of an existence. Only much, much later is this moment presented to Jane by Mr R—as the moment which explains his infatuation, gives credence to his willingness to throw over not only society, which has little sway over him in any case, but to actually throw over himself, his misanthropy and his power in that misanthropy. Only then does Jane come to know the power she has held over him all along. This is what Lubna too hopes for, that she may have lived her moment and has only to await the reward of its revelation.

'Why have you come back?' Mrs Mody from downstairs wants to know. Lubna doesn't know the answer. She smiles in reply. But that doesn't suffice.

'Do your children like it so far? Is it their first time?'

'No, not for my daughter. She was born here. My son—he was born there.'

Her daughter has been with her for nine years now but it still isn't easy to explain her. And she knows that Nathan's arrival in another eight days will raise more questions, not because he is American; there is plenty of that these days. Mrs Mody herself has just returned from Australia, where she has had the clearly pleasurable duty of providing what she refers to as post-natal care for her new grandchild. And Lubna has seen (been forcibly shown) pictures of the little family: a very young daughter Mody who is perhaps no longer a Mody and trails instead some other name that jostles awkwardly against mother Mody's choice of Alpana made in her own state of post-natal bliss, the little one fancifully made known by her parents as 'Nayantara', the 'star' of their 'eyes', and Mr?—Lubna still hasn't been told his name which, depending on what it is, may do worse than merely jostle at Nayantara's. Perhaps it is simply a Jones or a Smith; and perhaps it is some horror—a Barney or a Colfax.

Lubna has kept her own name, of course. Lubna McCray was, she felt, to be avoided at all costs. But she envies this little family: investment bankers with both the Australian salaries and the mother/mother-in-law descending from the home country to cook and clean and diaper and perambulate their child in Australian parks for all the months until Nayantara is old enough to be transferred to the nursery, crèche, day-care—whichever Australian English word covers the concept of holding cell for baby. Well, maybe she doesn't envy the total package—just the quality post-natal care of the powder-soft grandma variety, all coos and goos that Mrs Mody no doubt dispensed while in Australia to Nayantara Somebody, Alpana Somebody and Mr Somebody.

She wishes she had been the recipient of such beneficence nine years earlier on her last trip to India. Then she had held her new-sprung, dangerously undernourished, three-year-old mite whom she knew she shouldn't and in the end reluctantly didn't, bestow with what Nathan had laughed at and called a title as opposed to a name: 'Noor Jahan'—Light of the World. The adoption class instructor had strongly urged that they, the prospective parents, retain the prospective child's own name irrespective of whether, she added sternly, the name was given to the child by the birth-mother—whose paramountcy in the picture Lubna was always ready to acknowledge—or the orphanage, which Lubna was quite unhappy to see as anything other than an institution, and perhaps a cruel one at that.

The instructor's story of regret over changing her own daughter's unpronounceable Chinese name was pointedly tied to the story some hours later in class of the girl's troubled teen years, and the shockingly recent suicide attempt. But all of this only left Lubna with a strong sense of the hypocrisy of the adoption industry. To friends she said, 'They are holding me hostage.'

The instructions on naming, and the weight driving it pell-mell into her Noor Jahan plans, would have done little to alter the plans that Noor Jahan be Noor Jahan (after all Nathan's laughter had given ground easily to her tears) if it weren't for the fact that 'Asha', when she arrived, came equipped not only with her 'hopeful' handle, but also with three years of ferocious determination to remain Asha.

And so it was her 'post-natal' period was marked not only by the hellish loneliness of six weeks in a four-star hotel in Cochin—inclusive of the monotony of 5 a.m. bottle, 7 a.m. gruel (the instructor had also advised sticking to a diet familiar to the prospective child), 8 a.m. first potty fight, many more to follow throughout the day, 8:30 a.m. cable TV, a merciful nap or two in the afternoon interspersed with food fights, 4 p.m. at the hotel kiddy pool, 6 p.m. dinner, if courageous, in the hotel restaurant, weak smiles from the hotel's ridiculously turbaned waiters as Asha lay on the floor and wept, then Asha asleep, curled away from Lubna in the vast expanse of the hotel bed—it was also marked by Asha's unblinking refusal to answer to Noor Jahan.

Mrs Mody is still waiting for an answer to her question: 'Why have you come back?' Lubna decides this is the moment and brightening her smile and checking her envy, launches into the explanation that she has been preparing for the length of the two weeks she has been Mrs Mody's paying-guest. And she runs to ground, her mouth still open. No, the sorry tale of her 'post-natal' hell is an unexpected bump on the road to her prepared story. Rehearsed and derailed is not a new experience for her.

One afternoon, a week earlier, an autorickshaw driver had pulled up alongside her in the chaotic traffic that her own driver had seemed hell-bent on destroying, or being destroyed in. He stuck his head directly into her driver's cab and said with a leer, 'So where did she get them from? One must have come from summer and one from winter, one from hot and the other from cold?' This was followed by a particularly abhorrent 'Heh heh?'

Stewing, Lubna held on to summer winter, hot cold, on either side of her and rehearsed what she would say. What she said, and had to repeat twice to be heard, her Hindi, dormant for years, emerging a broken croak from her throat: 'He is mine and she, I took into my lap.'

This was not what she had wanted to say. In English she never would have made the distinction between the two children, never would have said, Asha is adopted. In English, they are both hers. But English is unsatisfactory. It does not convey the beauty of Asha being taken into her lap. And succumbing to the temptation to employ beauty in her defence, she had given away more of herself and Asha than she had intended.

Mrs Mody is far too genteel, and far too well travelled, and has the granddaughter who, while the star of her eyes, is also winter emerged, to ask which hemisphere the men Lubna has slept with may have inhabited. Or perhaps even cruder interpretations can be inferred from the autowallah's question. Lubna flushes hot then turns cold at the thought. At least Mrs Mody speaks English, though only with Lubna, and although it is of the variety that finds Lubna responding with 'Aunty, I also am too happy seeing you,' Mrs Mody's question in English is simple enough: 'Why have you come back?'

Lubna wants her understanding. Her living situation as Mrs Mody's paying guest is the best one so far this trip. It is a home, and eight-year-old Rashid is too active to be contained in a hotel, and Asha at twelve presents her own awkwardness. Lubna wants Mrs Mody's understanding, and in her rehearsals she has carefully chosen to forego her usual tendency to rushed confessions and pleas for sympathy. She has chosen to forego mention of the 10 mg of Prozac she takes daily to combat Asha's 5 mg of Risperdal, 5 mg of Strattera, and the a.m. and p.m. 5 mg of Triptafen. She has chosen to skip mention of the family therapist's galling prescription that she infuse her parenting with a greater sense of humour. This is advice that she has in fact undertaken to live by, by in fact careful tabulation of the number of times she smiles daily at her children, or is it with her children, well, just smiles—for her children, she supposes.

No, she is far from having plunged into the abyss for all that she believes she nightly glimpses it. She answers Mrs Mody with the studied straightforwardness of what she, in her dramatic moments, likes to describe to Nathan as her tightly held sanity: 'My daughter is adopted. My son came soon after. He is my biological son (*there is of course no translation for this in Hindi*). I probably already said my husband is joining us soon; he is American. We are just visiting.'

Mrs Mody is setting the tea in front of her. Her face is as kindly as ever. 'Oh, but I wasn't asking anything like that,' she demurs. Lubna's cup and saucer clatter as she attempts to raise the tea to her lips. 'I didn't want to ask before, but they don't look much alike, do they? I know of such cases. Something loosens,' and here Mrs Mody hesitates before adding, 'in the woman'. Then, lacking the English for what has loosened in the woman, she makes a swirling motion with her fingers, and Lubna, ever in awe of the complacent grace that is Mrs Mody, would have forgiven her even if she had not added, 'You are a good mother to both of them.'

The conversation moves to the morning's plans without Lubna baring her search to Mrs Mody's sympathetic eyes. This search, aborted nine years earlier by Asha's failure to be Noor Jahan, has nevertheless refused to remain buried—the search to seek if even today there isn't, somewhere in this land, herself still living, having continued with the life she imagined she would live—a girl, a bride, a woman, a wife, a daughter-in-law, a mother of neither winter nor summer, a mother of a pig-tailed, red-ribboned girl, or two, or three.

Oh, she is well aware that these days there is an alternative for women in India. Perhaps the life she was meant to have lived is a life she couldn't have imagined living, but which (the life, that is) nevertheless imagined her living it—viz. the life of the urbanite who does so much more than cook, instead makes policy, makes love, has a philosophical understanding of infidelity, makes money, has her nails done, is driven to her appointments, entertains reluctantly, as a duty, and only in her professional interest, launches a website which provides light but heartfelt advice in support of women like herself: the urbanite who does so much more than . . .

She knows of the alternative from the recently sprung correspondence with friends she has last seen twenty years earlier, at the age of eighteen, on the eve of her departure to the life she has ended up inhabiting. She learns of this hitherto unimagined life, this choice B behind door number two, from the sporadic responses she receives to the frequent emails she has taken to sending her old school chums, so that what she gains is a stuttering, stammering, staccato sense that, like hers, their childhood dreams too have long given way.

No, life doesn't always furnish itself as per childhood fantasies. Sometimes, it is even better, she thinks bitterly. These friends from the past have adapted to lifestyles unlike anything she and they imagined in the pre-infotech era that was the landscape of their childhood. But they switched from one imagined life to another as a group. In their possession is a collectively reimagined and collectively endorsed life. They, she argues, have the comfort of having done it together. I was forced to go it alone.

✳

Later that week, she argues this point with just this hint of pique with Sunil, whose baffled silence she now places in the Morse she has willed herself to decipher. He has responded to her 'Hello, I remember you, do you remember me?' plea and has obliged with a happy series of meetings culminating in this appointment at the Barista in Connaught Place.

Once seated, she is mortified to note that in the late evening hours the coffee shop is a play room for youngsters who suffer from the same familial and social constraints against open dating that she and her companions had strained against decades earlier but whose straining is so unlike anything she could have imagined. Disturbed by what she identifies as prurience in herself, she positions her chair so that she can turn her back on the spot-lit glow at each table where pairs of arms twine and intertwine and fingers grope their way to face, flutter at the entrance to mouth, and couple with the tongue within. With her back turned to them, she is sure she can hear days' worth of pent-up sighs, but actually the music is so loud that much of the time she has to strain to hear Sunil, who is soft-spoken. She in contrast is louder than she likes to be.

'You should have seen the Immigration guy at the airport. Typical. He never explained. Just kept barking at me to get my hair out of my face. I didn't know they needed a shot of my ear for the Green card. I almost cried that day. A big eighteen-year-old baby! Did you know that ears can be used for identification?'

Sunil knows. He is a doctor. Although they were in the same

year at school, the last they were in the same classroom and so in each other's consciousness, was at fourteen. After that the Board Exam results were posted and he moved with Zygote and Varghese and Neena and all the other brains into the science section. She spent the next years as an arts student and migrated to the US midway through her final year of schooling. He too left India after finishing that last year. He and two others were government-sponsored medical students for six years in the Soviet Union, and he spent an additional three years in Cuba. It makes her happy to think that these years spent away from home puts Sunil into the category of 'stranger and outsider' that she had believed was her lonely realm. This, she thinks, explains his interest in sipping coffee with her.

Others she knew far better in school have begged off meeting her. When she called, they were busy hopping from HK to Chennai, and Delhi was not on their schedule. Or they have met her a hurried once for lunch at Kwality's and spoken with forced enthusiasm about getting everyone together again.

Still others have invited her and kids home for elaborate meals and pre- and post-meal drinks and then waited expectantly for she knows not what so that the evening was quickly reduced to chatter about the Grand Canyon and New York City's subway system, both of them wonders she has failed to visit, and that the host has first-hand knowledge of. In the worst instances, her host's curiosity about life in the United States has run to 'the problem with the Blacks', and she has hurriedly reached for the safe topic of the US presence in Iraq.

Sunil, she knows, is interested in her. He is somebody who wants to know her and not the circumstances of her life. The first time they met was for lunch. Immediately afterwards he proposed a trip to the zoo for the children. They met again, and this time after lunch he whisked all three of them to the movies. It is at her insistence that they meet now without the children's ever-hungry intrusions on her attention and are seated across from each other, the children entrusted to Mrs Mody's maid's care.

He is a good listener, and when she finishes her harangue at the Immigration official she had encountered nearly two decades earlier, he makes sympathetic comments. He offers how hard it was for him in Moscow. But he also speaks with longing, though what he is describing is the boot camp weeks of intensive language study, his first year there.

'You mean the coursework was all in Russian?' she yelps.

He only looks surprised that she might have expected anything different. 'Yes, but we were provided with language classes. The professors were excellent. Actually their whole system, not only the education system but you know, the entire social system there, how they ran their hospitals, how they dealt with the poor, it was all excellent. I mean it's probably all different now. Back then it was something to learn from.'

'And it is not like that here?' she asks.

'No, here there is still no system. You would not believe the number of people I see here daily without any knowledge of history. Here we have no charts or records. Sometimes patients will give me these tiny scraps of paper with all this writing scribbled on it and tell me "The last Doctor wrote this." And that's all the history I get. Here we base all our diagnosis on clinical exams. Tests are for rich countries or rich patients. Still, no matter how much you listen to the heart and say it's a systolic or diastolic murmur, you still need an echocardiogram to really know. And if the patient can't afford the test, then we just have the clinical exam to go on.' He chuckles, but is not done.

'When I have to suture, I buy my own needles and suture material. Last night, I had to leave my patient and go out to the market to buy this fine needle. His lip was torn off. If I had used the needle they provided, I would only have injured it further. When I give injections, the syringes are so old, so blunt, you can hear muscle tear. Mostly, if they can, I send the patients out to get the disposable kind. Here, we are still using the old-fashioned ones. We autoclave the needles.'

She doesn't know what the term means. She decides to change the subject. 'Was Cuba like Russia or like India?'

'You people in the US probably hear a lot of rubbish about Cuba. That's where I would have liked to stay. But my parents wanted me back. They thought I should get married. There was a lot of pressure from them, you know. I was part of this fantastic team. The rest of the team was sent to Angola after I returned here.'

'Angola?' She is not sure why he sounds mournful. She cannot imagine what would make that a place to visit. Perhaps there was some professional gain that he missed out on by failing to go there. 'Angola?' she repeats again and then asks, 'So that's how you and Rani met?'

He doesn't reply. He's lost in Angola, she thinks.

'Happily married?' she asks and immediately realises how inappropriate this is, but doesn't want to retract. 'I mean you've been married a long time. You must be very happy, no?'

He smiles a little and tells her his plans for the two little girls, Meera and Mala. He wants Meera to study abroad. 'She's only eight now,' he says, and then talks eagerly about medical school in the US. 'I mean, if she wants to, of course. We've all changed here, you know. Now there is more room for kids to grow up and choose whether to be a doctor or something else. It's all right with me, whatever she chooses.'

Lubna is sure this isn't true, and she thinks he knows how untruthful he is being, that this is some formality he is engaging in, a disclaimer he provides because he is required to. She feels only affection for him. So much of her parenting is marked by just such formalities—the tabla lessons for Rashid, Kathak for Asha, the constant reminders thrown over her shoulder to buckle up, to do their homework, to not read in the dark.

'What about your marriage?' he asks

She is a little suspicious of the smile and then thinks he is just enjoying being mischievous; perhaps he is even being a little flirtatious. Right from the beginning, when she sent out that first group mail to her classmates and opened the first reply, his, they have, she thinks, connected. In an early email, she had shared with him the recurring nightmare that haunted her during the period of tension between India and Pakistan in 2000. In her dreams then, she wandered the hallways of her old school which morphed into the colonnaded corridors of Connaught Place. The dream always reached its end with her moving from one whitewashed pillar to the next, praising God with tears streaming down her face for allowing her to once again see the city of her childhood, whole and intact. She woke from these dreams with dry eyes and great sobs straining her chest. His email reply had been prompt, the vehemently pacifist tone of it sending a shock of recognition through her: they would be friends.

'Nathan will be here in three more days. May 10th.'

'Wonderful. You are counting down the days, possibly even the minutes. I am right?'

For the first time she feels nervous in his company. She wants to tell him about Nathan. How easily he had said that he married Rani under pressure from his parents. What would he think if she told him that she had married Nathan because one suffocating, hot night in the dwindling days of college, she had allowed him to hold her by the crook of her arm, to direct her around the grounds till they were climbing the dusty hill at the back end of the campus, to trap her there with his promises of the life he imagined them living together in Durham, North Carolina, less than half a mile from his childhood home. That night, she had allowed Nathan the truth that she had nowhere else to go and no one else to be with.

Forever after she has lived, afraid that there was another choice that she did not notice in the shifting, shuffling dark of that night, another voice that she failed to hear above Nathan's fervent pleas.

When Nathan had first proposed that they skip their annual vacation and save toward the heritage tour of India organised by the adoption agency, she had reacted with irritation. 'Why should I go on a heritage tour? That's for all the white women who have adopted brown babies.' She had known Nathan would not respond to this goad. He worked hard at maintaining indifference to her more practised provocations. Saving for the trip took them two years of skipped vacations and skimped Eid and Christmas celebrations. They drew together, just as they had a decade earlier as they saved, rehearsed their roles, and waited to realise the dream of a precious bit of humanity to stamp as their own.

She finds herself telling Sunil about Asha. 'You know she always wants to hug you. Do your daughters do that with your friends?'

'Well, no. I mean, I don't mind Asha hugging me. She must be missing her father.'

'But do your daughters do that?'

'Well, Mala is just an infant.' He laughs.

'You're lucky,' she says with reproving seriousness. 'Your daughters are yours from the first day. Asha was on her own for her first three years. Even now, she is still very much alone. She has us. But she just doesn't believe it. So she is always creating this buffer zone of people around her—people she can fall back on. So she hugs you. Just in case. Just in case, I decide to walk away from her.'

Sunil waits, quietly, expectantly. He doesn't understand.

She tries again. She tells him about the day she took Asha from the orphanage. She begins by telling him about the dogs kept chained and caged outside her grandfather's house, on the front grounds, at the entrance to the main road. She tells him about how they throw themselves from one side of the four-feet-by-four-feet space, pivoting on their back legs, their fore legs crashing into the wire mesh on one side and then the other, catching or failing, snout and teeth and saliva mixing into an insanity of anger and kernelled in the anger, the howling pain of fear. She tells him of the relief she experienced when she first saw those dogs and had finally the image with which to describe the abduction of her daughter, an abduction she had carried out herself.

Sunil has drawn back and is looking at her with the same quizzical look Nathan, her sister, her mother-in-law have all greeted this story with.

Asha had flung herself frantically from the window on one side of the back of that taxi to the window on the other side and back again. And this had been accompanied by her shrieking as she crawled across Lubna's lap and the expanse of the back seat to look for the exit that just wasn't there.

Sunil has tipped his chair back and his fingers are raking his hair. She pauses. It is her turn to wait expectantly. But his smile is embarrassed, strained even. 'I didn't know,' he says. 'I thought a baby could only be happy to be united with her mother.'

Lubna snorts out loud and thinks, or she can be angry—she can be angry for a long, long time. What she says to Sunil: 'Do you think Asha is beautiful?'

'Yes, she is a very lovable little girl. She is very lucky to have you for her mother.'

Lubna is angry now. 'Nathan thinks she is terribly beautiful. So do her teachers; my mother-in-law thinks so too but not my mother. All of the people we pass on the street on the way to school every morning. Over there. But none of the people here see it. No, not any of the Indians—they don't see the beauty. She is not beautiful here in India, is she?'

Lubna pauses and when there is nothing forthcoming from Sunil, she relaunches. 'Do you know what, my aunt, she's a paediatrician, and I took Asha to see her, straight from the orphanage and to the doctor's office, do you know what she said when she first saw Asha?'

Lubna forces Sunil to reply. 'No.'

'My aunt said, "Didn't they let you choose?"'

'Not everybody understands here about something like adoption. It's very threatening, you know, to their worldview.'

'Well, in America, everyone understands everything, and you should just see how people look at her. Their jaws drop. People sipping wine at sidewalk tables outside posh restaurants. They've seen Indians before. But you know Asha is straight out of some UNICEF poster. Not like the Indian doctors and engineers they are used to seeing. Not like the children of Indian doctors. No. She is all big eyes and black skin. They're fascinated. She's something they can't believe they are seeing in person.'

'Lubna, you know she is a very pretty girl.'

'Then why aren't people's jaws dropping here in Delhi? Sunil is quiet. 'Listen, I know. When I first started college in the US, I was fascinating too. People stared. They wanted to be my friend, to collect me. I was a collectible.'

'A collectible?'

'I had a friend who would always introduce me as: "My Indian friend, Lubna." Sometimes she would add "She's Muslim." This is after I told her to stop saying Islamic and taught her Muslim instead.'

'I had a lot of good friends in Russia who referred to me as an

Indian. It is true. I am an Indian. I never saw that they meant anything bad by it.'

'Listen, it's not good for her to grow up thinking of herself as beautiful—not if it's as a sort of collectible. It's bad. I know it. It's stealing who you are from yourself. I know this as her mother, and I can't even explain this to Nathan.'

Lubna doesn't know why she is crying. The distance between them is not that great and it takes him only a moment of watching quietly before he leans forward and places a hand on her shaking shoulders.

Her own hands are twisting the handkerchief he has offered. And now she doesn't know why and hasn't planned it, but her hand is moving on its own, crossing the same space his hand just crossed, moving through the air between them, a dark line cutting through the cone of light they are sitting under, and she can see in the rain-wet glass of the window that her hand, forefinger extended, is hovering near his face, and then tentatively her finger is touching the birthmark above his left, no, it is his right brow; it is a spot she recognises has been calling to her, a place of rest and repose for the tip of her finger. Outside, she can see through the glass, the streets are crowded even at this late hour with empty autorickshaws, turning home.

It is a long, long moment that he holds his face still under her fingertip and only when she feels its complete rigidity does she reluctantly move her hand back to her lap. The newest episode of *Star Wars* is playing at Regal Cinema across the street, and she thinks of seeing Luke Skywalker in that very theatre some thirty years before, holding his little hologram princess in the palm of his hand, her little hologram mouth pleading for a space of time before fizzling out. Just such a desert wind must have blown through his heart as she feels in hers now.

She thinks of what it is to fall from grace. She thinks about the times in her life she has placed herself on this stile, at this junction and waited for someone to ride up to her, to fall and to rise by leaning on her. She thinks about the possibility that she has not come into her moment yet or that it has passed her by entirely. Then, in a confused churning, she wonders for the first time if she isn't the one riding up to the junction, falling, looking for someone, perhaps herself, to lean on. She thinks for the first time that if ever there was a voice she failed to hear in the garden—if it wasn't perhaps her own. Perhaps it was a cry issuing from her own lips that got lost in the unstable dark, never finding its way to her ears and her heart.

Sunil breaks the silence with a sound like cloth tearing as he clears his throat. She slides his handkerchief to a spot on the table in front of him. He says, 'Rani will be back next week from her mother's. We are planning a celebration to welcome the new baby.'

She nods.

'Nathan will be here by then, won't he? Remember three days and how many minutes left in the countdown?' His smile is tender. 'You and Nathan and the children must come.'

Same Day

EVENING

The evening of that same day he sees her again. In the moment this is absolutely astonishing to him. And the moment after, he feels relief. It's as if he has been anxious about something, maybe her, maybe the question of whether he would see her again. He isn't sure what he's been anxious about since he doesn't actually remember feeling the anxiety that when dissipated should allow him to feel such relief. But the relief is certain, even visceral, more than a mere lightening of his spirit, or the lifting of a burden. Yes, he feels as if he could float, as if a burden has been lifted. But even more strongly he feels light flooding recesses of darkness in him, recesses that he had not known were dark or he had even known were there. It seems to him that if he were to unbutton his shirt and peer down at his belly he would see through the skin to his entrails which, just at present, feel as if they are shivering themselves awake from a long sleep.

And now he names the recesses one by one—Charu and Chuk Chuk, the old school building, the chink of yellow under the door somewhere (where?), the feel of the earth in the evening releasing stored heat, the feel of the earth against his cheek, the feel of the footpath releasing heat which isn't the same thing as the feel of the earth—furry or damp and packed. No, not the same at all. He stands on the footpath, bites into the guava she's given him and waits for the light to turn from green to red way ahead at the flyover. The man in the distance comes closer, his open shirt flapping in the wind, closer and the single button holding it together at his chest turns from white to whiter, and the handkerchief covering his head reveals its blue print. And watching and waiting Chottu Lal breathes into himself.

He hadn't thought of her after the morning's incident. Not to wonder if he would ever see her again, not to speculate that he might or might not, not even to conclude that he never would. But the evening of the same day as the morning, as Chottu flattened himself against the fence dividing traffic, pretending sales were what he was all about, which he knew they weren't, but he felt all right with the pretence since he hadn't yet figured out what else there was to him, as he leaned his head forward from the fence to mug in the rushing stream of mirrored car windows, as he caught himself hoping today Charu would show up with balloons, traffic slowed and stopped but not completely; it continued to lurch about.

He darted in. It was nearly dark, getting harder to sell magazines. Elly, he said into a car and the window went up tight. Elly, he thrust the spread-eagled pages at the window. He turned the magazine back to himself and with the idea of putting some effort into his pretence that a sale was even possible, he took in the passengers seated inside—mother and daughter, possibly—flipped to the back, to pages full of princesses, and turned these images to the car's interior: Beautiful bride, madam. Beautiful. Beautiful. He tried putting an entreaty in his eyes but felt bored and wanted done with it, pushed his nose till it flared against the glass and pushed again till the bridge bent and made a pleasant creaking sound, and pushed till the distant ache in the middle of his face was more glass than him, and boredom became the grease he spread on the window.

As much as he would have liked to go stand with the others, who had already received their evening jobs—balloons, jasmines, incense—who unlike him were free of the anxiety of wondering what came next, who like him were in that in-between time when it is too dark for magazines and cellphone chargers and too light for balloons, jasmines and incense, he knew he couldn't be seen loafing, or Charu would set her boyfriend on him. He loved Charu. She was his big sister, wasn't she? Or at least that's what she's been all these years cooking his food and cleaning his clothes for him. And hasn't it been a good thing for both of them that she has Mohansingh for a boyfriend?

✳

With the advent of Mohansingh, there had been a layer of protection added to the little enterprise that was Charu, Chuk Chuk and Chottu. But this protection which, at its best, meant their family had grown by one and a strong one at that, one who could keep at bay thugs and rivals, interested itself in studying the enterprise for internal weaknesses, found the primary weakness of the enterprise was Chottu's desire to develop his personality in areas other than salesmanship, cured Chottu of the desire. Chottu tried not to fear Mohansingh's beatings overly ahead of their occurrence. Because inevitable they were and it would mean ruining otherwise brilliant days to live in anticipation of them. On the other hand, he couldn't afford to entirely forget them. Because they were avoidable. Or at least Chottu thought they might be. It was a little confusing sorting this question out since even on the best sales days—four hundred rupees once—he has had to dart behind Charu or wail loud enough to turn the attention of the street or BRT guard their way.

If the mercurial nature of Mohansingh's temper was factored out and good sales factored in, then yes, there were days better than good. Days when Chottu was pulled into Mohansingh's brotherly embrace—samosas and tea at Krishi Vihar. Maybe an hour sitting idly, watching children at play on the DDA lawn. Mohansingh is a history buff, and in the time before he sold Chuk Chuk he'd taken the two boys to roam the grounds at Jantar Mantar and Qutab Minar. On such days, afternoon stretched to evening listening to Mohansingh's expansive talk. Jalebis turned everything sweet. And later than late, Mohansingh sent the bottle around the circle—the four of them, the circle. Four of them. A momentary confusion in counting as the fourth figure wavered. Chottu tried counting again but the hurt of his spread nose was not doing his thinking any good. He switched to his favourite line of reasoning: anything is possible. This was a thought that covered everything. It covered three, it covered four.

With a sigh of satisfaction Chottu turned away from the greased car window and to the woman in the auto. Only seventy rupees for new Elly. New Vog. New Maar Eclair. See see see see see. He must have repeated his Take it Madam—the whiny get-under-the-skin tone of which is the closest he comes to sleeping while standing in the middle of traffic—four times before she looked up from inside her purse and looked away. Too practised, this aversion of hers. No sale to be made here, just more of the same irritation shared by everyone else stuck in traffic; hers is expressed in the hair she shakes.

The hand that's holding out the guava, this is what she was rooting for in the purse, is empty and he's trying to see if he can hold the guava and magazine tucked between his chin and chest while he reaches deep into his pant pocket to pull out something for her. Because he recognises her now—by the rings on her hand, so many of them, they were amazing when he saw them in the morning, some of them flecked in red as was her hand and sleeve, the skirt spread on the street where she knelt. Not that he wouldn't have recognised her if he had looked her in the face. But he hasn't looked any more than she has. How then were they to know each other—the two of them who had met but not really met, just knelt side by side by the man and his leg earlier this same day? This morning. Amazing, is all he can think as he looks again at her hand. The rings. Then her face. Yes, he remembers her face, which is like all other faces, but since this morning so singularly hers it can't belong to anyone else. His voice is still whining, Madam. Please, Madam.

His thoughts are jumping in his head. Telling him to speak. Telling him to not. Telling him to do something. He searches. There is nothing in his pocket for her. She,

I don't read magazines.

And,

I don't read such magazines.

Frowning and shaking her head and hair at him, but not looking at him. Not seeing him.

I wish you would look at me. He doesn't have time to think this, just wishes it. He thinks, the light will change. The autowallah will turn hostile to break his boredom

He says, Madam this morning. The leg.

Now she looks at him. Sewage in his belly. He nearly heaves. She recognises him. She is embarrassed. Or is she? He doesn't know. Why would she be? He's not. Is she? The street has turned darker in the last one minute. He's right about the autowallah who's begun,

Didn't she say she doesn't want anything? Get lost.

✳

But Chottu's head is all the way inside the auto. He is so relieved she's here. He could let his knees buckle that's how weak he feels.

He could let some part of him rest against her. He could let his nose press against hers.

Madam, this morning. Remember the man.

His leg, she replies.

And they repeat this to each other: His leg.

He asks her shyly, Do you have any news?

She asks him, Where did you get the cloth from?

The spell is broken by something, maybe just the passage of those few seconds of their bewildered recognition into the next few seconds of time beyond the recognition. They turn together to the autowallah. They are both embarrassed.

This morning there was a terrible accident right here. On the other side of here. Going that way. Two cars, three motorbikes. On the other side, the fence is like this. She makes a curve in the air with the hand with the fingers with the rings.

He says to the autowallah, She helped. She was the only one who helped.

She says, This boy was the only one who helped. He brought a cloth.

She turns eagerly to Chottu. He, anticipating the question, is already answering it.

I bought it from the man who sells duster cloth. Twenty rupees. I paid myself.

What happened to the man?

✳

The ambulance never came. First the number was busy. I must have dialled 101 a hundred times. It was busy the whole time.

You should dial 100.

Well, yes. But by then I'd got through. And that was when a

police jeep happened by. I said as much to the ambulance people. They hung up on me.

Oh, what do they care. What happened to the man?

She turns the question over to the boy.

What happened to the man?

The boy shakes his head. He doesn't know what happened since they loaded the man into the police jeep. But Chottu understands the autowallah is asking something else and answers him.

No leg left.

Chottu tells the woman, Some different people have gone to his neighbourhood to say he's hurt. By now maybe his family's gone to the hospital.

The woman speaks excitedly.

One leg was crushed. The bone inside was so crushed I couldn't see any of it though I could see clear through to the inside, the blood and flesh had all . . . like a shirt inside out. But the foot and below and the knee and above was fine. He was trying to drag himself away.

Only as she says this does she realise what it was the man was trying to drag himself away from: his leg.

Not like a shirt, she thinks. Like a kite. It was crumpled like a kite, the frame broken. A delicate structure, given way. Between the foot and the knee. Something had given that should have stretched the leg smooth, but it had given, and the leg had crumpled and gaped. The skin folded on itself, the shine of it gone. She looks at the boy. She can picture him flying a kite. It is no effort. Seeking confirmation of this unexpected truth, something hidden from her till now, she nearly asks him if he flies kites.

This boy, she repeats, was the only one who helped.

She asks the boy, You paid for the cloth yourself?

He says, Yes.

She thinks, it doesn't matter if he is telling the truth.

He shakes his head and smiles. He thinks, it doesn't matter if I am telling the truth. The two smile, a secret smile.

Didn't she tell you she doesn't want any. You get out of here now.

The two smile, widening their smile to include the knowledge that the autowallah is jealous.

The boy pulls out the guava which has found its way to his pocket. She gives him a twenty-rupee note for the cloth he had bought, for the way in with which he had reached under the flesh that was a leg and wrapped the cloth twice around. She accepts the guava from him and returns it to him and accepts it back from him and this is where their fumbling finds them when the lights ahead change. And just before he runs, criss-crossing between cars, to the footpath, she thrusts the guava back at him. He re-pockets it. On the footpath he looks away from her, towards the light at the intersection. From far away, with his shirt flapping on either side of him, a great bird is approaching.

On the footpath Chottu notes the bird man's approach and makes a great show of eating the guava. He pops into his mouth the last bite, stem attached to a shredded leaf. Like a wave receding from shore the movement of vehicles igniting to launch travels back from the light turned green, reaches her auto and he, feeling between his teeth, tells her of his deep and abiding love. His leg, Chottu whispers, and she lurches forward, Then she is carried away.

MORNING

At the moment of the impact he was standing on the footpath making his sounds. Gawww and Heeenh. Nasal sounds, pitched to break the morning to tell the world about Gawww and Heeenh and much more that was not sound and so remained trapped inside him. The impact shot out the wealth of mucus from where he mined his sounds and afterwards he lay on the ground, his face wreathed in goo. What if, he thought, I have no sounds left to make?

He worried then about his one leg which very clearly was done saying. The foot at the end of this leg was planted firmly on the ground and the rest of him, supine. He turned onto his side, curled tighter in an attempt to pull himself to the foot, which done talking was apparently also done listening, would not come to him when he called. But his calling was silent. The foot could be forgiven. This foot planted firmly on the ground, he saw, was holding up the mass of his leg. Gawww and Heeenh, he thought: Jellied and Riven. The knee was good. A good knee. The knee and the foot were both good. Good knee and good foot. They held between them the flesh that skin and bone no longer wanted to. And the flesh was good. It wanted to remain a leg, his leg. It clung to itself. All the good in him conspiring to help the good flesh levitate between good knee and good foot.

*

The good in him welled up and he could no longer contain it. It pooled under him. It drew itself into spirals around him.

It rose from the ground, a stairway sprung from him. In starbursts of light his stairway materialised a few, then more, and many more. The many were good in their sounds.

Have you called?

Someone get that Bhatia fellow here.

The colony doctor, I said.

Don't move it.

If you move him.

What do you mean the tempo won't take him.

Get ten fellows together and that tempowallah will sing a different tune.

What does he mean he won't take this man?

Let's show him.

Who was the driver?

Yes you. Come here.

Here.

Here.

Here.

Who is it?

Here, give him water.

No water. Listen lady, don't give him water.

Is someone trying to get the doctor?

It's the Sadhu.

Yes it's him. I see him here every morning. These malas around his neck.

What Sadhu? That's no Sadhu. The man is mentally ill, and we call him a Sadhu.

The bloody incompetents. No one's picking up.

Busy. That's all I get.

Me too. Dialling for more than ten minutes now.

Get that driver here.

What do you mean he is gone?

Nothing left in that leg.

He watched these sounds of goodness. If only they were telling him what was known. Though he opened his mouth nothing came from within. The sounds were on the outside now. And he lay baffled. The woman who was patting him leaned closer and said, They are coming. Don't move now. The doctor will be here soon.

He rolled his eyes to let her know that she was his sound. She frowned at that. He found he could make crying sounds. Air went in and air went out with the crying sounds. It was good. He curled tighter and cried. The woman kept whispering.

Don't move. They'll be here soon. We'll take care of you.

Her sounds rolled under him, rolled him out from under himself. He thought, This isn't a bad way of travelling. He travelled on sounds.

Don't give him water.

Pick him up. Pick him up.

Bloody hell, there's nothing to hold onto.

Pick him up, I say.

In he goes.

Where will you take him?

Isn't there anyone of his here?

Got him good? Where to?

Isn't there anyone with this man?

I know this man. He's from the bustee near Khanpur.

Near Khanpur? Isn't that far from here?

You're not crazy are you? You want me to turn in that direction?

He wanders here every day. Stands around waving his arms.

He's not from Khanpur. He's from right here in Krishi Vihar.

He needs to be taken straight to the hospital. Sort out the rest later.

It will be all right. My husband's toe was the same way to the side.

Where will you take him?

Where else? Moolchand.

Isn't there anyone who'll accompany this man?

Bloody hell.

He's rolling. Green. Green. A lawn. He's rolling down a sloped lawn. Children watching. He's rolling through their days and nights. Green green rolls around him and a voice is whispering.

This is good. He can listen to this voice. It's telling him the sound of what he's wanted to say for so long. It's good to hear it. Amit, the sound.

DAY'S END

First the inert brown sack lying crumpled on the street. Then the car that rolls over the sack. Now the sack breathes life, a ripple travelling the coarse material, like wind travelling water. A hand emerges from inside. Chottu watches Chuk Chuk forming himself. The same old trick. How boring is this. And does it bore him: this ache in his throat?

Chottu dissolves into his shirt, pulling its dark around him. The comfort of his own warmth and smell are with him. A long time ago when Chuk Chuk replaced him as the magician's assistant, Chottu had repaid Chuk Chuk with a trick of his own. When tired, or especially sad, or just sick with the vomiting coming, when in the magician's embrace, smell yourself and instant happiness. Chottu Lal inhales himself then he turns the shirt front in with him and bending into his pocket, huffs the rag there. Out on the street the top of Chuk Chuk's head emerges from the sack and Chuk Chuk is borning himself through magic. Eyes and smile, white in the dark face.

✳

Come, Chuk Chuk says, breathe a little more. And I will talk to you. It is three-year-old Chuk Chuk who smiles and orders Chottu. When Chuk Chuk comes to him, it is always as he did the first time, as a three-year-old. Then, he had communicated with just his smiles and tears, and by pointing to the trains lined up on the platform. Koooo Chook Chook. And once he had your attention, faster and faster, Chuk Chuk Chuk. Chottu understood immediately. He turned to the magician and said, He came on the train, like I did. He spoke with awe. After all, he had been five, six, maybe seven when he climbed on the train. How did such a little fellow get on a train by himself?

The magician scooped up the baby and Chuk Chuk settled into the man's arms as Chottu had years before.

But he wants to go home, Chottu spoke anxiously. The magician paused at that. But Chuk Chuk himself never looked again at the trains. He pushed his nose into the magician's shoulder and wiped emphatically. At the end of a day performing on the platform the magician, carrying the now sleeping treasure, led the way out to the street, woke the baby, bought big glasses of sweetened milk for all three, fed Chuk Chuk by hand as Chottu looked on enviously. By then it was established the little fellow would answer to Chuk Chuk.

Chottu watches the competing images of Chuk Chuk and the man approaching. One, a rippling sack, the other equally a mirage, his outline rippled by waves of heat rising from the footpath. But moment by moment the rippling outline is clearer, closer—a bird flapping, then a building on the move, chest out and fists flexing. Chottu dives into his shirt pocket, inhales his rag and re-emerges to Chuk Chuk softening, sweet as sugar melting, We're brothers, aren't we? We're brothers, Chottu whispers. And the magic must be strong because Mohansingh is waylaid.

Chottu watches two men slap each other on the back, close enough to him for their thunk-thunk to clap his back. Now Mohansingh is slipping a friendly handful into the other man's shirt pocket.

The brother magic began for the two boys when they met Charu. She told them, You are brothers. She told them she was their sister.

What a slut. She's no sister of mine, Chottu thinks. And he knows he's right because how else to explain the heat blast of her scorching him.

Mohansingh's all right. He's freed Chottu up as never before. He no longer feels it necessary to watch Charu around men—she is characterless, she is, the way she grinds her hips when she walks, and sways—as if the effort of all that grinding has left her too weak to simply stand—when she stops. There is nothing very still about her, is there? Even in sleep, she sends her arms and legs every wild way. Chottu squirms. That business of her acting shocked if a fellow were to lunge for a handful. Nothing but pretence. With Mohansingh around she is a considerably cooler Charu. No longer free to induce anything, neither an inducement to anyone.

And, Chottu thinks, he is no longer the one responsible for defending her—in the past the most he had managed was to take the beatings of those who stepped over him, asleep next to her on the footpath, then awake to protest them having their go with her, then silenced by the blow the footpath struck his cheek.

Too ugly, that Charu, to be a whore till twelve, one or two when the drunks come looking. With traffic dwindled and the city dead, the street lights, though they do nothing to enhance her, casting her in blue and cratering her skin, allow the right notes to exchange hands—from the customer's to Mohansingh's. And she's gone, into the dark, over the wall, and amongst the trees of the jungle park. Mohansingh, Chottu's turned a sleepy eye and seen, stands a respectable distance from her, but still well within the apron of the street light, so that Charu's finally a professional with backing, and not merely the girl wrenched to the ground and taken for loose change or nothing at all. Backing. It's a word Chottu understands is stronger magic than brother and sister.

Chottu ignores Mohansingh's finger crooked at him. He crosses the street to the middle divider and leans his back against the fence, studies the younger children. None of them bring back Chuk Chuk's face. A brother is what he wants. His one arm lifts in the air, reaches for a shoulder to throw itself over. He lets this arm land on the fence, picks the other arm up and throws it over the fence as well. Now he tucks one foot flat against the fence and waits to catch the eye of any one of the older boys. One by one they look his way and look away till he's found by the one. Chottu ducks his head, takes a hasty wipe at his face and looks back to catch the boy's eye, to nod. The boy has turned away but in the aggressive self-consciousness of his squared shoulders, in the way the other boys have stepped away from him, Chottu knows he's not mistaken in thinking he's been picked.

✳

He waits another moment at the divider, hoping Chuk Chuk will come again. But he doesn't. He doesn't crawl out of the sack the magician spreads in the middle of the street for the car to run over. He doesn't take a bow while the crowd applauds. He doesn't turn the money over to the magician. He doesn't grow too big for the magician's sack as Chottu once grew too big for it. And he doesn't join Chottu in running bottles of liquor for Mohansingh. And he doesn't get caught by the police. And he doesn't get sold somewhere far away. (Where?) And he doesn't crawl into Chottu's bed at night when he wets his own. And they don't lie side by side. And Chottu doesn't feel in Chuk Chuk's cheek the soft earth releasing the heat of the day. And as sleep takes Chuk Chuk, Chottu doesn't prop himself on his elbow to watch the fluttering lids, the place where a light shines under the schoolhouse door.

And Mohansingh is upon him.

How much?

Chottu shakes his head, dumb in the sweet he is swimming. He giggles in reply.

Having a good time, eh? Good good, you stay alert. Get sexy.

Mohansingh ploughs through Chottu's pant pockets, lifting him as he pulls the various coins and notes out. A cuff to the ear and the building moves on down the street. When Chottu looks again for Chuk Chuk, even the sack is gone.

He checks his pockets. How much was in there? How much in there now? The twenty rupees from the lady? Is it still there? No. He checks his shirt pockets. He takes the rag out from the plastic bag, searches in its every fold. The twenty-rupee note is nowhere. The magazines are gone with Mohansingh. His longed-for break is here.

Briefly he remembers the woman. Evening and morning on the same road. Surely she will return. And then what? He can't remember what comes after that though the story is one he had only recently been telling himself. The guava, he remembers, was perfect—the skin astringent, the flesh mellow. He sucks at the seed bits, still there, hard between his teeth. A better world, he thinks as he chews at his teeth.

It's a long wait for Charu. When she comes, she is trailing a string of buoyant hearts.

Once in 1982

He is determined to climb the tower now while construction on the stadium is ongoing. Once construction is complete the towers are sure to acquire gates, chains and padlocks. In the dark, outside the lit zone of construction, it is possible to search for openings in the wire fence, to select a path through the acres of building material, to run with sister loaded on his back into the lit area, uninhabited because tonight construction is focussed elsewhere in the complex, to arrive at the metal monster he wants to climb and whose neck he is determined to ride.

The lights up top are blazing and the heat from them is palpable. Alok climbs toward them. It is important to keep his head down and eyes on the steel rungs of the tower he is climbing. If he looks up, it will be to scorch his eyes. Then there would be blind groping down to safety. He would have to lean on the five-year-old below, and she would somehow have to take the weight of his arm on her shoulder and all of a sudden learn how to cross Lodi Road. This picture gives him satisfaction. If he were to be struck blind today, she would be his eyes. It would be him and her. A flicker of light as he throws the switch in his head illuminates the forward flight and conclusion of their story: he still blind, but now old, she still somehow a child, as they squat on a red polished floor, an orchard rustling outside, and her hand directing food to his mouth.

He ignores her calling from below. 'Bhaiya, come down.' Then he thinks he should look, and looking from under his arms, he sees her framed in the curve of his armpit—standing below, only a speck; a speck in a frock which glows in the light. The washerwoman hasn't come in a week and he has washed on the sly a pile of clothes each day, doggedly imitating the motions he has seen her make. Crunch the clothes tight into a bucket with water and soap, crunch them with fists on the bathroom floor, then the exhilaration as each garment is unstuck and smoothed in the flow of water run endlessly from the tap. This is his devotion to her who must soil dress, socks and underwear daily.

The dress she is now wearing which is swelling white as she pirouettes in the light will have to be washed tomorrow. She looks like the Nirma Washing Powder girl, who wears a similarly flared and similarly white dress on the box of detergent at home. But outside supernatural stadium light, his sister Maya's dress is red and has blue roses with brown-green leaves, enormous ones, scattered all over. At present, he is happily aware, the dress is also terribly stained. His own shirt sleeves which are light blue and yellow-striped are also bleached out in this light, and in the breeze of this upper altitude his arms are covered with cockroach-antennae-hairs that wave so silver-white they have the lucidity of glass. He would like to brush his hands over their filamentous light, but he is afraid of loosing his hands from the steel rails they grip.

'Come down. Bhaiya, come down.' He hears the unhappiness in her voice. He climbs some, looks down again, and again refuses to reply. But knowing she will cry soon, he shakes his head at her. The ladder shakes with a singing metal quiver, its vibration making the blood jump inside him so he almost tastes the red in his inflamed nose and swollen throat. It's too late, he thinks, to answer her. His voice, he knows, will not make it past his tight throat.

He can hear that she has begun crying. He can hear it in the glimpse of her halted pirouette; in her one leg up inside her frock as she crane-bird balances in the loneliness of her own rice field, in the thumb she has stuck in her mouth and is sucking hard, and from which he is convinced she will through her exertion soon slip the skin loose. The thumb in the mouth is usually a precursor to the sort of crying which requires his lap, comic-books and promises of 5-Star bars.

Alok has brought Maya to the foot of one of the four light towers at Jawaharlal Nehru Stadium, trailing her there with an offer of walnuts cracked between his back teeth. She is one to appreciate his displays of strength, and he is sure on arriving at the stadium that the announcement of his desire to climb the tower will be met with handclapping, and that his struggle with her will be getting her to not follow him; to wait below. But the moment they arrive at the foot of the tower she turns to him in panic. 'Bhaiya, don't do it. You'll fall and land on me.' 'I should have left you at home,' he replies. He leaves her his handkerchief and a store of walnut kernels. Before he climbs he instructs her, 'Eat them one by one.'

Midway up, the tops of his thighs and knees burn and there is grit in his eyes, ears and nose. This grit invades his mouth. 'Maya,' he calls. 'You have to think. Are walnuts salty or are they sweet?' This will occupy her for a bit. He calls out the question three times and segments of it fall to the ground below and other bits fall to her ears. The bits that reach her she reassembles, and when she calls back up to him he is satisfied that they have cohered. 'Salty or sweet walnuts, Bhaiya?' He knows he has time again. And although he has never seen an escalator, his father has described its unfolding, upward movement and he thinks if he can only imagine he is on one then he will make it to the top. He races the steps, counting, '112, 113 . . . 118 . . . 134,' his palms wet, the metal hot. He forgets to imagine he is on an escalator. The lights closer now are overwhelmingly hot and what he thinks he is climbing is a stairway that will pull him into the sun. Hotter it beats, hotter on his head, beating him down, down, back down.

He has not thought through getting down. The descent takes him the better part of an hour during which his legs shake, shaking the steps, which shake him, which he shakes. His sister's wail is a pleasant weaving of sound through the rungs till eventually he ceases to journey the steps and instead allows himself to be carried along by its strength.

'Salty,' she wails. 'Sweet.' And he agrees she has solved the riddle correctly. He holds her and sits, unable to stop the trembling in his legs. Then he laughs to soothe himself and tells her when she is older he will take her on a journey to the sun. He points up at the lights.

'But Bhaiya, you said you can only climb now. Before Asian Games comes. Afterwards, police will stop us. Will I grow up before Asian Games comes?' she asks slyly.

'No,' he tells her, irritated by her pretend-voice. 'You won't grow up any time soon. I'll be washing your clothes and your bottom and your teeth for a long time.'

'If you are supposed to be taking care of me why did you leave me here, alone?'

'Did you eat the walnuts?' he asks. She nods and opens the handkerchief to show him. He mops his face with it and still irritated, snaps at her, 'You have nothing to complain about. I am the one who didn't reach the top because of you.'

'Mumma will scold us.'

'No. What makes you think she will know?'

'Then Daddy will scold you.'

'Maybe.'

'I'm going to tell Mumma.' She stops to think: will Mumma hear me? 'Okay, then I'll tell Daddy.'

'Idiot. They are busy. You go ahead and complain all you want.' Then he softens to her continuing hiccupping—a sound sweet to him from the days when her infant mouth first rewarded his crooked finger with sucking-hiccupping end to tears. 'I'll walk you through the peacock forest. We'll count how many there are. Okay?'

'Idiot you,' she counters. 'The peacocks are sleeping. It's night and even the trees sleep at night.'

'It's only 7.30.' He turns his wrist up to his face pressing the button to illuminate the digits strapped there. No one else in his class has a watch like this. His father has purchased it for him in that faraway place called Bonn, where maybe he has given a similar one to that other boy, the brother who is only a half not a full brother. If he is only half then why does he get to have a watch like Alok, and why does he get to have Alok's father for whole lengths of time?

No one else in his class has a half-brother or a father who has another wife in another country, and a briefcase that spills foil-wrapped condom packets that look like foreign chocolates. Alok, who has opened the briefcase behind closed doors recognises them for what they are only after ripping one open.

'Come,' he stands and beckons. 'Even if we won't be counting sleeping peacocks,' here his scant-haired upper lip twists, 'we still have to go home. Mumma will be watering the garden. We can help her.' His mother, he thinks, is always watering the garden. The heat requires it. Again his lips twist, his soon-to-be-adult face insinuating itself. There is a frightening mirth there. The watchful Maya throws her arms around his hips and buries her face in his thighs. He tries to laugh but something else yelps out of his throat. Close behind are words spoken in a fierce tremble: 'She doesn't want us. She only cares about Daddy.'

'Bhaiya,' his sister whispers. He squats, hoists her on his thin back, his knees knock hard and he rises and jogs to the row of fences they have to get past. He forgets his handkerchief, lying gleaming at the foot of the tower. The tower itself recedes reluctantly from the departing pair; pulls with an elastic pull which Alok is free of only when he steps from the apron spread of its light, into the dark.

*

Alok feels the familiar pull, driving by Nehru Stadium. How tame the towers appear to him in daylight. And, with the padding of years that has come to rest in his paunch and thighs, how distant his dream of climbing them. He would not now make it even halfway up the tower, he calculates. His Maruti suffers up the Defence Colony flyover, the stadium and its four towers throbbing in the corner of his eye. He begins the drop down the other side of the flyover, and the vision and its power is banished. Ahead the blue and white signboard says 'Nehru Place Chirag Dilli Panchsheel IGI Airport.' Distributed among these place names are arrows he must negotiate. In obedience to one of the arrows, he scoots the timid creature at his command to the right and prepares for the turn. But it is early yet. The turn, right, to IGI Airport is a long way in coming. A maddening rush goes by all around him. He cannot fathom why he has to be so slow on this of all days. After the turn there are more turns, and he is nearly late picking Maya up at the airport.

On the journey home with her he has even greater difficulty negotiating the roads. His head turns again and again to the passenger seat where she is—his sister. 'Maya', he breathes. He knows it is absurd but nevertheless feels as if he has hustled into his car some rare creature.

'Look ahead, silly,' she laughs. 'Hey, isn't that Nehru Stadium? Remember?'

He is staring at her belly which does not look any different to him. But he knows from the fuss being made about it by his mother that his sister is pregnant and her return home is so that she can get married. Not that this will make the pregnancy business go away, but even with the order of everything being all wrong, it is still better according to everyone that at least now she is getting married. He is angry, but at who? At his mother for even saying Maya must marry, at the baby who is now a little turning creature in Maya's belly (on exiting customs she had reached over the barrier railing, grabbed his hand and thrust it on to her middle, and he had withdrawn, scorched and muttering), or at the man who in another week will be turning up at their house on Tilak Marg to marry her?

'I will send the driver for him,' he tells Maya.

'For who?'

Maya looks at him, and clearing his throat he tries again. 'When Frank comes we can send the driver to the airport. That way we can be sure everything is on time.'

'Alok, we'll all go to the airport.'

'That's true, that's true. Frank possibly won't know the driver.'

She shakes her head, bemused.

At home he hardly sees her. Number 6 Tilak Marg is full of others. Sometimes a sense of her in another room, fleeting but present, registers and he looks up and sees she is sharing the breakfast table with him; her teeth wolfish, and white. She has grown sharp, he decides. But suddenly, his father is also at the table. Maya turns to her father and they begin talking. A chair screeches across the floor, and it is he who is dragging it from under himself.

'Done, Alok?' she asks.

Why does she have to be so polite? To me? 'I don't feel like eating.' This is as much as he dares to say.

'It is hot, isn't it? Why did it have to be at this time of year?' she murmurs.

He is confused. What is it that has to be at this time of year? Oh yes. Yes. The baby. The wedding. Frank. He retreats to the balcony outside the dining room. It overhangs the front drive. The three cars below, his father's collection, are being primed for display, a pack of children going over the details. Later today the entourage will set out to bring his sister's man home.

He looks around the balcony and thinks: There used to be trunks on this balcony. Where have they gone? When their father had first settled this house on their mother and moved them into it, Alok had been confused by the many sudden changes in his life. His friends disappeared overnight and so did his nursery school teacher whose name he was wont to taste with reverence before dropping into sleep: 'Baljeet Ma'am.' He had choked this name to his mother and she held him, comforting him. When he made note of his father's absence his mother rewarded him with a slap.

Alok could not say whether his changed life was good or bad. The new house with its too-many rooms lost him on a walk from bedroom to kitchen. Fogged corridors yielded an occasional glimpse of his mother. Alok made adjustments: allowing the fog inside his head, letting Baljeet Ma'am fade, forgetting what it was to ride horse on his father's lap. But then his mother would sharpen her eyes on him and he would find himself pulled to her lap, and her words—'left us for some whore'—would set him adrift to walk all over again the corridors of fog.

His father returned to them and then came the new baby, Maya, and after that they had all learned to share. But before it was established that his father could be shared, before when Alok and his mother had been left alone in the new house, she had refused to unpack, leaving trunks scattered on the lawn, verandah and balcony. The ones from the lawn, those that had successfully withstood the elements were eventually delivered of their contents indoors. Then the verandah trunks had made the trek just in time to save themselves from the January rains. But the boxes and trunks on the balcony had not shown similar foresight and once understood to be rotting, had stayed rotting on the balcony. He remembers playing among them, reordering their rectilinear silhouettes into a space station. He remembers Maya questioning him.

'It fell from the sky?'

'Yes, one in 1977. Just before you were born. That one was Soviet, and another one, an American one, when you were two.'

'Before I was born? Weren't you scared it would fall on you?'

'A lot of people were scared,' he informs her solemnly. 'The Skylab when you were two just almost fell on us. On India. But actually in the end, it fell in the Ocean.'

'You mean it fell on all the fish? Did they all die?' and she begins to cry.

He cherishes her for this great capacity of hers to sympathise. He hugs her tight even as he scolds her, 'You are so silly. Space stations have to re-enter orbit. They have to fall somewhere, and the ocean is always the best place for a landing.'

That day, he goes straight from the space station game to hovering on the edge of the cricket game convened evenings in the field near his house. The game pauses when an older boy, Vaibhav, sweeps the ball into the army camp next door. The boys mass and trail Vaibhav in the ensuing search, which finds them not a ball, but a crow that hops in the undergrowth. Alok watches the chase that ensues. He is too shy to join in. But he lets the cry of the clan echo in his head: 'Catch it, catch it.' Bound in twine and packed in dried leaves the bird is held to lit matches. He cannot turn his head but must watch the boys roast the bird till the stench of it drives them giggling back to their side of the wall where the ball is waiting for them.

'Where was I before I was born?' she asks.

'Always with me,' he assures her. Alok rubs his palm meditatively. The wet of her thumb no longer lives there. His jaw thrusts and he exclaims in irritation at the absence of the trunks and resolves to ask where in the house they have been dispatched. His sister's voice breaks in. 'Where are those trunks we used to play with?' She has followed him to the balcony.

'Do you remember playing space station?' he asks.

'Space station?' She cocks her chin and he thinks she will chirrup. He wants to press her from top of her head down till she squats into the little bird he carried everywhere with him. 'We played space station? Yeah. Yeah I remember. You were always the astronaut who flew it into the ocean and saved India.'

'Actually it was an unmanned operation,' he mumbles.

'Nooo?' She starts laughing and he decides that it is okay for her to laugh at him. He laughs with her till asthmatic coughing takes over. She knocks him hard on the head with the flat of her hand when he begins choking. 'Look. Look up. Lizard. Lizard.' She laughs provocatively. He swats her hand away. She looks hurt. 'Well, you always did that when I was little and choked.'

'That's for kids,' he reasons earnestly. 'To distract them. When they look for a lizard that's not there, they get distracted and that stops them choking. And the way you stuffed your mouth and ate. No wonder you always choked. I would have thought you would grow up fat. But look now at you.' This last, he says with a sense of despair.

She responds briskly. 'The trunks. The trunks have something in them I want. Mumma's wedding stole. I am sure it is a mess, but I know a place in Hauz Khas, and if it's still there, they claim they can restore anything. They reweave. They do everything. I am sure this will just need some polishing, unless the moths have gotten to it. Come Alok, help me find it.' She heads into the house.

✳

From somewhere inside the house the children are calling, 'Mumma.' Mixed in with their voices, Alok can hear Frank's murmured shepherding. Alok hurries to pull Maya away. They follow the turning corridor's ruined lines. The walls here are pocked with pictures, bred overnight it seems to him, like the sudden sprouting of mushrooms under the tree fallen in the garden. What rainstorm has facilitated this malfeasance? The pictures will all have to go. As he passes, he plucks them from the wall, leaving them stacked on the floor for the workers from the moving company to handle.

He struggles for a length of time in front of a grouping of nine that are smaller than the rest. These don't pluck as easily. Devoid of ornate frames that curl away from the wall these simpler black and white photographs—only so much bigger then postage stamps—are neither matted nor elaborated in any other way, but simply framed in wood so thin, they are flush with the wall. He peels them and piles them from his elbow to wrist on his forearm from where the weight of their accumulation slides them to the floor. Glass crunches under his feet.

'Alok.' She is an unwavering light at his side. 'Those were pictures of us as kids. First day of school pictures.'

'That's nothing,' he says, waving lavishly. 'There are so many more in the drawers. But if any of them are important then we can set them aside before the auction. What I am going to show you is something else I found.' He sweeps on.

'What is it? Slow down.'

They pass the dining room empty of all furniture on their right and he turns to the stairs. But she is no longer following. 'We have to go upstairs.' He sounds too authoritative, too loud, to himself. 'Sorry,' he says. 'I don't mean to scold. I always had to scold Mumma and the servants or nothing worked here.'

'It's all right, Alok.'

'No, no. I have to learn to stop. I won't do that anymore. Not after I pack it all up. Then the servants will be gone too.'

Her eyes rest on him and he shifts feeling peevish that she is witness to this mayhem. 'Come up,' he says abruptly and makes a grab for her hand. He thinks again, I mustn't scold her like I used to Mumma.

She withdraws her hand. 'Alok, I'll wait downstairs in the garden. You can bring whatever it is there. Mumma took such care of her garden. It will be good to sit there for a bit.'

'It's something I have to give you, upstairs. Come up.' Then he relents, 'All right then. You wait in the garden. It's not all that cared for at this point. But I'll bring it there. I found it yesterday for you.' Breathing heavily, he turns himself up the stairs. When he returns, he is surprised she is not waiting on the landing. It takes a moment to remember she will be in the garden. Heading down, he notes the banister is loose. Have to get this tightened before the sale. He tacks that thought to all the other thoughts fluttering unquietly around the house.

He is not sure where in the garden she might be. He hopes she is alone. Somewhere in the house the children are still calling, 'Mumma'. Somewhere in the house he hears Frank's voice answering them. He steps out quickly, shuts the door behind him, jerks a key out from the assortment on his ring and grapples it into the lock. Satisfied, he secures the package which is sliding out from under his arm and heads to the back of the house. Away from the house, he has direction. He knows where Maya will be.

*

When Maya is five, the day they return from the trip prowling the stadium, Alok is feverish, his forehead and forearms blistering and peeling. His father rages and Alok in his delirium can only manage, 'I was looking for the sun.' His father belts him then for taking his sister out in the dark. During the scene of this agitation, Maya stands on the periphery of the drawing room rug and watches, thumb in mouth. Alok fixes his vision on her through the chinks of space between the arms he wraps around himself. But somewhere in time his vision slips to the tower he has almost surmounted, and she slips free. When his father is done his mother scolds him to buy time with him. 'Alok, you are a big boy. Your father relies on you. And I rely on you. This is no way for a grown boy to behave.' His father listens to this for a moment and walks out of the room. She pleads with renewed vigour, tears gathering in her voice, 'Why do you make him so angry? He wants to love you. Why do you have to make it so difficult?' Alok hates her for it—this apology. It betrays him more clearly than the anxious intake of her breath, between the snap of his father's belt in the air and the laying of it on his skin. When his mother finally leaves Alok goes looking for Maya and does not find her.

He wakes the next morning exposed and chilled. Maya is at the foot of his bed, spinning, on her bottom, gathering to herself radiating spokes of his cover. 'Hey,' he warns her. The socks he has left paired on the bed, climbing into sleep without bothering to put them in the drawer, his mother's imagined 'never finishes anything he starts' giving him secret satisfaction, are coming unpaired in the bunching of the sheets.

'I have something to show you. Quick, you have to be quick before it disappears.' Downstairs in the garden he obliges her by covering his eyes, and pretending not to see, he is led by the shirttail pulled from his waist. The garden path unspools under his feet; the garden bench approaches from the periphery to the centre. She spins him by the bench as if in a game of blind man's bluff and sensing from her laughter they have reached the final spin he lunges to wrap his arms around her ('caught you'). She pushes him back into the bench, where he lands, with her in his lap.

'See,' she points to the star jasmine bush, 'It's like the sun you were looking for.'

In what his mother calls her white garden, this bush is allotted a meagre role as backdrop—the tulips his father brings from that other place, the tulips no one else in Delhi presumes to grow, occupies the foreground. He looks to where his sister points and thinks, a bush, a bush. And he shrugs, so what?

'You have to squeeze your eyes,' she says.

He does, and sees: burnished by April morning, a pulsing globe, seething with white bloom and green leaf. Each white flower blooming not its habitual single-petalled, star-shaped bloom but something hinged and also white that lays flat to the petals then flick-folds upright. Alok watches these bits of white-gold separate from the darker mass of green, take short flight, and settle back into the fold. He opens his eyes and the bush is once again its spindly branches, pruned into an unconvincing sphere.

'A sun for you. A sun for you,' Maya continues her chanting.

Happiness is a hammer blow that he bows under. He wants to tell her that he sees it is like a sun. Then he realises he doesn't need to. She is perfectly satisfied with what she has given him. He feels her settling in his lap, her head pushing hard into the cave of his chest. Pressed against the bench the stripes on his back open and weep into the cloth of his shirt.

Alok knows where he will find Maya—on the bench facing their bush. She rises when he approaches and he takes the roll from under his arm. Uncovered, it is thin and flat in his upturned palms. He frees it from tarnished folds, and the perfect span of his arm spread, it emerges, a length of pale silk. 'This is it, isn't it? You tore this place apart looking for it. Somehow Mumma remembered. Told me where to look.' He brings his arms together and the cloth accordions back into stiff folds.

Maya does nothing to bring herself forward to receive the cloth. Alok pulls and collapses the cloth a few times, then it tears with a whispering sound. He rolls it up and thrust it at her. She opens her mouth, seems to think better of it and then as if the words require speaking, as if they own her and not she them, 'You've been living in the past, Alok.' Then, 'What will you do next, Alok?'

He tries to make her laugh. 'Not many jobs for a grown man who has never done anything other than administer insulin shots to his diabetic mother.'

'Alok.'

'Well, I know how to turn on the heat lamp and point it in the right direction. Very good for arthritic pain.'

'All right then.' Maya is brisk. She takes the roll from his hands and bends to pick up crumbles of cloth. 'You don't know what you will do next. It takes time to figure these things out. A job. People. You need to meet people. Frank and I were thinking it would take you time and of course we would be happy if you stayed with us while you thought things through.'

He is surprised at his sister. When did she start thinking of him like this—as a problem for her to solve. He feels a faint sense of outrage. 'I was with her till the end, Maya. That's not living in the past. Daddy has not been here in five years. I was all she had. I was living with her here. Not in the past. Here.'

'Grow up,' she says.

They are approaching the borders of a brutal country. A border he has seen before in the scar on the kitchen girl's face—a scar travelling her laugh line, curving beautifully white on her black face. He would have touched the scar to let her know that he has travelled this country, if he had known how one set about touching another creature. Now he puts a hand on Maya's cheek. His hand has grown in the years since he last touched her. The fingers alone fill her face. They are fat.

And though the idea is only just arrived within him he fully expects she knows what he is thinking. 'Maya,' he tries to tell her, 'I can't live with you'. Was it when the cloth tore, or was it when she bent to pick the crumbles of it from the ground? He doesn't know when it came to him, the room empty and lit, the room he has never been in but has suddenly imagined into being.

'I have a place,' he tells her, speaking with the strictness which as an older brother he really should have adopted a long time ago. 'The details haven't been worked out. But I have it in mind.' And again, he can see it. It is empty and lit. 'No AC,' he tells her. 'It will burn up in the summer.' And the room is licked by flames. A smile spreads over Alok's face. 'An architect friend of mine—yes, I have an architect friend,' and he can picture the friend—told me the solution was to place those clay water pots, without water of course, upside down. Cover the roof with them. A sort of insulation against the heat. Cools the place down. Oh it's one of those rooftop affairs, a barsati,' he adds happily. 'And I don't want an AC. Hated the way we kept this place chilled year around. All that water dripping for years from the different ACs has just ruined these walls.'

They sit on the bench. He tells her the details of the repairs he is undertaking on the house. The banging sound grows louder and Alok stands up, realising it must be Frank at the back door that he left locked; the children come running from around the house. 'The front door, Dad,' they yell. Then they attack Alok, 'You locked us in. You and Mumma thought you could have a secret meeting without us.' He sits hard on the grass and they hurl themselves at his frame, bruising their ribs as they strain to unseat him. The littlest one, Alok's niece, grasps his chin in her two hands and fights the head which he lowers like a bull's. She gives up when the scruff on his chin becomes too much to bear. Her two brothers take over from her. It is like playing with a wall, which makes him their favourite toy—a toy whose opaqueness rules out the distorted reflections that are forced on them when pulled into games with other adults. 'You are a cheeky one,' another adult might say. Uncle Alok does not describe them to themselves. And Maya's children, who don't know themselves as cheeky or smart or even funny or agile, without exactly knowing it, love this about their uncle. They especially like it that they are the ones who are free to declare a game at an end. Which they do now by careening away to race around bushes.

Frank emerges from around the house and the three of them move back toward the bench. Alok sits between Frank and Maya, who begin arguing. It's all a jumble. Maybe it is about the house. He strains to listen to the words colliding overhead and a pleasant feeling of being lifted towards these words comes to him.

'I don't know what I will do next.'

He is not sure if he has said this aloud. In any case the mild tinkling of their words continues rising from either side of him. It makes him think of the pairing of crows that he has been watching from his mother's bedroom window these past many days. They hop in the grass, whispering in each other's ears, feeding each other from their dark beaks.

With some astonishment he realises that Maya thinks his life is not a good one. It is a bit tattered, he acknowledges. But there's the room now. And this time when he pictures it he sees tattered curtains, crumbles of them needing to be swept up from the floor. The room widens in his mind, gathers coherence. It is easy, he thinks, to live within small details. He is in the room and sweeping it. He hasn't held a broom in his hand in the years since his childhood. But he can feel how one stoops when holding one. He can feel that stoop stored in him since childhood.

'I called her, Mumma. Twice. She was slipping away. At least the nurse said so. Her pulse was barely there. It had been two days since she spoke. So I told her you and Daddy were coming soon. That's how she went then. Happy enough thinking you two would be here soon.'

Maya seems to want more. He doesn't think it makes sense to talk about the rest of it. The body drying up on the bed, the skin turning dark, breaking into sores, the mouth itself another sore, the endless hunger for ice, the ice slippery in his hands. And even when all the fluids in the body dried, when she left off excreting, there was still hatred, held unmitigated by the approaching end. Before the silence of the last two days set in she periodically called to Alok, 'Come see where it all began.' The nurse responded by placing her hand on the pelvis his mother was trying to lift from the bed. Alok held to his seat by the bed. His mother's words were not ghastly to him. If he turned his face it was from the nurse's scolding, 'Enough now. You will hurt yourself.'

There are only two ways to go about things. He doesn't know how he first made this discovery. During the beatings he suffered in childhood the realisation was already his—the options were to howl or to not howl. Now he can tell Maya that their mother's end when it came was horrible or he can tell her it was good. And he can tell her a little about the room he will find somewhere in this city. He hopes his sister won't ask him what he means by any of his words. He has so few words with which to explain his happiness.

This late season, only a sprinkling of white, like small and few stars in a cloudy night sky, remains on the bush surrounding the bench. The bush has not held to a globe. It is as tall and outspread as a small tree. A stray butterfly, a gaudy orange, lights on a low branch. The tulips once forced to grow here are long gone.

Passage

Tuesday, early a.m. The sound of the man clearing his throat outside her bedroom window then retching to signal four o'clock gives way to the scrape of the sweeper's broom, then to the clang, rise and abrupt halt of shop shutters, and finally to the muezzin calling '5 o'clock, ohhh 5 o'clock'. In half-an-hour the alarm will ring and Susheila will rise, turn on the taps and begin the musical buckets game, sliding the green, the blue, the red bucket under the rusty spitting, then clear and steady, then trickling stream. Which bucket will lose in this game and remain empty when the tap dries up? The alarm must first ring; she must rise, line up the buckets, sternly admonishing an end to their impatient jostling, and check periodically between the preparation of tea and cornflakes, between the laying out of the school uniform and the search under the bed for yesterday's school socks, to see whether today it is the green, the blue or the red.

The echo of the muezzin hollows into her ears, continuing its ringing for her alone. Tinnitus. She shakes her head, flops back and bangs against the bone of Jacob's shoulder. He scoops her tight into his sleep but there her muffled breath condenses and soaks his chest. She inhales, protests the forced recycling of spit, then the embrace itself. She is half-irritated with Jacob, half-dismayed at herself for this bit of early-morning drama. He tightens his hold. She is entirely won over. Contrite now, she offers him mock-drama: 'I am a woman who cannot be comforted.' He comforts her quickly, brusquely, then tenderly, then hopelessly. Reduced and enlarged in each other, they sleep briefly then wake, she to fling herself from bed to buckets, and he to arrange himself in front of the computer screen.

Across town and across many more towns and the country and the ocean there is a time so far away it is another time, that yet remains the time Susheila wakes to retching. In a different day and date and hour that is yet the same one Susheila is ticking to, her beloved sister's chest too lifts, to fall. And before it fails to lift again this sister senses the cold outside rushing in and she knows no flicker of responsive fear. It comes too quickly and she is gone. By the time Susheila discovers it is the green bucket's turn to lose today, but mercifully not before it is at least a third full, the doctors are flinging gloves aside and one is saying, 'Triage should have caught this . . .' Another has this to say: 'We should review . . .' At which he is torn into by his colleagues and driven from the room and out the door by their baying-barking, his bloody gloves only half peeled from his hands, still joined at the first joint of each finger, so his strange, pale, powder-dusted fingers extend out to a second set: luminous yellow. All twenty fingers useless, useless in the service of saving the woman behind the swinging door, which swinging in ever smaller arcs ushers out the detrital puff displaced in the last heaving of the woman's chest. For seconds it lingers, cohering to itself then dissipates in the corridor.

The door yawns suddenly wide and disgorges five more, some of whom are thinking ahead to home and sleep and others who remain lost in the body now sewn temporarily shut, within whose cavity organs are yet bobbing: didn't realise . . . thought a standard D&C . . . just a miscarriage . . . they should have caught it in intake . . . if the husband had said . . . damn tube bursting . . . should have hurt enough for her to kick up a fuss . . . or him, why didn't he . . . waited out there too long with her flooding like that . . . damn near emptied into herself . . . these women from God knows where, always so damn quiet, why?

✳

Susheila sends her son off to preschool, crammed into the van that ferries him daily. Yusuf is crying as he boards the van. Susheila has searched in all the inconceivable places pity dictated—under mattresses, behind the gas cylinder, between Ammachi's dust-basted suitcases—but the card Yusuf made for his teacher the night before is simply vanished. She looks at her email one last time then begins the shut-down process, noting as she closes the series of windows that she is travelling back through Jacob's morning—his Google-searched 'Delhi Schools' has produced a list the length of which seizes up her back, the *Reader Rabbit* he promised to leave on the desktop for Yusuf to find on his return from school is still downloading when she 'X-es' it forcefully. Then comes the MSN news and the record of his gmail chat with his sister, sprinkled, it seems to her suddenly self-conscious eyes, with enough ellipses to warrant a second look. Jacob wouldn't be discussing her with Annie, would he? He wouldn't. No, he wouldn't. Besides she has last chores ahead of her before she exits the house—lights off, fans, balcony doors bolted, at least the dining table cleared.

And here is Yusuf's card on the seat of the chair, which is slid neatly under the table; it is an action she has repeatedly urged Yusuf to undertake because, 'if Amma and Appa have to do everything for you then what will you do when you grow up and become an Appa and have to run your own house?' To which her son likes to say, 'You will live with me and do all the work like Ammachi did for you.' To which she never replies, assessing instead her mother-in-law's role in the household prior to her death with an easy charity she could not muster when the old lady was alive.

Now twenty minutes into the journey and still crying in the nursery van, this child who Susheila calls her 'waah-waah kid' for his incessant whining and general tenderness, prefers to bypass these periodic back-and-forths about chores and his grandmother, a fierce loyalty to the dead forcing him in this instance to prefer

Ammachi to his mother. He most often answers requests for chores by reminding his mother that his destiny lies in Hamilton, Ohio, where his Cuckoo Aunty has promised him he can come and live with her, and where all cleaning is done by robots.

Far away from her nephew, where she was not anyone's Cuckoo Aunty, the process of reopening temporary stitches and conducting an autopsy on Laila Habib is underway. Because it is known there will be no one to raise uncomfortable questions—the man they had first thought a husband is after all only a boyfriend— a solemn but relaxed air prevails over the signing of the death certificate. Two of the doctors, from the earlier scene of hasty surgery undertaken too late, make a note to share the findings of the autopsy with those of the team gone home. Everything points to the need for a quality assurance review of ER intake procedure. The staff physicians are in agreement that their performance at the moment of discovering on dilation that the woman, Laila Habib, was awash in her own blood, and their subsequent speed in opening her up, is a case of textbook adherence to best practice. Still, there is the internal murmur, disquiet, the senior doctor feels speaking to the man standing in the same spot he has occupied for the previous six hours, disquiet which carries the doctor's words back to himself: 'You couldn't have known. When the tube bursts there is so little external bleeding. People don't know how serious it is. It happens.'

Susheila does not open her email till late in the afternoon, during a tea break at work. She reads the words of a stranger writing from Cuckoo's account. A succession of moments overtake her, each moment delivering words, the flash accompanying each word illuminating her from within. She reacts with a quickening exhilaration and simultaneous faintness to the fearsome rush of these words. '*My name is Alex. You don't know me although I very much wanted to meet you,*' is something she attempts to rub from her eyes, then careens past, allowing herself to breathe heavily while holding back panic. From *'She had quite a bit of internal bleeding and was in a lot of pain when we did the ER. But we only knew about the pain,'* Susheila understands a need to weep. Then, *'We had known she was pregnant about ten weeks but she had spotting and we had known something wasn't right'* lights in remote reaches the nastiness that accompanies Susheila's pride in all her sister's accomplishments—a baby? A baby without a wedding to precede it, a baby unannounced in the family? Quickly rising and choking her is sympathy for the baby who didn't make it and sympathy for the loss her sister is suffering. *'Laila died at 6.30 p.m. our time'* charges every vibrating mote of her with bafflement. Who died? Susheila thinks.

She pushes back her chair from the screen, stands up, speaks over the partition, 'Who died at 6.30 p.m. our time?' Her colleague is not in the next cubicle. Susheila sits back in her chair and pulls forward to the screen and tries to bargain first with Alex, and then she doesn't know who it is she is bargaining with. To Alex, triumphant at having caught him in a lie, this stranger who Cuckoo had somehow let into their lives: 'It is not 6.30 p.m. our time.' And then to the unknown: 'But you already took the baby. Leave her.'

Back at home, she frightens Jacob, telling him, 'Don't come near me. I don't want you.' Trusting no one else, she addresses herself, 'Make it not real, make it not real'. She repeats this to exhaustion. When she turns to Jacob it is to tell him, 'You would have to die for me to want you again.' She is trying to shock herself. She wants to be shocked; she wants to say and do ugly things that will undo the ugliness of what she has read. With her own self, the negotiations are exacting and leave her feeling she is close to swinging a deal: an eye, an arm, a limb of any kind, two limbs are all easy to give in return for Laila.

She once danced with Laila, exciting interest in the men circling their sister-act on the dance floor. Then, afraid of the attention that was pressing in, afraid to see who it was really meant for, she had turned silly, dropped to hands and knees and tangled herself there between her sister's legs, barking and biting the creamy skin of Laila's calves. People had laughed. Laila had scolded with tears in her eyes. The lesser sister, Susheila had thought then, and always. Why shouldn't the lesser sister be without a limb or an eye in return for life in the holy and good body of the sister who once knew to scold the lesser out of Susheila?

When she wakes up the house is quiet. Jacob has not told their son. He is waiting for her to tell him how to do it. He whispers when he speaks to her and she asks him, 'You think I am unwell?' He offers, 'The homework is done. I thought maybe if you felt like getting up we could talk to him. I still have to give him his bath. Maybe not now, if you don't feel like it. We can tell him after his bath.' All that night and for the next three she repeats, 'Make it not real, make it not real', and 'It's not real. Don't let it be real.' She thinks dully through the crimes of her past: the envy, always the envy that had accompanied her love for her sister. And lesser crimes: 'I counted her calls versus ours. I thought, she is making money so she should call us more, more often than we called.' Jacob soothes her and she is not soothed.

On the fourth night, after Jacob puts the phone away, having spoken to the man on the other end, Susheila tells Jacob to call back. 'Ask him, if Cuckoo knew. Was she scared? Did she say my name?' On the phone she cannot ask this man, Alex, any of her questions. Instead she tells him, 'When we were little she said every night, "Don't go to sleep till I go to sleep." She was so scared of the dark.' The man, this stranger, who she knows from his voice is also mourning, inspires only anger in her. 'Did she sleep with you because she was afraid to sleep alone?' Jacob takes the phone from her hand and over many more phone calls the arrangements are made without Susheila's participation to fly home the package that is her sister.

Two days, and the package arrives. Her son greets it with what looks to her to be the same greed with which he had once greeted other packages filled with Sunday comics from American newspapers and little boxes of tic tacs, cheap and colourful pencils with erasers attached to their ends. She is useless to her son and leaves home that night.

✳

She walks past the guards outside the large homes in the neighbourhood next to hers. She is sure the guards are staring at her. She is sure they know she has committed a terrible crime. They have guns; and unlike the rusted rifle toted by the guard outside the bank she works at, these guns that guard expensive homes look to be expensive themselves. These guns look like they might do successful battle with any number of marauding thugs. She walks swiftly with a growing fear she welcomes. Perhaps there will be a mob, like the one that came when she was twelve and Laila ten, to drag out the owner of the taxi-stand across the street from her home. Soon perhaps this mob will materialise, the guns will be fired and she will die shielding Laila. She reminds herself that the taxi-stand owner who lived to rebuild the stand incinerated by the mob and who still serves her neighbourhood was only slashed at that afternoon. He survived, losing the tendons of his shoulder. Perhaps, in the event a mob materialises, here and now, she won't necessarily have to die for Laila; she might live with some sort of disfiguring wound. She allows a sympathetic pain in her shoulder and walks on, past more houses, bougainvillea bushes, artful windows, stretches of empty footpath, stray dogs waiting in sleep for the hour that will see the streets theirs. A mob, she thinks, is a good thing for her to save her sister from and refuses to think of those who might die in the inferno she imagines engulfing this neighbourhood, these bushes, this house with flame-licked decorative urns flanking these steps that lead her nowhere.

She turns on reaching the lit-up sounds of a wedding that had earlier been in the distance. This is the Mayfair Garden neighbourhood. Did she cross Khel Gaon Marg to get here? She doesn't remember doing it but re-crosses to escape the raucous joy of men dancing ahead of a chariot: horse-drawn, and seat for a man garlanded in a thick rope of rupee notes. The groom has come for the bride. But no one came for Laila. Here on the street, hurrying away from the hissing kerosene lamps held aloft to light the groom's way Susheila remembers schooldays singing under the guidance of Mother Mavis; she remembers the wide-open and enthusiastic ugliness of Laila's voice next to her own, singing, 'Give me oil in my lamp, keep me burning, give me oil in my lamp, I pray.' Mother Mavis had snaked the long cane—kept only for slicing the air in front of her but which nevertheless preoccupied the singers, all of whom sang with their heads jerking and eyes keeping time to its rhythm—over suddenly stilled heads and trailing voices to tap Laila on the head. 'Everyone else, quiet. Let me listen to this tuneless child.' Laila sang then, spilling such an unexpected jangling into that beautiful morning, she was swiftly demoted, this pet of all the nuns, to singing with her mouth opening and closing but without ever her voice emanating.

Her mother's grief is Susheila's now: 'We should have married her before sending her there. At least she would have known the happiness of being married.' Her mother knows nothing of the ectopic pregnancy and the burst fallopian tubes. Susheila has prevailed in this matter, arguing that her mother's spotty grasp of the real would never be able to handle the additional complication of Alex and the baby. A reluctant Jacob had handled the story, describing a burst appendix from his own experience of being rushed to the hospital, clutching his eighteen-year-old middle, which in the unmoving traffic of Delhi's major arteries seemed that day unlikely to see a nineteenth year.

Now Susheila sees clearly that they should have married Laila to someone, anyone, but not as her mother claimed for Laila's happiness. For one thing, she thinks fiercely, it would have put Alex and the pregnancy out of the picture. And another thing, she starts to think, but her face splits open and her hands, which reach to cover the gash that is her widening mouth, are soaked in an instant. There is no other thing. Remembering Laila's ugly singing she is sure death was present that schoolday morning, inside the sky-blue blouse, inside the box-pleated steel-gray skirt.

If only, she revises her thinking, we had married Laila before allowing her to go there then we would have had at least that happiness. She thinks of the selfishness of wanting to squeeze this additional bit of pleasure out of Laila. Anything, she feels, even selfishness, is justified with Cuckoo gone. Susheila searches to feel the pleasure of the chariot-driven groom, the pleasure of the lamps burning to light Laila's face. She fails.

Jacob had said on the phone, his mother-in-law's lamenting having been duly and silently listened to so that the old woman could finally put her phone back onto the receiver, 'Thank God she wasn't married. Think of leaving someone behind, maybe even children.' Susheila had nodded her agreement into their second receiver. The child that burst in Laila, excavating her, and the man left hulled in a hospital corridor were not real to them, that afternoon. The fabrication of the burst appendix, rooted in the story of the harrowing ambulance ride—'Life and death, man, and no one stops for you on these streets'—told at many a dinner party, and known even to Laila, was so much more real. They would never meet the man. They would, of course, never hold even the remains of the baby. Jacob, one to systematically think through details, envisions the embryo at ten weeks as a collection of cells and tissue disposed of in the American hospital's bio-waste. He has not communicated this to Susheila in words. What is known to him is also known to her—a simple function of years of nestling, one into the other. But this once, it is after a lag of days that Susheila comes to the knowledge: the child is not in the unopened package at rest on top of Ammachi's stacked suitcases.

Susheila crosses the street. She is not back on Khel Gaon Marg. This must be Hauz Khas Enclave, on the other side of the Mayfair neighbourhood. She circles the squat tower that is Chor Minar, not sure which lane will ensure she remains on the course she is meant to take. She circles, following the traffic sign that directs her to keep left, trying to listen for inner direction. When that fails to materialise she approaches the rubble of the tower itself and strains in the dark for direction from among the words on the sign describing the importance of this thirteenth-century national heritage monument. Thieves were beheaded, she reads, and their heads displayed in the towers' windows. She looks up and picks out in the dark the darker openings of these windows. There are many of these darknesses pocking the night. She cannot imagine the heads. She can only imagine the secret mourning of women who she is certain are circling this tower with her. Why else a tower, circular, why else the circular path, but for them to tread endlessly?

She is terribly tired but the thought of sleep brings guilt. She should keep walking: this is the lesson for her in her mistaken crossing of the wrong street. All around, the blurred lights of moving and pausing traffic pass on in the unrepentant motion of a tide travelling in and out of shore. The pain in her shoulder, when held in her consciousness, grows to such prominence that her whole body swivels on the action of this one joint, so it is not her feet that propel her now, but the pivotal shoulder. Crushed by the dizzying sense her shoulder should meet the footpath, she stops and squats, and holds her head till she can reorient herself. This she does with the aid of various smells that converge to converse with her. The tender solicitude of footpath smells— mustard oil and mustard shit—tell her she is in the company of her own kind. She walks on, pretending to the vendors packing away their food-stands in Green Park Market that she is an exercise fanatic out for a late-night walk. She rehearses lines in her head: It is so hot to be walking in the day. Much better to walk at night.

An hour later her waah-waah child wakes crying that his mother is dead. He is inconsolable, passing into hysteria when his father fails to produce evidence of Amma asleep, elsewhere in the house. Jacob rings her mobile repeatedly; she sees it is eleven o'clock as she holds down the key to turn it off. He rages from one room of their home to the other, forgetting that he has a son, forgetting that his wife's sister is not dead a week yet, remembering only in some place within him, deeper even than the place where lives the remembered pain of his appendix bursting, that the woman is his, and so her grief should be. Baffled and unable to sustain the anger he passes back into sleep on the drawing room divan, his son's steady hiccupping striking a syncopated note in the ragged rhythm of his heart.

Susheila crosses back over Khel Gaon Marg, but far north of Mayfair Garden, north even of Defence Colony and Jangpura. Here her feet turn and she climbs up then down one flyover, and another, and finds herself listening in the dark to the past midnight sounds of metal pots being washed in restaurant alleys. These sounds, old friends from nights of insomnia, tell her she is somewhere close to home again. Under the Chirag Dilli flyover, dogs come up to her, licking their smiles and wagging their hindquarters. They only want to be touched but she is afraid of the craven confidence that brings them so close. Hurrying away she walks among the ironmongers and the fishmongers arranged head to toe, and where the footpath is afforded any width at all, side by tight side. She chokes against the musk of their trade. One of their children cries and a woman turns and swats from sleep a man next to her who wakes and grips the wailing child to his chest. He meets Suheila's eyes over the child's head and the hard love there nearly buckles her to her knees. Instead, she feels her feet turn again looking for another way. He knows he is happy, she thinks. She cannot imagine that she will ever again grip her child in such pure happiness. Did I know, she wonders, that I was happy then?

She can see her home now: three lit windows strung among tree branches. She cannot imagine what life is held in that light. Inside, 'Global Priority Mail' spelled on slick white paper is a slippery surface for the mating of two moths. One crowds against the other; the other from under, wings spread for stability, thrusts the curved tip of its tail. In the crucial instant they slide apart, inexpert on this ice. They try again. Again the slippery slide and again the renewed charge at each other, till a dozen more attempts are made fuelled by the night's own charge. Finally, they tumble to the floor where scratched concrete gives them the necessary friction and leaves them with crippled wings. Another thousand instances bloom into being in the house dreaming and sleeping. The letters on the package confined to dreams of the past begin by dreaming of the moths' visit.

Susheila trails one hand behind her, scratching it on the bark of trees and the decoratively hobbed metal ropes that surround the little park outside her home. Her fingers snag and tear on something sharp. The rope has given way to barbed wire. She turns to the wire and hangs her frame against its yielding support. She brings her face tentatively to its kiss and the elbowed barbs bear her, cradling her. She pushes a little harder and sighs when they don't enter her skin. Leaning, she sees the little square of grass on the other side of the fence. Leaning, she thinks of her son's wail as Laila turned to wave from between the sliding glass of airport doors. 'I am saaaad,' he had wailed and Susheila wishes to wail this too. Leaning, she asks: 'How long will I be here?'

Jacob turns in his sleep. Something is pulling him awake and something else pinning him to sleep. He opens his eyes into the soft darkness of his child's cheeks, realises he is sealed to Yusuf in a wet and pungent embrace. With difficulty he frees himself from under the boy. The hollow impressed into the divan mattress by their collective weight now swallows Yusuf whole. Jacob's outstretched legs sing the joyful pain of blood coursing again through muscles. He hobbles to what is pulling him and circles back with the unopened package.

There is no real dining room in the house. In the catch-all hallway off the front door and adjacent to the drawing room is a table which when not in use can be lifted and latched back into a niche in the wall. As it is they keep the table down at all times, cantilevered from the wall. It serves as the anchor to the emotions surrounding the doings of the household. Here on the table he resets the package and opens the front door, certain that the door needs to be open. He sits at the table and listens hard to the muezzin call: 'Come home, ohhh come home,' '5 o'clock, ohhh 5 o'clock'. He imagines his wife, a ship tossed in the sea of the city at night. He is ready to tell her about safe passage—that it can be known only once treachery is navigated. He wants to add this crucial ending to the story of his crawl to the operating theatre, siren blaring for years afterward the danger of his time coming to end without having known her, without having known the joy of sleeping puddled in his child. He sits at the table signalling her where the rocks are and where harbour lies.

Los Angeles

What comes wrenching out of Ashima Jain tastes of Saturday-afternoon *fideo*, but is saltwater-thin, has no substance. An earlier bout had filled the toilet with chunks of tomato and marvellously intact lengths of noodle. An old habit this—one forsaken for some years and yet so close at hand it is readily picked up in the frenzy of self-abnegation. In the bathtub to get cleaned up, the business of retching and heaving begins of its own volition; too tired to pick herself up and over to the toilet, she leans over the drain, pukes saltwater.

In this room, built on the scale of an airline stall, the door opens only far enough to allow her to wiggle in. Once inside, she must shut it to access the toilet, where, when seated, her knees bump the sink cabinet. The tub sits aside the sink and toilet. A strange creation of her landlord, it is more deep than it is long or broad: a square, tiled box sunk into the ground, with a built-in sit-ledge, which no amount of scrubbing has rendered fit for contact with her seat. The tub was so unlike anything she had ever seen; on her first tour of the place she decided this was the kind of tub newscasters were referring to when they reported meth house busts. Yes, the tub was paraphernalia for cooking meth. Which made complete sense to her since the landlord, straggly bearded owner of the two Dobermans kept chained in the backyard strewn with shit, looked to her to be the LA version of the meth-cooking white trash she had left behind in Klamath Falls.

The neighbourhood was the kind her father had warned her to steer clear of. But the neighbourhood came with the internship at the clinic. And nowhere else in East Los Angeles was there a place so tidily her size at a rent so within her means, $250 per month plus utilities, one month refundable deposit. And before the home tour was over Graham explained the tub. 'Japanese design. I love the Japanese. Brought one home from my service days. Built the tub for her. She was a knockout.' He repeated himself, punctuating each word with a pause. 'She . . . was . . . a . . . knockout.'

Ashima's eyes traversed the thin leather cord wrapped across Graham's forehead, gathering a line of oily black to itself before disappearing into the hair hanging in chopped chunks of gray-blonde. Graham laughed to himself, 'Poof. Left me as soon as she passed her nurse's licence exam. I drove her to Sacramento for it. Smart people, the Japanese. She passed it the first time she took it.'

His face moved closer to Ashima's. 'Wonderful hair like ink she had. Kind of like yours,' and he reached as if to touch her hair, winked, and withdrew his hand. 'Inca blood. Am I right? What did you say you were? Nineteen?' And when Ashima, in some confusion over what she was assenting to, nodded, he smiled and handed her the keys. 'Well, here's wishing you some of the fun I've had in that tub.' The heat from her cheeks rose to mist the air in front of her eyes. Briefly Graham wavered there. But Ashima smiled as politely as she had seen her father smile into the phone while negotiating payment plans on the electricity bill.

✳

A stretched web of drool drapes from Ashima's mouth into the drain. '*Pendejo*,' she curses Marvin, who taught her to cook the fideo she's just upchucked, who taught her to curse in Spanish 'because,' he said, 'teach you the right words and you'll make one cute cha-cha'.

Now look what you've done to me. I was doing so well, so

well, she cries to herself. I was just getting the hang of it. Why did you have to ruin it like this? 'You've ruined it,' she cries out loud and subsides.

It was late in January when she arrived in Los Angeles. Her first triumph was the discovery of her apartment. She settled in, covered the door-less closet with a thumb-tacked bedspread—Indian print—and promised herself other home improvements, in time, once her first paycheque came in. In not quite two weeks Dr Takanaki, half-smile on his face, handed her a half-paycheque in an envelope accompanied by a card wishing her the best. Her talents, he could say this confidently, having known her for nearly two weeks now, were better suited elsewhere.

There was no question her father would have stepped delicately in welcoming her home. But returning to Klamath, to her father and her sisters, was just not an option. Going back would have been like the time her third-grade teacher sent her to sit in kindergarten for the day. Ashima doesn't remember for what infraction. She remembers the humiliation.

In the days after she returned from the clinic, half paycheque in hand, this was the explanation she offered herself for remaining in the city: pride. True, there was pride to contend with. They'd seen her off, her Papa sending to Medford for a pundit to perform the puja, blessing this new beginning in her life. The expense of feeding all those strangers who showed up from everywhere! Who knew there were that many Indians in southern Oregon? And why did Papa have to boast like that? Making her internship out to be more than it really was. She couldn't go back. Not now. Not so soon. Not even a full month since leaving home.

In the dark that descended she was careful to pick her way, to avoid stumbling across a truth kept hidden behind piled-up furniture: the loneliness of life lived within her family. Ship-sized truth, hulking, yet hidden, the tug of its undertow is a constant in her life. The flight from her family was undertaken without her ever admitting to its presence. Flight was disguised as a grown daughter moving out into the world to see what the world had to offer. It was flight she had prepared for all her life.

*

It is January again. Nearly a year after her arrival in Los Angeles the flight still shivers in her. For the second time since her move from home she is fighting the urge to turn tail. 'I can't,' she talks to the faucet, then to the hands holding onto the faucet. 'Hold on,' she instructs her hands. If they obey her they will not reach for the phone. She will not speak into the receiver, ask to return.

Her loneliness is a gift from a man who hoarded it till it grew too large for the home of his youth. He rolled it then into his bundle and let a dust wind pluck him up from amongst the refugee lanes of Kotla village in Delhi and set him down in the still streets of Klamath Falls; from the hollow of one village to another, this man was flung and came to earth, bundle intact. He became a man with a smile affixed by years of greeting strangers, a man who came noiselessly when summoned by the buzzer to the front desk of Haven Inn, from behind which he threw a switch, illuminating at dusk the neon squiggles of Welcome Rooms Available Free HBO Single $24 Double $38.

Kitchen, bedroom and bathroom—the manager's suite—located a swivel of his body behind the front desk, a place for Prasant Jain to raise his daughters. Asima and her sisters grew between plywood walls, escaped their father to play hopscotch in a lot fenced on all sides by freeways, overhead by sky. There, loneliness found the daughters, set them to play chase with their shadows, a game of spinning and falling. Whole afternoons were spent alone in hidey-

holes. When their father called them to dinner—
AshimaSunitaBhawna—they remembered their names, set the
dinner table, crowding the edges of their plates with shiny gifts of
freeway litter the wind had blown their way. And each year the
time left to them to grow lengthened, yawned wider. They grew up
afraid they would be pitched into it, as their father was every dusk
pitched from them into his vacant smile. The two younger ones
looked to Ashima to show them the way to leave home.

✳

Ashima cashed the half-paycheque and counted it out under the
newspaper lining of a kitchen shelf. Daily, she walked, moving
slowly, glaring at the few on those mostly empty streets who
ventured to look at her. A long walk, seventeen blocks to the
Safeway, deposited thirty-five cents in the coin slot of the news
rack outside the grocery store and sat herself down on the bright,
empty sidewalk strip, pored over the contents of the paper. She
read about the recession. The news was much the same here as in
Klamath. But the claims of disaster were much larger. Undaunted,
she turned to the classified section which she saved for last, and
with aid of ballpoint-ink circles and arrows she trawled there
among the jobs teaching English, the jobs answering the phone at
legal firms and bath houses, and the jobs providing 'residential
support' to the inhabitants of groups homes meant variously for
the emotionally disturbed, the developmentally disabled or the just
the plain old incarcerated.

For three months she charted a respectable course through the
crumpled and re-smoothed words of the pages spread before her.
Then she readied herself to concede the lure of oilier waters. Here
was a section she had refused to ink, but now let herself doodle

closer to—here were jobs that required only that she answer the phone at night, to whisper companionship to the lonely in the City. And what of her own loneliness? What of nineteen years of loneliness? She went to a glassed-in building, where they handed her a script, asked her to read from it. The mystery of what she was to whisper solved, she turned to the other dilemma.

'Bitiya,' Papa liked to begin when he was imparting those items she knew he knew she would not want to listen to. 'Bitiya, like it or not, in this country, especially in this country, girls cannot allow themselves every freedom a boy can. Living away from me you will have to be the one to remember when it turns dark. Dark is not a good time to be out visiting friends, shopping. Ashima Bitiya, have friends, but call your friends to your house.' Listening to this Ashima yanked with her free hand at her hair. When had she ever called friends to her house? There was a pact among the sisters: no one was to see their kitchen-bedroom-bathroom arrangement. 'Don't have to be alone, you know.' Her father continued, 'You need to buy groceries? Don't run out constantly for this item and that item. Do it all together in one trip. If you keep a list on the kitchen counter, you keep adding to it all week; then on Saturday or Sunday morning you do it all in one go.'

What trouble Prashant Jain had imagined his daughter getting into he had forbidden her gently, hesitantly; his voice that of a man rousing himself years after the fact to his daughter's maturity.

Ashima suffered but not tortuously when she read over the script. Hers was a bit part, requiring little more than silent acquiescence. That the phone needed to be answered in the glassed-in building and not at home as she had hoped, that getting to the glassed-in building would require boarding the bus at night, that she could hear her father entreating, 'Bitiya,' finally stopped her from accepting the job.

*

In the heavens above, angels sometimes interested in the beautiful and frightened daughters of widowed fathers made note of this rather tame turn in Ashima's story.

✳

In April of that year Ashima found employment. Her afternoons loitering on freeway overpasses indulging her vague attraction to the pitched drop below came to a relieved end. The job at the hospital was nothing to boast about. But it was at least marginally related to her avowed passion. And so what if the passion was more her father's than her own? She told her father on the phone, 'Medical Records today, maybe med school and UCLA tomorrow. And Kaiser Sunset, Papa, is the flagship facility. It's huge, Papa.'

Her father was placated by this vision of his eldest, his secretly-held-as-favourite child making good. 'Ashi, you know I don't like you working when you can be home and attending a good school right here. Anytime you want to come back, your Papa can afford that for you.'

She allowed him this grace, taking on herself the burden of rationalising her move from home. 'Yes, Papa, I could have stayed. But for what? So I could head to LCC and spend another two years with the same clowns I've spent the last twelve with? You didn't raise me to do the same old, same old.' She knew this was the right note to strike. He replied, pleased, 'I trust you Ashima. What you are doing is what I did when I left everything and everyone I knew to come out here. And I was right to do it Ashi. Such daughters I have. I am so proud. So proud, Ashi. You are doing what I did once.'

She did not want to hear this story, spent from endless retelling. She had her own story to make. Her father, sensing this, rushed to close before she cut him off. 'Just you don't forget we Jains may not have been in this country very long but we come from a very old country. Ours is an old culture. You be careful who you mix with out there. There are all kinds of people in the world, Ashima. And I am not saying anything against the Blacks. I have nothing against them. And the Mexicans. Nothing against them either. Every kind of people stays here at Haven Inn. They all get treated like guests. They all leave the same dirt behind for me to clean. I am just saying if we know ourselves and our quality then we have nothing to worry about anywhere in this world.'

Ashima lowers her bottom till it makes contact with the tub's sit-ledge. She tucks her hands under her and tells herself this will occupy them. Yet again, and helplessly, she thinks ahead to the sound of the phone ringing at home. What frightens her most is the picture of her father, phone to the ear, eyes glued to the television screen, and the moment of his attention shifting, turning itself completely to what she is saying. 'But why, Ashi?' he is bound to ask. And then, will she simply lie? That she might wield power such as can turn him fully toward her, such as can reveal her fully to him is an idea terrifying to her. And then, will she simply lie?

'I am a fucking idiot,' she mutters to herself. The rest is a snarl of words festering in her in the weeks since she said all the wrong words, in the weeks since she left the one word unsaid. I deserve this. What was I doing?

She can hear her father's voice: 'Remember our quality' and 'Careful Ashima' and 'Games are for children'. But she knows that's not why and how she and Marvin got started. It wasn't a game. It was her curiosity, her wanting to know, not who he was or even how he could be—so different from her. It was her curiosity about how he would see her, so different from him. She had hoped he would see something new, unearth a talent which would win her the crown: Ms Ashima Jain, the newly-crowned Ms Jain. Applause.

Oh no, but Ms Jain is declining the crown. Ms Jain, ladies and gentlemen, is just not daring enough. Queen of what, Ashima thinks sourly. Maybe if I had been told what I was being crowned for.

She swings back to cursing Marvin. '*Pinche Cabron*! You did this to me. I never wanted it. You forced me to.' Even in her anger, she is incapable of the word 'love', but she thinks it. You forced me to love you. And she remembers the night of the strike, the night weeks ago now, the word almost bolting from her, a frightened bird exploding from tree cover. I almost said it. Oh God, I should have said it. No, but then Papa. Then she is left to think of what she actually said. All the wrong words.

It's been two months since the night of the strike. She had thought she would avoid the cafeteria, the hallways, the parking lot, the street, anywhere she might meet him. She had thought she would arrive at work early, leave late. She had thought she would eat at her desk. Instead, the day after the strike she went looking for him on her lunch break. He was at their usual table in the cafeteria. He looked at her, then past her, then turned to someone next to him. Ashima put her tray down at the nearest empty table, sat a moment, got up and nearly ran from the room. She's eaten alone every day since. Those who once said, 'You two' and 'Enough of that' have nothing to say to her now. It doesn't matter to her that others know. She can't bring herself to avoid the cafeteria, the hallways, the parking lot and the street. Everywhere he might be, she is. What drives her to it? She can't say. Whatever it is, just as surely weights her eyes when they find him so they look nowhere but at her tray, the hallway floor, her table, the tips of peoples' shoes.

Ashima lets her bottom slide forward on the tub's shelf. The lip of the ledge cuts under her thigh, the back of it cuts into the bump of her spine. Her belly has ceased rippling. She cries for all she believes she has lost. Queen of his heart. Silly, but that's what she would have crowned herself. She pummels her stomach. Then she whines, 'Please, when will this end?' A little later she is nearly asleep, wandering in her mind past the word, past the silence she has inflicted on herself, past life without Marvin.

Tidily lined up next to Ashima on the bathtub's sit-ledge is the phone receiver. I will call Papa, tell him I am coming home. Tell him it's the wrong place for me. And if he asks me why then I'll go away again, somewhere else.

Then she is in a dream of herself bent over and cooking a concoction in a bathtub. Marvin comes to her in the dream, asks her if what she is cooking is sweet. They are in a park. The palms arch over her. Marvin's face rears up in front of the palms, blotting them out. There is him and a sky more beautiful than any she has ever seen. She sees his face in bits that travel in and out of her view—bits of forehead, replaced by bits of chin and then back to forehead and then chin and back to forehead and chin. His lovely face. His face. His loved face. How beautiful his face.

*

Above Ashima's shower-matted head, the angels weep a collective tear—a behemoth droplet that hurtles to earth, elongates as it gathers velocity, spins, flinging salt from its centre, so it acquires in passage a crackling shell; lands crashing hard, spreading salt glitter on Ashima Jain's tin roof.

*

Leaves from a pair of young avocado trees by Ashima's front door rain in the wake of the deluge that has torn through them. Ashima's eyes open. But it takes a slowed second before she registers the sound of a wave followed by a rat-tat-tat drum roll. She yanks hard to the left the volume dial in her head, stretching the Marvin-loving, self-loathing monologue that white-sounds her every waking moment. Bweeeeeep. The sound pulls long and smacks shut. Inside her head and overhead there is silence. She decides she has not dreamed the disturbance. A quick assessment: the crash above is too loud to be that of late-night squirrel revelry. Nor can any number of weakened-stem avocados slipping free of parent tree effect such a shattering and clattering. A raccoon, she tries to convince herself, refusing to allow the ninja image of a burglar entry into her head. The burglar horror exits easily enough but is supplanted by a bigger fear. She scrambles from the tub. Earthquake! Her first LA quake and she is naked and cannot remember the details of the drill she has only read, never practised. But the slight tremor recedes into the earth's thick skin. It is, she concludes, the shaking of nearby HWY 134, and pictures the highway passing under the thundering charge of late-night cowboys stampeding their eighteen-wheel rigs west. Oh for the highway to be repoured so it heads north, would she then crawl into one of those rigs and home to Papa. No, she wouldn't. Yes, she would.

✳

Angels, benevolent and malevolent, and angels somnolent, pause in their fornicating. This business of sympathising is getting to be a habit, think the dourer ones. The last intervention they, any of them, can recall was a mere blip ago in time. The most cynical of them are quick to draw a parallel. On that occasion as well, the favoured one had been young and beautiful. They remember the randy fellow, too frightened to tackle his sheep, who had amused them when he made use instead, of sun-warmed, foamy flesh of watermelon. Later, the stripling David, the clumsy shot with the quailing heart, had elicited something akin to their pity. The stone, poorly chosen and misshapen, destined to arc too early, and land well short of its mark, to be anointed along with the rest of the surrounding plain by David's own heart-fuel, needed but a momentary realignment, a nanosecond suspension in earth's gravitational field, and it had soared to immortalise the thrower.

He had, they justified their intervention, amused them to the last. They had loved the boy turned King, condemned to drench his pillow in maudlin psalms, searching forever for a return to that early stroke of slingshot genius, thinking to find by force in Bathsheba's arms what he, failing, searched shivering for under heavy coverlets and in the company of a daily ration of freshly-gotten virgins; shivering as hopelessly in the end as he had in the beginning on that stone-strewn desolate plain.

There are angels unwilling to strain themselves in actual argument, who simply mutter: 'It's the landscape, stupids.' It is not her beauty nor the beauty of that earlier boy—coincidental, this extraordinary beauty. It is the speck of him against that vast plain and the speck of her in the vastness of the city. It is the landscape and not the humans themselves that interest the angels. And it is play to reach down, pick up the globe and give it a shake. Los Angeles. The angels shrug away the memory of David. Their pity once elicited cannot be denied. And all ends as it is conceived to in the beginning.

So it little matters to them that their single teardrop—having landed on the corrugated cover over Ashima's 400-square-foot home, and having spread there to travel in creeks its rutted ribs, is now reconvened in the gutter pipe from where it gushes out underground with such force that little-creature-burrows are collapsing and burying alive all within. They are little interested that their saline solution to Ashima's bit of minor tragedy is now travelling deep within the earth; is looking for the exit west where all points meet and where the continent ceases to be; is intending to assault there at 2.08 a.m. the incoming tide, and turn back time. Even the most curious among the angels lose interest in their shed tear, in the intentions of that tear, and in Ashima, well before the earth ceases to tremble from its impact.

The earth's reverberations and the half-wakened mutterings of Angelenos
still. The tear meets the Pacific Ocean, raising the sludge level and toxic spume
of Santa Monica Bay. The Pacific Ocean, no small backwater satisfied to allow
co-joining tear, angel-shed or otherwise, upstart entry into its bowels, rears
sky-high, flaring a watery serpent hood charged with venomous rage. The moon
pulls hard in aid of her lover. But sorrow, tear-encased, is insidious and merely
wends its frictionless way past rage, pulls back the tide and starts time over
again. It is once again that morning.

✳

The morning of the one-day strike, Ashima arrives at work in a
new yellow blazer. She is the union steward for the sixth floor and
it will be her job when the noon hour strikes to blow the whistle
around her neck, to distribute the armbands and process out her
co-workers. The Banana Republic store tag is still attached to the
inside lining of the jacket sleeve and from there it pokes at her. She
is not bothered by its stiff paper prick. It reminds her as she gets
up from her station and moves among the stations of her co-
workers that she is a leader, dressed as a leader should. Tomorrow
the strike will be over and she will return the blazer to the store.
But today she will look sharp as she marches out 100 per cent of
medical records.

At 10.30 she takes her morning break in the basement cafeteria
where a Stewards Council is being held. Many of the women are
newly known to her. But the identities of many others are still
contained only in the Kaiser nametags hung from their necks or in
the case of the professionals, clipped somewhere on their fronts
among a litter of other professional affiliations. There are at least
200 of her fellow Stewards here and she knows the meeting will
run past her fifteen-minute break; might even last an hour or more

as meetings have of late. But who cares, she tells herself. The Boss can't say anything now.

On the edge of the crowd, pushed against the dish-conveyer belt, Ashima bends over to tie the laces of her shoes and Marvin bends next to her. 'You look great,' he whispers. 'But if you stay bent like that, the rest of my crew gonna faint.' There they stand; the four of them in their Transportation blues. All four have assumed the thumb hooked into elasticised overall waist, front unbuttoned, legs-cuffed attempt at grace which the uniform is designed to deny them. All four hang their heads and Marvin's 'Girl, you just sooo' results in four hidden smiles.

He had pursued her in the halls for months. Once he understood her schedule he took to parking himself near the cafeteria doorway on her lunch break. She could have switched to the cafeteria most workers avoided because it was the one the doctors favoured. But why, she had thought. He was handsome. He had never once pushed for her number; never seated himself uninvited at her table; never, in fact, asked to be invited to sit. If he had, she, easily bullied, wouldn't have known how to say no. She would instead have switched cafeterias. When she volunteered for Steward there was a teddy bear, one of the larger ones—dark fur and red bow— from the hospital gift shop waiting for her at her station. She took the teddy bear home with her. Then without a whole lot more fuss she took Marvin home one evening. She told herself she liked the attention. Her life after work would otherwise have been empty enough.

Lately though, she finds she likes more than just the attention. She likes him. Bent over so she can hide her eyes, she thinks, I like him. She thinks this before he slips her the single rose, before the woman ahead of Ashima turns to stare. This woman's hunger plants in Ashima, quick blooms with the force of what Ashima had a second before tossed off with nonchalance as her 'empty enough' life. But the larger drama of strike preparation sweeps this Michelle or Felicia back into its fold, and Ashima acting to clamp down on her heart hisses at Marvin, 'Marvin Judkins, this is not the time.' He ducks and grins. Then he punches lightly at his chin with balled up fist and whispers, 'Knock Out,' continuing the drama by buckling his knees and swaying for a second in front of her before he turns to run the empty gurney to the service elevator. She can hear him whistling above the clatter of wheels as he and the rest of the crew disappear down the hall.

Ashima turns and faces the back of the crowd. The meeting lasts only ten minutes. The Union Representative asks a woman to speak. The woman forgets to tell the crowd her name, saying instead: 'I'm from 4600. I work the reception there. I had to turn away a mother with her baby this morning. *Pobresito*. The little one. His arm was broken. You don't got to be a doctor to see that. His arm was bent crooked. He was just limp. And they told me to send the family to County. Why do I got to do their dirty work? That's what I want to know.' The crowd loves this story. A visible joy breaks through the tension in the room.

Back on the sixth floor, her co-workers crowd around her. 'Sups gone,' they yell. 'Are we going out? Is everybody else with us?' Ashima stands on a chair to speak over the 163 heads in the room. That is the number of signatures she collected the previous week and that is how many there should be present in the room. If there is time, she thinks, she will re-count and make sure no one is sitting this out at home. She finishes the story about the baby with the broken arm adding the bits the Union Representative had provided downstairs. 'See, they can say we are selfish and we are abandoning the patients. But we know, don't we, we are doing this for the patients. If they cut our healthcare today, tomorrow we are the ones going to get turned away with our babies and told to go to County.' This is as long a speech as she has ever given in her life, and she feels exhilarated.

Up front Beryl Bemis nods her head, the glasses bob with her fleshy face, winking 'yes, yes' at Ashima. Joey Leyva has been nothing but trouble, questioning the one-day strike strategy—'Why not just do an all-out? What is this one-day crap?'—refusing to sign the petition till the last minute. Now he looks on quietly.

At noon the march out to the sidewalk is orderly and anticlimactic. The building empties out and when the sign-up sheets are tallied at four o'clock, 100 per cent turnout is claimed. '2,400.' For a bit this becomes the chant of choice. The crowd yells out the response: 'Strong.' An awkward chant, soon abandoned.

At six o'clock the line outside the Administrative Building opens for the Reverend Jesse Jackson to enter. When he exits the building a half-hour later, the lines from the six surrounding buildings have converged onto Sunset Boulevard and the police are calling for reinforcement which arrives spectacularly mounted on horseback. 'The LAPD has horses?' the question is raised and answered within the crowd. "Course, they have horses. Whaddya think? The LAPD don't have horses? They got everything. Why wouldn't they have horses? Jeeesus!' Jesse Jackson leads the crowd in repeating, 'I am somebody.' Ashima knows this is an old speech and that he has given it many times. But she is moved, and standing between Joey Leyva and Art Lozado she weeps, repeating the words: 'I am somebody.'

Midnight. There is confusion. 'Aren't we going back in?' 'Hey, one day is supposed to be over.' And from Joey and a handful he has managed to pull around him: 'No way in hell are we going back in.' Ashima and the other Stewards fan out to work the now-thin picket line that straggles in the dark along the six blocks of sidewalk fronting the hospital.

Few day-shift workers remain. Ashima's crew, which works only the day shift, exited in mass at the end of the Jackson show. 'Who's gonna feed my kids if I don't get home to do it?' Other workers who stayed to mug for the TV cameras at 8 and 10, 'Got to make the numbers look good,' abandoned the line by 11. Nearly everyone remaining is from graveyard. Besides Joey, Ashima recognises no one.

Buckets of fried chicken are littered everywhere. They are easy to see; their white stripes schemed in red gleam under the street lights. But running hard, Ashima nearly misses seeing a pile of crumpled brown paper, on a stretch of sidewalk left dark in between the street lights. She swerves around the pile, fails to avoid it completely, and the brown paper skitters apart, grating and tinkling. The sound tells her the bags are cover for bottles recently emptied.

Rumour has it that in the parking structure between the two main hospital buildings there is a regular party going on, and that Union Representatives who have gone over to bring picketers back to the street have themselves failed to return. But she has no time for rumours. She is running to 4460, and her orders from two senior Stewards are to keep people from entering the building: 'Get there quick. There is no picket line there to stop those scabs.'

'Scabs,' she mutters to herself; psyching herself to confront them. Her yellow blazer flaps behind her, irredeemably grimed by her day of leadership. Just as she reaches the edge of the building, she runs into the sound of a shopping cart coming around the corner. She knows the purposefully loud sound of this shopping cart. It belongs to the Sunset Lady. Wheels don't propel this cart but drag behind it. The rubber on the rims and the rims themselves in the case of two of the wheels are long gone. The spokes are bent into mangled claws and screech on the sidewalk, alerting all to steer clear of the outcaste trundling this monstrosity, which today is laden with more cardboard buckets of KFC than can be consumed in a week of 'finger-lickin' meals.

The Sunset Lady stops at the corner. Ashima thinks she looks like Beryl Bemis but larger, 100 pounds larger, and not as friendly. The woman blocks Ashima's path and stands quivering there. Her face is strained and shiny; her forehead and eyes bulge, then slowly relax. Her legs spread, and Ashima's eyes travel to the massive thighs which unstick from within rags, and allow to drop on the sidewalk a thick rope of brown. Ashima pushes herself against the wall to let the cart and owner scrape by. Then she runs to the entrance through which management personnel are ushering in a group of twenty or so workers dressed in clean lab coats.

'Are you crazy?' she yells. 'You stupid Blacks. You stupid assholes. We don't go back till tomorrow noon.' She grabs at someone's coat. The man turns and shoves her from the door. The Security guards standing with Management personnel start radioing something into their walkie-talkies. A man entering the building turns and brings his face close to Ashima's, and she can smell how clean he is. He bares his teeth and snarls at her. She thinks for a crazy instant that he is going to bite her. But he gets in the building and the guards start to pull the heavy glass doors shut. From behind her she can hear the sound of feet running toward her. Help is coming. 'Thank God. Thank God,' she sobs and yells to them, 'Hurry, they are locking us out.' She shoves her foot and then body into the last inches of space between the door and frame and from both sides a tremendous pressure briefly collapses the breath from her. The pressure lifts, the doors open, and she is pulled into the wrong side.

From outside the chanting is audible: 'Let her go. Let her go.' A little later the small crowd takes up 'Shame on Management.' Inside the brightly-lit lobby she feels exposed. She doesn't know what stance she should take. Defiance, she counsels herself. When two of the guards lift her from the polished lobby floor it is done so swiftly, the scream catches in her throat. A hand brushes gently her cheek and she briefly sees it splayed on her breast before it bunches, gathers nipple into cloth of blazer and twists hard. She forgets the existence of the crowd outside and shakes her head to free it from the weight of the guard's other arm which is preventing her frantic search for the one woman manager she remembers seeing at the door.

The door is opened by two more guards and she is swung out and set gently on the concrete ramp. She doesn't recognise the faces of those who rush to pull her up and though there is a half-hearted attempt by the crowd to find out what the story is, she is too incoherent to respond. Then someone tells her to just sit, which she does; seconds pass and she sees Marvin standing in the light coming from the front of the glassed lobby.

She clings to Marvin, keeping her head down. He takes her to his car and they sit for a long time. He digs in his jacket pocket for something and brings out a pouch, extracts paper and rolls a cigarette; licking its seam shut and tapering it as long as his own lean fingers. He hands it to her and then rolls himself one and tidily returns the pouch to his pocket.

She watches the motion of his hand lifting to mouth and then tapping the cigarette on the car's open window. She can't summon the thinking necessary to understand the meaning of these gestures. She is sure they mean something. She wants desperately for him to speak. He depresses the car lighter and when it pops he holds its glowing face to her. She flinches. She hasn't the courage to ask him what he heard. If he heard. She doesn't smoke. But he already knows this. Silently she acquiesces to his lighter and tentatively holds the smoke in her mouth and lets it out.

'You want me to take you home?'

'No, that would look bad, if I left now, don't you think?'

He doesn't reply to this. Afraid of his silence she babbles, 'You think it's okay? The way it's going is okay, don't you think?' She cannot allow the silence to stretch and ploughs ahead, 'Some people are not for the strike. But they're in the minority, right?'

He speaks then. 'Before LA, I'm from Fontana. Born there, grew up there, was there till I left there.'

'Oh.' He is saying something important. But she doesn't know Fontana. She knows Marvin but not enough to know what Fontana means and what it means in his story. Doesn't know what it is doing in her story. She tries to listen. Hears: 'smelting steel' and 'in the '40s, thereabouts' and 'selling scrap. He works in scrap.' Then she hears 'Kaiser' and 'striking Kaiser, just a family tradition for us'.

'There's a Kaiser in Fontanta?'

'Yes,' he says, his voice patient. 'But in steel. Kaiser Steel. What about you? You never explained all this time why you are in this?'

'I don't know.' She is bewildered by the question. Which 'this' are they talking about? 'I don't know much about Unions. My father manages a business. It's small. I don't even think he likes Unions much.' She pauses, forming her words carefully, 'He's not a joiner. He doesn't have time to. He's raising my two sisters and till this year he was raising me as well. He wouldn't be very happy if he saw me running around here.'

'Ah,' he says and the silence presses between them. Very slowly he asks, his words clear, 'Probably wouldn't be a good thing for you to be running around with me now would it?' He turns his whole body to face her better. 'A stupid Black like me?'

She thinks, this moment will pass. She thinks, it's already past. But it hasn't and it doesn't. She thinks about getting out of the car and walking away. She would have to hide at work, avoid the basement cafeteria. Maybe she could just quit the job. She almost begins to pretend confusion; starts to ask, 'But how did you . . .?'

Ashima stares hard at the empty street outside the car window, at the buildings that stay lit all night. She moves in the car seat, an imperceptible forward motion. She almost opens the car door, can picture herself tumbling out into the glitter. But the coins of light caught in her lashes are not the city's. She pushes herself into the seat and takes his hands into her lap.

She feels how nervous his fingers are; understands how nervous they have been all along. Nervous fingers had rolled her the cigarette. When she lets herself raise her eyes from his hands, she sees the corners of his mouth, gone grey. She says very softly. 'You heard me.' He nods, and she says, 'I'm sorry. You hear things growing up and they stick inside your head. I didn't even know it was in there.'

He says something in response. She hears his voice, but not the words. When she drops her face into her hands, he lets his fingers prise hers apart and extract the cigarette which is dangerously close to burying itself in her forward flung hair. 'You don't know how to smoke,' he says. 'You let it go out.' The sense of a small catastrophe lit and defused, a minor tragedy averted makes them goofy.

'Around Fontana we say sorry when we fuck up.' He is teasing her and smiles to soften the 'fuck up'.

'I already did.' She is whining or pouting, she is not sure which. But the teary feeling is still there snagging in her. She pulls herself as far away from the car door as she can, pushes herself deeper into the seat and closer to Marvin.

She has little memory of her parents together. It makes her shy, the years of wondering how people are together, the years of being everything to her father, the years of no aunts-uncles to show her the way, no older cousins. I've had to learn everything myself, she thinks, allowing herself self-pity. She doesn't ask again for forgiveness. Offers him the bloom in her heart. 'Love,' she says. It sounds so hideously mangled, so never-heard and never-said before; she hides her face again.

'Love,' he says.

In a different life, she thinks, she wouldn't have the courage. If there had been a mother, or aunts or cousins, she is sure she would fail this moment. She doesn't know how she will explain Marvin to her father, is glad there are no aunts and cousins who will also need explanation. He has to ask her twice: will she please take a break from the line, come for just a quick ride.

They don't go very far. He takes her to Echo Park and she agrees the lake is beautiful. He tells her it's dangerous to be there at this hour and watching the word 'dangerous' form in the mouth she saw so recently hurt, she counters with, 'It feels familiar.' But she can't for the life of her explain the sense of familiar that accompanies these new sights. And there is everything new in the sense of expectation she feels. They lie down in the wet grass and she sees the dark silhouettes of palm trees arching over her and beyond them the great bowl of the night sky in which the stars are holes burnt black by reflected city lights. While he works his hands under her clothes, the palm trees talk to her. 'Have we seen you here before?'

She tells him about the sky vs. sky fight she and her sisters have fought for years with their father. 'When we say the sky in Klamath is the most beautiful in the world he always says no sky is more beautiful than the sky where he is from. If we ask him if it's bluer, he says, "Brighter, stormier". If we ask him about thunder and lightning, he says, "Still and Empty". So we ask him if there are more stars. He says, "No, more crows."'

'What about Los Angeles?' Marvin asks. 'We don't even have a sky here, just the lights.'

'Papa would hate it. Delhi is always the most beautiful to him. But you know I think this is the most beautiful. These lights.'

She is hungry to transmit her life to him in this one night but lying there next to him she has just enough strength left to tuck her face into his neck. Words continue slipping from her mouth for some time after she is asleep. She dozes and wakes to his fingers exploring inside her. The trees above are no longer there. There is a dark mass. It is his head rearing over her. He kisses her urgently and she tells him about the time she was eight and made to sit in kindergarten for a whole day. The memory of why she was punished comes to her. It was for pursuing a boy, for sending him a card in which she drew the two of them together, he flanked on his side by his family and she on hers by her father and sisters. 'You got sent to kindergarten for that?' She's not sure. She thinks, yes. But has to admit it might have been that eight was the year she continually peed in her pants. 'You what?' he asks, not suppressing his laughter.

His back is turned to her he pulls on his shirt and begins buttoning it. She sees the sweat dried dark on the cloth. That he sweats beautifully, raising a pattern of paisleys on his shirt, is something she has not seen till tonight; it is something that does not surprise her in the least. A breeze circles them, lifts a stray lock of her hair and tucks it behind her ear.

✳

Sometime before innumerable instances accrue to the rest of their lives, and sometime after Ashima and Marvin leave the park and return to the last hours of the one-day strike at Kaiser's flagship Sunset facility, that is to say, somewhere in time between the present and the future, somewhere where the past intersects, there is a Sunday morning in January when Marvin peers out of Ashima's bedroom window and shouts, 'Snow. God almighty, snow in LA.' When they step out they find it is a strange snow, crusting only their roof and no other, frosting only their avocado tree's suddenly withered branches; a snow not in the least bit cold, a snow which glitters, which Marvin tastes, makes a face, and touches to Ashima's tongue. She creases her forehead over the unfamiliar. 'But it tastes so sad.'